© Claire McNamee

About the Author

SUZANNAH DUNN is the author of eight previous books of fiction, including *Blood Sugar, Venus Flaring, Tenterhooks, Commencing Our Descent,* and her most recent success, *The Queen of Subtleties*. She lives in Brighton, England.

The Sixth Wife

Books by Suzannah Dunn

The Sixth Wife

The Queen of Subtleties

The Sixth Wife

SUZANNAH DUNN

HARPER

NEW YORK • LONDON • TORONTO • SYDNEY

HARPER

First published in Great Britain in 2007 by HarperPress, an imprint of HarperCollins Publishers.

HarperCollins books may be purchased for educational, business, or sales promotional use. For information please write: Special Markets Department, HarperCollins Publishers, 10 East 53rd Street, New York, NY 10022.

FIRST U.S. EDITION

Library of Congress Cataloging-in-Publication Data is available upon request.

ISBN: 978-0-06-143156-2

10 11 12 OFF/RRD 10 9 8 7 6 5 4

Here lyethe Quene Kateryn wife to Kyng Henry the VIII and
last the wife of Thomas Lord of Sudeley high Admirall of
England and onkle to kyng Edward the VI
dyed 5 September MCCCCCXLVIII

Inscription scratched onto Katherine Parr's coffin

I can say nothing but as my Lady of Suffolk saith,
'God is a marvellous man'.

Katherine Parr, in a letter to Thomas Seymour

This day died a man with much wit,
and very little judgement

*Princess Elizabeth – later Queen Elizabeth I –
on hearing of Thomas Seymour's execution*

The Sixth Wife

One

I won't testify. They'll get no help from me. Not that they need it, the trial being a formality. It's over already for him. No need for this investigation, the intimidation and confessions. And anyway they should have left him to it, saved themselves the bother. He'd have ended up doing the job for them. He'd have got nowhere, in the end. Got away with nothing.

It seems they have little better to do, though, than rubbish the memory of a good woman who's barely cold in the ground. That's what's happening: it's making her look bad, what they're digging up on her widower. Making her look as if she was beguiled and hapless.

Kate?

Listen: she'd dealt with it; it was all dealt with. She'd dealt with Thomas and the mess he'd made. She'd saved everybody's skin.

One mistake: that was all Thomas was in her life. Could just as easily not have been a fatal one, that mistake; just the turn of events made it fatal.

I won't testify, and if they come for anyone in my household, they'll have me to reckon with.

Which they know.

Which is why they haven't.

I'll tell you something about Kate; I'll tell you what it was about her. She always made everything all right. That's what she did. That was Kate.

And now she's gone. And now look.

I didn't go to her funeral. I arranged it, the day she died, that long, long day of her death. Then, when the next day came around as suddenly as a drawn curtain, I didn't go. I couldn't watch her lowered into that vault.

You could say that I didn't need to go; you could look at it that way. I'd made the arrangements, I already knew that funeral from first moment to last. I'd dressed the chapel, lain drapes over the altar rails and then supervised the men struggling with the black, embroidered hangings. I'd planned the procession, right down to the servants at the rear. Well, someone had to do it. I'd selected the four knights to walk hooded with the pallbearers, and the two torchbearers to walk with them. Then would come Jane, tiny ten-year-old Jane Grey, chief mourner, and I'd coached her maid how to carry her train, forewarned her of steps and loose slabs. The psalms and the sermon: Reverend Coverdale had gone through everything with me.

I'd dressed Kate for her burial, chosen the dress, a dress

that I'd loved on her: holly red, running with gold stitching. Kate had colourless eyes like a dawn sky, but she had sunrise hair and I turned it loose for her burial as if she were a girl again.

While the funeral was taking place, I stayed with the baby. I couldn't believe she was our compensation for Kate. Such an unequal exchange. She was like something skinned; she was nothing like my boys had been, born big and with frank, focused gazes. But, then, they were boys: from their first moments, the world was theirs for the taking. The baby was unsettled, so I walked with her. With everyone at the chapel, the house was deserted and I'd never been so alone. It might have been that everyone had died. Everyone in the world, even, so that I could have walked from the house and kept walking but never found anyone again. Just kept walking until I, too, died. From starvation or exhaustion or perhaps sheer loneliness – can you die from loneliness?

I was bone-tired when the baby finally gave in to sleep, so I sat down where I was, nowhere in particular, on a carpet-draped chest in a hallway, my back uncomfortable against the linenfold. Suddenly a nearby door was opening. Who on earth wouldn't be at the funeral? But then I knew. There was indeed one person in the household who wouldn't be there. The one person I didn't want to see. I should have thought of that. Of him. And so there we were, facing each other. My heart was furious, each beat nipping hard. His beauty rankled; he'd always been everything that Kate wasn't, and never more so than today. It was an affront, that bright beauty, on this darkest of days. I wanted to strike it from him.

A frown snatched at his eyes. I knew what he meant: didn't I want to be in chapel?

I said, 'Someone has to look after this baby.'

He looked back at me with no look at all; his incomprehension said, *There are nurses for that.*

I could have said, *I don't have to explain anything to you.*

Or I could have said, *The nurses are all there, they wanted so much to go, because everyone loved Kate. Everyone, that is, except you.*

He said, 'Cathy . . .'

I hugged that oblivious baby to me and turned, walked away.

If she'd never married Thomas, Kate would still be alive. She should have stayed a widow, that last time. The king's death had been her third widowing, and had made her dowager queen. I'd been around while Henry was dying, in case she needed me, but it just so happened that I wasn't with her when they finally came with the news. I'd gone into the gardens to take a few minutes to myself. When I returned to her room, unaware, she asked everyone to leave us. In her hands was one of the pairs of spectacles – silver rims, Venetian lenses – that she'd encouraged Henry to buy and which he'd tended to mislay all over his palaces. She watched everyone leave the room as if their leaving was of some interest to her. Always so polite, Kate. Not until the last of them had gone and only her dogs remained stretched in front of the fireplace did she look at me, and that was when she sighed and closed her eyes. The mildly interested expression went from her face – indeed, all expression went from her face – and she covered it with her hands and began to cry.

I'd never seen her cry. All our years of best-friendship and I'd never seen her cry. She'd never seen me cry, either, for that matter. Should she ever, though, I realised, she'd know exactly what to do. I couldn't even guess, myself, what that would be, but *she'd* know. She'd rise to it. She'd comfort me, I imagined, without making me self-conscious. For now, though, folded forward there on that huge chair, she looked awkward. It was usually well hidden, that gawkiness of hers; she tended to turn it to her advantage, turn it into something else, walk tall with it. I crouched beside her – awkward, too – and rubbed her bony shoulder. She cried harder and I didn't know if that was because I was doing something right or something wrong. Exasperation dizzied me. Tell me what to do, I wanted to say, and I'll do it.

Just two years before I knelt there with my arm around Kate, my own husband had died. My husband of twelve years. I was widowed at twenty-six. Charles had been a little older than Henry – sixty – but in good shape and could have passed for forty. His death – a sudden illness one weekend – was a shock, whereas no one could claim that Henry's death had come as a shock. It wasn't shock that was causing Kate's tears.

Four years, they'd been married. Kate had known him fairly well when he was gorgeous and big-hearted, but those days were long gone by the time she'd been persuaded to stand at the altar and think of England. During their marriage, he'd been a cantankerous, backwards-looking monstrosity. No sense in pretending otherwise. It couldn't have been the loss of Henry that was causing Kate's tears.

Queenship, though: the loss of her queenship. She'd loved the role. Not just the work that was required of her – the easy but tedious meeting and greeting – but the bringing of changes. As queen, she'd been able to champion certain people, albeit quietly, Kate-like. How suited she was to all that: the talk, the confidences. She'd always had people's trust, but as queen she had the ear of anyone who mattered. Careful work, for which I'd never have had the patience. My view is: what a time this is to live – it's *the* time to live – because the world is opening up to new ideas and the truth is here, now, for the taking, if you just look. And if people don't take it, if they don't look, don't make the effort to learn, it's because they're lazy, self-interested, they're cowards. But Kate's view was that people are slow to change because they're scared, or misguided, misinformed. And people trusted her. No one trusts me. That's not what I'm for. Kate used to say to me, *We all have different strengths, Cathy.* I don't know if she omitted to say what mine were, or if I just can't now remember.

Queenship had been Kate's big chance and now, suddenly, one January day, through no fault of her own, it was being taken away. Over, for her, before time. Just four years she'd had, and there was so much more to do. No wonder she was miserable. I'd never before seen her miserable. Frightened, yes. Impossible – foolish – to live through our times and not be frightened. Even I'd been frightened. And I'd seen her angry, too, beneath her considerable composure. But never miserable. Because that's something that you feel for yourself, which wasn't Kate, she didn't do that. Or hadn't done, before now.

A month later, something happened that made me see her dejection on the day of the king's death as perhaps having had rather less than I'd imagined to do with her no longer being queen. At least some of those tears had been because she was in her mid-thirties, still childless, and once again unmarried. And who'd marry her now?

Two

A month or so into Kate's widowhood I went to stay with her in the Chelsea countryside, at the old manor that Henry had left to her. I set off from home later than I'd envisaged because my friends the Cavendishes, en route to their Hertfordshire manor, stopped by for longer than they'd intended; and when they did eventually depart, we saw that one of their horses needed a shoe.

'Go,' Bess Cavendish dismissed me, 'or you'll be on the river in the dark.'

'It's February,' I countered with a laugh. 'Half the day's dark; dark's unavoidable.'

Then, back indoors at last, I had to see a local shoemaker whose home and workshop had burned down, because my steward wanted to discuss with me how much assistance we should give the family.

We didn't launch the barge until the evening and, despite

hard rowing by my men, arrived at Chelsea too late for dinner. I can't say I minded. I sat cosily at the fireside in Kate's room with my two accompanying ladies to eat excellent pigeon pie, and peaches that had been bottled in lavender-infused syrup. I'd brought Joanna and Nichola, my youngest ladies, knowing they'd fit in best at Kate's. We all have girls in our household, of course, come to us to learn the ropes, but trust Kate to have *only* girls, every last one of her attendants a fledgling under her wing. There had been some changes, though, now that she was no longer at court. A couple of new faces. One was Marcella, who, Kate told me, was married to one of Thomas Seymour's men; the other was the Lassells girl – Frances, 'Frankie' – an eager twelve-year-old.

It was an easy, gossipy evening, Marcella playing the virginals beautifully in the background. I wasn't late going to bed, to the room that was mine whenever I was there. I hadn't been there for long, though, when Kate turned up, nightdress-attired, barefoot, hair down, unattended by any of her girls. There was never any bustle to Kate, just this walk, loose, light, and tall. She sat on the edge of my bed and switched those big clear eyes of hers to my maidservant, Bella.

'Bella,' I said, 'that's fine for now, thanks.' She was unpacking for me. 'Why don't you take a little time to yourself.' Bella wrapped herself in her cloak and made herself scarce.

Kate scooped her hair behind one ear and said, 'I've something to tell you.' She held my gaze steady with her own and told me: 'I've married Thomas Seymour.' With a brief laugh, she turned her eyes to the ceiling, or just upwards, somehow both nervous and bold, as if taking pleasure in admonishing herself.

Thomas Seymour? They were friends, he and Kate; had been for years. Odd little friendship, theirs: a friendship that I'd never understood. Well, never even considered really. I couldn't remember ever having seen them in each other's company. She'd mentioned him sometimes, over the years, in a manner that might in retrospect be said to be friendly, but Kate was friendly with everybody. Her close friends, though, were reformers and scholars, people who believed in and worked for a better life for everyone. From what I knew of Thomas Seymour, the only life he was keen to better – and he was very keen indeed, from what I'd heard – was his own. But there I was, thinking about her friendship, and hadn't she just said 'married'?

Married? That was impossible. She was married to the king. Well, no, widowed, but only by a month. She was the king's widow, still. Not some other man's wife. And certainly not – *certainly* not – Thomas Seymour's.

She got up, moved to the window. 'No one must know, though, obviously, for a while.'

She *had* said 'married'. 'Thomas Seymour?'

She laughed, delighted. '*Yes*, Thomas Seymour.' Then, less boisterous, 'It's been so *odd*, Cathy. Such an odd time. And I couldn't tell *any*one.'

You, she meant.

Me.

It was an apology, but I was glad I hadn't known. And wished I still didn't. Because this was madness. Married to Thomas Seymour? *Kate?* No one must know? *Oh, don't worry, Kate, I won't be the one to tell them.*

Thomas Seymour had been away – High Admiral – for at least a couple of years. I'd had the distinct impression that he was regarded by those in power as someone best kept busy. The polite word for him would be 'colourful': a colourful character. Not only in character, though. I'd only ever known him in passing, but I remembered exactly how he looked. Because he was a good-looking man. No point in denying that. He certainly didn't; he dressed the part. Fiercely cheekboned: that was what I recalled, now, of him. Sulky-mouthed. Moved fast, talked fast. Well, he'd certainly done that in this case, hadn't he. Moved fast; fast-talked Kate. *Kate*. I looked at her, really looked. Those big fish-eyes of hers. She had a gaze – unlike his – that rested on people. And on books: those eyes of hers spent a lot of time resting on books. Thomas Seymour had the reputation of being quick-witted, but that, I gathered, was the extent of it: quick. Too quick – seemed to be the consensus of opinion – for his own good. Here's the truth: I can't claim that it was hard to imagine why some women would go for Thomas Seymour. Not, though, a woman such as Kate.

That was only half the puzzle, though, because what on earth had attracted him to her? I'd have sworn that Kate would have been Thomas Seymour's very last choice. The very last choice for a man such as him. But, then, I knew nothing of his choices in women, did I. There *were* no women, was how it seemed. Somehow he – forty, now – had managed to stay unmarried. And he was the kind of man of whom I'd have expected to hear rumours of women, but I never had. Except, that is, for the very recent one. The big one. Big enough and recent enough to make me very worried.

He'd had his eye on the Princess Elizabeth, only weeks ago, and had been warned off: this I'd had from a reliable source, namely his brother, to whom it had fallen to do the warning. He had to remind Thomas that it's treason to make such an approach to someone in line to the throne. Certainly the princess was Thomas Seymour's type. In line to the throne. Sitting on a fortune. The latter, she had in common with her stepmother: both princess and dowager queen had been amply provided for by Henry. Was it the money, for Thomas? And the status? He was, after all, in the unenviable position of not being on the Council supervising the new boy-king. Sixteen men, none of whom were him. Worse: sixteen men headed by his own brother. Marriage to the dowager queen would be a smart move in the face of such a snub. Suddenly, he'd be husband to the kingdom's first lady. Was it, then, Kate's money and status? Well, let's face it: what else could it be? Kate was going into her mid-thirties, three marriages behind her, with no children, so there'd almost certainly be no heir in this for him. And as for her other assets: you wouldn't look at her twice, if looking was what you were about. And good-looking men – like Thomas Seymour – do look, don't they. It's a luxury they have.

If Kate wasn't for looking at, though, she was for listening to. And she spoke so well that it was easy to overlook that she did it at all. A few quiet words from her: that was how she worked. Oh, and a kind of twinkle in her bulbous eyes. That's all it took, for people: that wide-eyed, steady gaze of hers, and nothing much said, or so it seemed. And then whatever needed to happen would happen as if it had been that person's own idea all along. Clever, that. Made her a lot of friends. So, you *could* say it was the money, for Thomas – and I will say it – but there was more to it. Kate took people on. She made their lives. I should know, because I was one of them. Kate made everything all right, and I now know there was a lot that wasn't all right with Thomas.

Three

The next day, she was all for telling me how it had happened. Except that, it seemed, she couldn't. Which was, as far as she was concerned, somehow part of it: the magic of it. 'It just *did*,' she insisted, exhilarated, trailing frosted breath. We were riding with a few of the household children – the doctor's and falconer's sons and a couple of excitable pages – and some liveried attendants in the parkland beyond the manor. Kate was a very good rider, a daily rider, a natural in the saddle. I'm probably as at home now on horseback when I have to be, but for me it comes from years of hard practice. From having two horse-mad boys and wanting to join in with them.

It just did? Well, yes, and quickly.

'Mind you,' she was calling back to me over the pounding of hooves, 'we've always been friends.'

No, not 'always'. The Seymours are relative newcomers.

Compared to our families, they are. If it hadn't been for their sister, Jane, the two boys would have got no further than that creaking old manor house of theirs in the West Country. Poor plain Jane, dull as ditchwater, around for a mere couple of years in which she was required only to be everything that Anne Boleyn hadn't been. In other words, nothing much. And to produce the son that Anne Boleyn hadn't been able to. Which she did, just, before draining away into that childbirth bed. By that time, the brothers had got their feet under the top table. They were uncles to the future king, no less.

I didn't know them in those days. I've never been one for court. Best to leave them to it has always been my view – confirmed for me by the Anne Boleyn years. If you value your freedom, you're better off away from court. Too much bowing and scraping. Kate was like me in that respect, so I don't know how – where – it ever developed, that friendship of hers with Thomas. His brother, the elder of the two, I did get to know. I've had various dealings with Ed Seymour, and we've become friends. I like Ed in spite of himself. He has fingers in a lot of pies. It's not hidden, though, that feathering of his nest, and I like that, I respect it. Being on the make isn't bad if it's honest. It's subterfuge that I don't like. Ed's nothing like his younger brother. He's even the opposite in looks: pallid, thin-lipped. Hardly fun, but straightforward. And despite all that – fingers in pies, feathering of nests, no nonsense – he's somehow also a man of vision, full of interesting ideas. Whereas I wouldn't want to think about any visions Thomas might have.

'He makes me laugh,' Kate yelled of Thomas as she thundered away from me.

I didn't come back at her with, *Yes, but my dog makes me laugh and I haven't married him, have I.*

Nor, *Yes, but* I *make you laugh*.

People underestimated Kate in one respect: kind but serious, was a lot of people's opinion of her. Maybe it was as simple as that, it occurred to me as I trailed in her wake: maybe Thomas Seymour truly appreciates her.

Yes, but why *marry* him, and so *soon*?

Well, that was quite simple, too, in the end, it seemed. He'd asked her, she told me later. Marry me, he'd said: that's what she told me. Marry me, marry me, marry me: he'd said it a lot. So that it seemed less and less ridiculous, presumably. Why not? he said. I've been away for years and you've been – well, you haven't had an easy time of it for years, for your whole life, in fact, so . . . and then that smile of his.

Enough. That smile. I didn't know what she was talking about at the time, but now I can well imagine it.

We were back at the stables, dismounting amid rowdy dogs, when she said, 'So, the boys are fine?' She was all lit up from her ride. And not only from her ride: it was how she seemed to be now, which, despite my misgivings, was good to see.

'Yes, fine, thanks.' A measly word, though – 'fine' – for my wonderful boys.

'You should bring them again, sometime.' Then, as she handed the reins to one of her grooms, 'Thomas is so good with children.'

Well, we'd see about that, wouldn't we. 'Next time.' A second groom staggered away with Kate's saddle and gold-tassled, crest-embroidered saddlecloth. I handed over my own horse and began removing my gloves.

'Elizabeth's coming to live here,' Kate added, 'did I tell you?'

'No. No, you didn't.' Was my wariness audible?

She enthused, 'She's a good girl, you know, Cathy.'

Well, to be honest, I *didn't* know. All I knew of Elizabeth was that she was thirteen, had the Tudor-rose colouring and was clever. That's what Kate said: very, very clever. Kate had great hopes for her. Couldn't bear to think of her shut away in some country house with any so-so tutor. Nor did she like her having to do all that kneeling at her brother's feet on her rare invitations to court. Elizabeth was very much looked down upon by her sister Mary, too. Of Henry's three children, Elizabeth was definitely the poor relation. Which was, of course, down to who her mother was. But Kate had been working on Mary. It disturbed me, Kate's bond with Mary. I don't like catholics at the best of times, but Mary's fervour feels to me like something else altogether. Like grief, in fact. As wilful as grief. But Kate was friends with everyone and, anyway, she and Mary had been at school together. Now Kate was telling me, 'I said to Mary, Elizabeth's incredibly bright.' Well, that was a good move, because Mary would hate to think of any clever girl going uneducated; I'll say that for her. Kate was saying, 'I said, she needs to study here with Jane.'

Little Jane Grey. 'Jane's all right, is she?' Earlier, I'd unwittingly made the mistake of asking Jane if she'd be riding with us. Her expression had been one of incomprehension as she'd declined and shrunk away, presumably to lessons or prayers.

'Oh, Jane's Jane,' Kate said, diplomatically, with one of her wide-eyed twinkles.

Jane Grey: that tiny, serious girl, top-heavy with brains. Jane must have been so pleased to be at Kate's. I'd had nice parents, if rather absent, but Jane's situation was the opposite: parents not nice, and far too present in her life.

Walking from the stables, I puzzled over Elizabeth's impending move into Kate's household. Because there *was* something I knew about Elizabeth, wasn't there: something that Kate didn't seem to know. That Thomas Seymour had, only months ago, been pursuing her. But, then, I reminded myself, he'd left her alone, hadn't he. Kate was the one he'd married, and as quickly as possible. So perhaps I should give him the benefit of the doubt. Perhaps it had always been Kate for him. After all, Elizabeth was way out of his reach and surely he couldn't have ever seriously imagined otherwise. Council would never have stood by and let him marry her, and he'd have known that, wouldn't he. He must have known that. Anyone would know it. Perhaps, then, sensibly, he'd been covering up his interest in the king's widow. In that way, it made sense, his play for Elizabeth. It was the only way it made sense: Elizabeth as red herring.

Four

A week or so later, when I was back home, Thomas's brother turned up at my Barbican house. 'Cathy,' he said, and gave me a cold kiss on the cheek, somehow both diligent and absent-minded. Offered a drink, he requested warm milk and I suppressed a smile: England's most powerful man, sipping warm milk. Bella fetched our drinks and a bowl of roast almonds, and Ed and I spent a while exchanging the usual pleasantries and making enquiries after family and mutual friends. Not Kate or Thomas, though: my best friend, his brother. Notable absences. Looming absences.

Presumably there was something that he felt would be best said if and when we were alone. So, I suggested a stroll in the garden. I'd probably have suggested it anyway because Ed is rather dull – he'd take no offence at my saying so, it's something he seems to cultivate – and half an hour in his company is improved by there being something else to look at. Even a wintry garden. He hunched himself back into his luxurious cape and down we went to the terracotta-tiled terrace, then further down into the garden. At the bottom of the steps he launched in with, 'My brother's a bloody fool.'

So much for no one knowing.

He explained that he'd learned the news from the little king, who'd learned it from Thomas himself.

'No one's supposed to know,' I said.

Ed's smile was a sneer. 'Thomas doesn't keep secrets about his own good fortune.'

I asked how little Eddie had taken the news.

'Thinks it's nice: his favourite uncle and his beloved stepmama.' Then he dropped the sneer and worried, 'It's just . . . too soon,' touching his forehead as if placating a pain. His velvet cap didn't disguise that he was more grey than when I'd last seen him, which was only weeks ago. No longer greying, but grey. The same thick, sleek head of hair, though.

'Yes, I know.'

He gave an apologetic shrug: of course I knew. But then a double-take: 'Did you . . . ?' *You didn't know beforehand, did you?*

'No! No. I'd have told her . . .' Told her what exactly? Any number of things. I voiced my doubts, or, more accurately, my incomprehension: 'It's not just that it's too soon, is it. It's that it's *him*.'

He stopped, almost smiled. 'But I thought you'd have been all for that.'

'For what?'

'Marrying "for love".' He handled the words with a show

of reluctance but it was clear that he enjoyed saying it. Probably the biggest thrill he'd had in ages.

I've never made any secret of my opinion. And if anyone fails to understand quite why I object to arranged marriages, a good start would be to have a look at Ed's wife. Nasty piece of work. Or, indeed, look at Ed himself: pallid and shadowed.

'It helps,' I said, sarcastically, 'if both parties feel the same.' We walked on, alongside joyless, brittle lavender.

'So, you don't think my brother is in love with Kate?'

'Do *you*?'

Wearily: 'I suspect he's up to his usual tricks.'

I brushed my fingertips against a rosemary bush – the dusting of flowers, tiny knots of brightest blue – and enjoyed the sting of its deep, dark scent in the air. 'What was all that with Elizabeth?'

'Exactly what it looked like, I should think: an attempt to marry a princess.'

'Has there ever been any other interest in women?'

He admitted, 'That's what puzzles me. If it wasn't too premeditated for my brother – who's nothing if not impetuous – I'd suspect he'd been waiting for the princesses to grow up. We're lucky that his faults don't include being Catholic.' Mary would never have him.

I said, 'It's Kate who's the mystery here, though, isn't it. Not Thomas. What is *Kate* doing, marrying *Thomas*?' Sensible Kate. Probably the most sensible woman any of us have ever known. Strong-minded Kate, though: it did fit, in that respect. And Kate who keeps her own counsel, likewise.

Ed nodded. 'It's Kate I'm concerned for. You know that.' He was fond of Kate; she was his kind of person. 'It's not that I'm objecting to their being married. In fact, there's probably no one I'd rather have as my sister-in-law –' He stopped, gave me a look that meant *Besides you, of course*, although he didn't mean it – he thinks I'm trouble. I laughed, but actually something serious occurred to me. I was remembering how Kate had said cheerfully to me, 'But I don't have to explain this to you, do I. You of all people.' And how I'd thought, *Yes, but I'm me, Kate, and you're you.* Possibly, just possibly, this was something I'd do: marry someone whom others saw as unsuitable, and marry him quickly because I considered myself in love. Even though I had never, in fact, done any such thing. Had never had to. But Kate? Had I led her astray? By giving her ideas? She'd been the one giving me ideas, all my life: that's how I saw our friendship. It felt odd to me that it might be the other way around, for once.

As we walked past my sunless sundial, Ed broached something else: 'If there's an heir soon, there'd be a question as to whose,' and he clarified, unnecessarily, 'Thomas's, or the late king's.'

'Ed, there hasn't been an heir in all these years. She's been married three times since she was fifteen. To men who'd already had children, so there was nothing wrong with *them*.'

He checked: 'So, she isn't . . . ?'

'Is that why you came here? Not to talk this over – two friends putting their heads together, concerned for a mutual friend – but to try to press something out of me?'

His turn now to take offence. 'No. No. Don't bite my head off over this.' He sighed. 'It's genuinely that I don't know what to think. Don't know what to make of this.'

'Yes, well,' I said, 'that makes two of us.'

Five

I went a couple of weeks later, at Kate's invitation, to dine with the newlyweds. This was to be it: Thomas's formal introduction to me as Kate's husband. No point in my putting it off; every point in getting it over with while making as little as possible of it. It had to be done. When my barge drew up, it was Elizabeth – unmistakable hair of Tudor gold – who greeted us. She just happened to be sitting on the riverbank steps. Holding a lute. Beneath her scarlet, ermine-edged cloak was a gown of deepest, plushest black; beneath that, a kirtle in cloth-of-gold. Oh, very picturesque. How had she managed to slip away alone, unattended? The gems on her hood's border winked as she stood to give me a huge smile – 'Hellooo!' – but those Boleyn-black eyes searched my face. I was careful to show just as much enthusiasm as we chatted. You want to know why I distrust Elizabeth's familiarity? Because it's calculated.

Those scanning eyes. Oh, I understand *why* – she's spent her life on the outside, special to no one – but that doesn't mean I have to like it.

Her standing back from all the bustle of mooring and unloading our barge gave the unfortunate impression that she owned the place. 'Oh, well,' she said eventually and offered up her lute, raised her faint eyebrows. 'Already late for my lesson.' Watching her go, I did soften a little. Because there was also something genuine there. Excitement. She was obviously pleased to be at Kate's. Understandably. Quite something, it was, to be taken on by Kate.

It was something, though, to which her elder sister was objecting: this I discovered a little later, when Kate came with me to my room. Her old friend Princess Mary was refusing all contact with her, she confided dolefully. 'Doesn't like my having married Thomas so soon.' So soon after her father's death. She shrugged, helpless. It crossed my mind to say, *I'm sorry to hear that*; but then it crossed my mind that I wasn't. I was pleased; it was a relief. That friendship of Kate and Mary's was unfathomable to me. Mary is from the dark ages.

It was predictable that she'd have voiced an objection: she's famous for her sense of protocol, as well as for her horribly complicated relationship with her father. Understandable, the latter: think of his adoration of her as his precocious little princess, then his savage rejection of her along with her mother before he welcomed her – minus dead mother – back into the fold. Poor Mary never knew whether she was coming or going, whether she loved him or loathed him. Her confusion persists and she's touchy on the subject, to say the least. I don't like her but even I'd say that, given how her father treated her, she should be dancing on his grave.

'She'll come round, I think,' Kate said, cautiously. We could speak freely; my two ladies, Joanna and Nichola, were reacquainting themselves with Kate's; Kate and I could barely hear each other over all the chatter. Bella had gone to the laundresses with my gown, which had snagged on something when we'd disembarked.

'And Elizabeth herself has no problems with your having married Thomas?'

'No, none. Although Mary suggested she should have. Wrote to her and said it'd be best if she didn't live with me.' Kate permitted herself a wry smile. 'Well, you can imagine. Elizabeth knows her own mind. She answered to say she'd be staying.' Now, a burst of enthusiasm: 'Elizabeth loves it here, you know. And I love having her here, Cathy. She's a real joy to have around. Such a clever, grown-up girl; it's so good to see her flourishing.'

I felt she was going to say, *She's more like a daughter to me than any girl has ever been.* Or perhaps, *I see a lot of how I was in her.* She said neither. But she could have said either. It struck me that I was envious; of which of them, I didn't know.

I didn't meet Thomas until we went into the hall for dinner. And then there he was: across the expanse of jewel-like tiles with the cavernous fireplace ablaze behind him. Kate took my hand, led me towards him, presenting me to him and getting away with it before I'd quite noticed. He kissed the hand – my hand – and greeted me with just one word: 'Cathy.' My own name, yet somehow it made me shy.

When had I last seen him? Five years ago? He was forty

now but looked no different from when I'd last glimpsed him. His years of being cut loose from England seemed to have done him no harm at all. On the contrary. In the candle-light, his face looked sculpted, his eyes adamantine and his hair like cloth-of-gold. Impeccably tailored, too, he was, with even the smallest pieces of fabric slashed to reveal, underneath, as linings, fabrics that were just as fine. A performance in itself, how he looked. Kate never stinted on clothing – her gown was cloth-of-silver – and to my surprise they made a good-looking pair that evening.

He was bowed over my hand when he said my name and never during that whole evening did he once look me in the eye. I'll be frank: it's not something I'm used to, not being looked at. Ours was an intimate gathering, too, or should have been: just Elizabeth and me at the top table with Kate and Thomas. Jane Grey had gone from evening prayers to bed, having one of her headaches, and all Kate's ladies and my own two were assigned with Thomas's men to a separate table which was set at an unusual angle from ours. As was the table for the senior members of the household such as Elizabeth's governess, the men of the church and the girls' tutor. Kate's consort of viols was practically inaudible. Uproar, though, heralded the subtlety brought to our table at the end of the meal: knowing, congratulatory laughter for the sugar-sculpted, goldleaf-tabbied pair of cats – the bigger one presumably a tom – which were arching their backs, rubbing against each other.

For all the supposed intimacy of our table, Kate seemed like a stranger to me. Was it, perhaps, like when a girl sees her older sister with a friend? I wouldn't know, sisterless as I am, but that's how I imagine it. A whole new Kate was conjured up in front of my eyes. A Kate who was somehow more than Kate. Not the one I knew, and surely the one I knew was the real one. But this one was so convincing. Pretty much perfect, in fact. Looking back, I suppose I felt as if something was being kept from me and something was being shown to me. I felt betrayed and tolerated and favoured, all at once.

And as for Thomas . . . Well, Thomas is always Thomas, I've learned. That, if nothing else, can be said for him. He was good company, that evening, telling stories and making us laugh, me, Kate and Elizabeth. If you know no better, that's how he seems: fun. Daring, even, because he tended to tease Kate and this was something I'd never seen. Kate, I realised, had never been teasable. For all that she could do for people, all that she could be, she wasn't teasable. Not due to lack of humour or humility – she had both, in spades – but because teasing's for taking, and Kate was a giver. But this, now, from Thomas, she had to sit back and take. I watched her warm to it; watched her rise to it, as required, then submit to it.

Kate wasn't the only one to fall in with him. Elizabeth and I must share some blame, too. Thomas was a good judge of when he'd taken more than his fair share of time and attention – as storyteller, joker – and that was when, to keep us on an even keel, he'd switch our attention to Kate. That's what he was doing when he teased her, turning us away from him so that we could return, minutes later, refreshed, ready for more. He was also calling up our affection for her and offering it to her on his terms, in his words alone: *Our Kate, our girl, our queen*. We were giving up our say in who she was, to us, *Our Kate, our girl, our queen*. We went along with him. I can see it in retrospect but at the time, as I say, he seemed good company, telling stories and making us laugh. Now I know that's what Thomas does: he charms; he tells stories. To women.

Six

I don't remember ever having *met* Kate; she was always just *there*. My earliest memories of her are probably when she was thirteen or fourteen, when I would have been five or six. She was the daughter of my mother's best friend, but more than that, to me, at my age, knee-high and wide-eyed, she was one of a crowd of girls of whom everyone at court spoke with such approval and enthusiasm. Very clever girls, they said. Of course, it wasn't a crowd, it was a mere handful of girls from a few favoured families. *Tall* girls, to me, although that might only have been true of Kate and her sister, who did grow up tall. If the Princess Mary was tall, back in those days, she stopped growing, because she's no bigger these days than a twelve-year-old. Something else: they were all so light-haired. Well, compared to me, they were. That's what I'd notice: flaxen, auburn and gold tucked into those dark hoods.

Perhaps all this makes Kate sound striking. What was

striking about Kate, though, if it's not contradictory to say so, was her plainness. There should be a word for it – striking plainness – but in English I don't think there is; if there is, I don't know it. Kate probably would have known a word or expression for it, in one of the four languages she spoke. *Fish's eyes* was what came to mind, and still does. It might not sound complimentary, but actually they had an arresting glitter to them, those pale, protuberant eyes of hers.

For all her bookishness, gangliness and pallor, there was nothing off-putting or overawing about her for the five-year-old me. She was never anything but a comforting presence. I'd say that she always made a fuss of me, except that somehow she did it with no fuss at all.

And then she was away, married, and I thought no more of her, I suppose, or not much more; and then I was away, too, and then married and having the boys. My boys were part of Kate and I later becoming friends. She adored them and they adored her.

Now there was Thomas, and Kate seemed to be right about him being good with my boys. They came with me when I next visited Chelsea, for my first visit of a couple of days with the newlyweds, and on the first evening they were gone for hours with him. I don't remember now what they'd gone to do, but eventually it was close to midnight and they hadn't reappeared. Having had enough of Elizabeth's strenuously sophisticated chatter and Kate's indulgence of her, I made my excuses. The dogs were too sleepy to rise and I made it outside alone. The courtyard was balmy, horse-scented, under a blunted moon and a span of stars. The gardens were what made the old manor so special. Behind me, its roofs were sheathed in moonshine. Ahead, the rosebushes lay in wait, hunkered. Beyond them, at a stone's throw, was the river, still and silent yet somehow very much a presence, a body of water at ease but vigilant.

Kate had told me that this was how she and Thomas had managed their clandestine meetings: in darkness in her garden. He would ride across the fields from London and the night porteress would admit him. It made perfect sense now: I could imagine it, even though I'd never in my life done such a thing. Before long, I heard the boys' voices accompanied by a more certain male voice. I crept up on them; but where I'd expected to find them, there was unbroken darkness. It took me a moment to fathom: they were on the ground. Flat on their backs on the flagstones. Stargazing. Thomas was telling my boys about the stars. He'd had years away but under these same stars. Unanchored, star-trailing years during which this immense, peep-holed blackness had had to be his home. I heard how intimately he knew it, every faintly star-brushed corner. How he revered it. Earthbound me, I know so little of the constellations. I stopped at a safe distance, undetected.

It could have been an echo that I was hearing: my boys as little boys again, agog as Charles told them a bedtime story or told them about their day or the days they'd go on to have. Charles had already had families; we were third time around for him, but he never stinted with us. He had the time by then and the patience. I didn't have much of him – twelve years – but I probably had the best. That's what I have to remind myself.

What I was thinking, as I stood there in the darkness, was how well my boys had done in their two fatherless years. They'd done Charles proud. Their worries, I knew, were for me, for my happiness, however much I wished it weren't so.

And standing there, listening, was the first time I wondered if I was being too hard on Thomas. Perhaps Thomas, like Charles, had simply chosen to marry the woman he loved and would never waver. That kind of thinking – a forgiving kind – is what happens when you stop in a sparkling darkness and listen to a man showing your babies the stars. I doubt now that I was undetected; I think he knew I was there.

Seven

There's a myth about Kate: that she found happiness at last with Thomas. Until, of course, it all went wrong. It's a nice idea but it's a myth. 'I've always been happy,' she'd said to me, during that first visit of mine, and was laughing as she said it. She sounded surprised that I'd made the remark, the one that would gain currency over the following months: that it was nice to see her happy at last. I'd succumbed already to the myth. Or perhaps, even – who knows? – I was the first to say it. Myth-making. Not like me; I don't go in for myths. I can't think why I said it now, can't imagine how I'd fallen under that spell, except that's how it is with myths, isn't it: they're persuasive. Myths, spells, lies – all the same, powerful.

This, then, is the truth about Kate, as I know it; this is as close as I can get. She had a happy enough childhood, growing up with a brother and sister, the three of them close.

And if her mother wasn't exactly merry . . . well, who *would* be, widowed in her early twenties with three small children? I barely remember Maud but she was, as far as I know, a woman of careful, calculated steps, dedicating the final decade of her life to her children's education and inheritance. And who does that sound like? Except that Kate failed in the end to follow her mother's example in one crucial respect. Maud chose to stay a widow.

Maud stayed at court, lodged there with her children and began working long and hard to secure future marriages for her children that would keep the Parr fortune safe. In the meantime, she made a job for herself organising the royal school, a benefit of this being that her own daughters could attend. That's how Kate had come to have an education fit for Catherine of Aragon's own daughter. Consider just how good that education had to be. Priceless were those lessons that Kate took alongside Princess Mary from the wonderful Señor Vives. *Beebis* was what I used to think his name was when I was young, before I realised how it was spelled. *Señor Beebis* and his glamorous Belgian wife. He was hawkish and sallow but handsome; she was big and blonde, with a habit of affectionately cuffing him. They'd both had heavy accents, but different ones. Juan Luis Vives wasn't only a man of ideas: he *had* ideas. One of them – a big one – was that education didn't come from memorising facts but from asking questions. The biggest, though, surely, was that education was for girls. *Especially* for girls. Because, he reasoned, a woman needed her wits about her. His school was soon world-famous: its pupils, by the age of twelve, debating with lecturers, lawyers and bishops. In those days, the Princess Mary – heiress of England, studious half-Tudor and half-

Castilian waif – hadn't yet turned into plain old Mary Tudor, narrow-minded Catholic.

Just as I was ready to move on from nursemaids and governesses to the school, it closed. Anne Boleyn was coming to the fore, and Señor Vives had unwisely been persuaded to say a little something in Queen Catherine's favour. The consequences were worse than he'd anticipated. His services were no longer required. Whatever I've learned, I had to learn from Kate: a hand-me-down education, with which she was unstintingly generous. Which wasn't how she claimed to see it. Once she claimed that it was from me she'd learned what mattered in life. Incredulous, I'd challenged: *Learned what?* This was how she put it: to have the courage of her convictions. I couldn't see it. She was courageous, she had convictions. Whereas me, I follow my instincts and I'm stubborn: it's as simple as that.

She'd tried to explain: 'What's your dog called?'

'*Which* dog?' And, anyway, she *knew* what my dogs were called.

'You *know* which dog. Gardiner.' My lapdog, named after our principal catholic bishop who also – bad luck – happens to be my godfather. Our principal catholic bishop, preaching celibacy whilst installing a succession of mistresses in his palace. 'You called him Gardiner,' she said, 'so you could make us laugh by calling him to heel.'

'That's just me being silly.'

She gave me her wide-eyed look. 'You're never just being silly.'

I was determined not to let her take it seriously. 'It was nothing.'

But she wasn't having it. 'Well, here's something that isn't nothing then. I was there, remember, that evening, at your house, with all those people, when Charles said every lady had to choose the gentleman they'd most like to take in to dinner, and what did you say?'

Oh, she had me now; I couldn't suppress a smile at the memory. What a good pair we'd made, Charles and I, if an unlikely one, me being half his size and half his age. (Lucky that I could never have been mistaken for any daughter of his: him, a genial, greying bear of an Englishman, and me a snub-nosed, sharp-tongued half-Spaniard.) The evening in question, I'd gone up to the repellent Stephen Gardiner and said, 'I'll do things a little differently; I'll take the man I like least and that's you.'

I said to Kate, 'It was a joke.'

'He didn't find it funny, though, did he? He laughed along with everyone else, but you could see he didn't like it.'

'Yes, which is why he's the butt of jokes like that.' *Pompous ass.* 'Look,' I said, 'you're nice, Kate, and I'm not, and that's all it is.' I didn't like the way the conversation was going, her implication that she was somehow lacking. Something I loved about her was her quiet certainty. And why, in any case, should she want to make cheap jokes? That was for me to do.

'You make your point, Cathy,' was what she replied. 'You make people think. You go out on a limb to do that. And I've never in my whole life taken even the smallest risk.'

I wonder, now, what Señor Vives would make of what happened to her in the end. Advice to his girls was something he'd undertaken seriously. Yes, there were languages to learn and translations to do, there was astronomy and maths and music, but he was keen, too, for his girls to do well in general. In life. To be happy, no less. Kate told me that he'd advised them never to marry for love. For a man, it was of no consequence, he'd said: a man could marry for love. But not a girl. Because it would render her vulnerable.

Of all the pieces of advice from him, Kate chose to ignore this one.

Eight

It was this, with Thomas: he was often onto something, but he never knew when to stop. That was Thomas's problem. He was unstoppable. Take that night of the stars. Was he content with a few special moments that arose there in the dark garden? No, because next morning – barely morning, barely even dawn, a mere few hours later – he decided it was the turn of the girls.

I was awake, just; must have been, because I was unaware of being woken. How early was it? Very. I'd heard the clock strike four, but couldn't recall it striking five. Not dark, nor light. What I'd heard was a girl's voice, outside, in the grounds. Not the voice of a resentful servant on some extra-early duty, perhaps in the bakehouse, half asleep and matter-of-fact. This was someone wide awake, excited, momentarily forgetting herself before being hushed. And from my window I spied them: Elizabeth – it had been her voice – with little

Jane, being led through the garden by Thomas. Only nightgowns beneath their cloaks, the three of them, and the girls' hair was down; I'd never before seen Jane with her hair down. Her walk was brisk but she was well behind the other two, her reluctance clear. Elizabeth's hair was like a fox fur. Her lolloping sideways canter was keeping her abreast of Thomas while she chattered at him in a theatrical hush. She loves drama, I realised as I watched. Why do people say there's none of her mother in her? Her father would have either woken the whole household to join him, or he'd have genuinely enjoyed the secrecy. But her mother would have done exactly as Elizabeth was now doing: making a show of stealing away. The old king had been a showman but Anne Boleyn had loved show, and there's a difference: Henry had drawn people in, Anne had wanted them to see what they were missing.

Unwittingly, I was Elizabeth's audience. I'm all for high jinks, believe me, but this? A grown man prancing around in his nightgown in the early hours with two girls entrusted to his wife's care? A man who had been suspected of having had too close an interest in one of the girls. A girl who wasn't just a girl but a princess. Was that why Jane had been drawn into the escapade, as alibi, chaperone? They slipped from view and I attempted to follow them, leaving my room without waking Bella, but then I saw Elizabeth's governess, Mrs Ashley, in her nightdress, at a window far down the hallway. 'Mrs Ashley?'

'Oh!' She slapped a steadying hand over her heart. I apologised for unnerving her and asked what was happening.

She glanced at the window as if she had to look again before she'd know, and answered slowly, flatly. 'He says it's going to be a beautiful morning.' Then she sounded anxious: 'Do you think they'll be all right?'

It was her job to know that. Or in Elizabeth's case, at least; Jane's nursemaid would be held to account for Jane. I quelled my irritation. 'Where's he taking them?' She shrugged, which frankly wasn't good enough. I answered myself: 'To the river.' Because that's where I'd go on a beautiful dawn.

'He woke her before I could stop him.' She chewed her lip, contrite.

'He *came into her room*?'

She, too, now sounded surprised. 'Yes. But he does. That's what he does.' The surprise seemed to be at my not having known. 'In the mornings.' She half laughed. 'Just not usually so early.' And then when I said nothing – flummoxed – she continued, 'He likes to come in, get her up, play with her.'

'*Play with* her?'

She shrugged. 'Tickle her. Tease her. Chase her around the room.' She must have realised how it sounded because she explained, 'That's how he is: friendly, very friendly, never on ceremony. Everyone's favourite uncle.' She gave a quick, worried smile as I turned away, gave up on her and returned to my room.

I raised it with Kate later. She was having breakfast in her chamber. Who but children ever have breakfast? But there she was, with eggs. I declined to share. Since when had she been sitting around in her bedroom in the mornings, eating breakfast? She checked whether I'd slept well and I lied that I had. 'Thomas, though,' I added, 'he was up early.'

'Oh, he woke you,' she concluded. 'I'm sorry, Cathy.'

He didn't, I reassured her. I was awake, I said; half awake. 'But he woke the girls.'

'Girls?' She was unfolding the linen in which her bread was wrapped.

'Jane and Elizabeth.' I declined her offer of some of the soft, white bread; picked up, instead, one of the mound of cushions from her bed, hugged it to me. This particular cushion I recognised; remembered her embroidering it, back in the days of Henry. Stunning embroidery. Was there anything Kate didn't do, and didn't do perfectly? I'm a poor needlewoman, don't have the patience. 'That's a habit of his, is it?'

'Waking early?' Before I could clarify, she said, 'I don't think Thomas has "habits".' And flicked her gaze skywards. 'He just . . . does whatever he wishes. I lose track. I didn't realise he was up early but . . .'

Kate's response – if it could be dignified as such – was not as I'd expected, not as I'd hoped. Irritated, I persisted, 'He was taking them to the river, as far as I could see.'

Chewing, she frowned. It was a question.

'Said it was going to be a beautiful day.' I put the cushion back. 'Said to Mrs Ashley.'

She looked at the window. 'Well,' she began, dreamily, 'it is.' Her eyes caught the light, shone.

This was no good, she was letting herself get carried away and this could well turn out badly. She should be extra-careful, in charge of a princess; she should realise that. Especially this particular princess, but presumably she didn't know what I knew about Elizabeth and Thomas.

'Bet the girls'll be tired,' I said, because I was uncertain what else to say. 'It was very early. Before five.'

'Before five?' That had her attention. She seemed to stop and think. 'Well,' she continued, 'they should have a good, long nap after lunch. I'll tell William,' their tutor.

I almost laughed. The girls, *miss a lesson*? And Kate herself rising late. What was going on? I tried to look merely mildly interested. 'Does Thomas do this often?'

'Wake the girls?' She dabbed a damask napkin to her lips.

I shrugged. 'Wake people.'

She stood, indicated to her maid that she'd finished. 'Well, he's always waking me,' a quick smile, 'but not to take me to the river.'

I was shocked, to be honest. Which in itself shocked me. Because I'm unshockable, aren't I? Everyone knows that. Yet there I was, feeling flushed and – deeper – chilled. That's shock, isn't it? But why? What on earth had I been thinking? That they didn't sleep together? Newlyweds? Happy newlyweds? In truth, I hadn't been thinking about it at all. There was so much else about them that was a puzzle. Was it, then, Kate's mention of it that shocked me? Her direct mention of it? No, because sex wasn't a popular topic of conversation with her, but it certainly wasn't unmentionable. And, anyway, it wasn't direct, what she said. But nor was it coy. I didn't quite know what it was. An aside, a quip; it had felt like a brush-off. I realise, now, what it was that shocked me. It wasn't what she said, but how she said it. As an aside, while she stood up and turned away. Allowing me a glimpse, but only so much, as if it were nothing of significance.

It was something I thought about as I lay in bed that night. Kate, like me, had probably had only one lover. Three marriages, but probably only one lover. Ted, her first husband, had been too old; I remembered now that she'd told me, 'There was none of that.' I hadn't known her really in those days, the brief time of Ted; not properly. 'It wasn't a bad life for a girl,' was what she later told me about it; and indeed she *was* a girl – fifteen, sixteen – in those days, younger than her own stepchildren. Her next husband was John and he, too, was a lot older than she was, but he wasn't *too* old. Come to think of it, when they married he was probably younger than Thomas is now. John and Kate were married for fifteen years. John had been her lover. And then Henry, the king: nothing much doing there. I'd wanted to know, of course; everyone had wanted to know, but she actually did tell me. He'd tried, was what she whispered; he'd tried, a couple of times, and then given up. She gave me a look, and I pulled a face, said, 'Thank God,' to which her response was nothing more than a wan smile. Because the less said, the better. Not that it was news in Henry's case. Anne Boleyn had famously decried his stamina – it was one of the misdemeanours for which she died – and, frankly, the record had been poor since then, with his fifth queen, little Catherine Howard, too stupid to realise that it didn't mean she could take her pleasures elsewhere.

Pleasures. Me, like Kate: just the one lover. My husband. I bet people assumed that Charles and I were lovers for all twelve years of our marriage. Because we were clearly in love; because Charles was what they call a full-blooded man, a ladies' man, he was so evidently all man; and because – I know what they think – I'm what's known as hot-headed, headstrong, which is taken to mean hot-blooded. Well, people know nothing, do they. I spent the first couple of years of our marriage having babies. And then there I was, sixteen, with two babies under two. Enough, as far as I was concerned: I'd done my duty and was anxious not to get pregnant again.

Really anxious. And Charles was anxious not to hurt me. I hadn't recovered from the second birth, no doubt because I hadn't healed from the first. Charles – much married, good at women – understood. And what they don't tell you – unless they're Anne Boleyn – is that the all-jousting type of man doesn't actually have much energy left for the bedroom. Not when he's over thirty, certainly.

Charles must have considered that he was doing me a kindness by mostly leaving me alone and of course in a way he was. But months became years and then it had been so long – practically all my adult life – that I wouldn't have known how to start if I'd had to. That was something I pondered that night: how had Kate *known how to start*, when it came to it? I had to conclude that Thomas – resolutely non-jousting Thomas – had taken the trouble to show her.

Nine

The day I set off back home from that first visit, Kate was up late and then at prayers, then talking with the girls' tutor. Having sent word that I'd like to be fetched when she was free, I remained in my room and helped Bella pack up. Or tried to, but Bella's too capable to need or probably even welcome my help. I had none of my own ladies for company; I'd come unattended, this trip – Joanna being due her first child, and Nichola having returned to her family home. I used the time to tackle some correspondence. When I finally got to Kate's room, she was treating herself to a bath. Her ladies Marcella and Agnes seemed to have exhausted themselves preparing it, and were reclined on cushions by the fire, reading. I ducked through the canopies, brushing aside bunches of lavender, and there was Kate amid more lavender in a tub of deep oats-creamy water.

'Bath time,' I said, pointlessly – a mere envious purr – and she smiled in response, closed her eyes and smiled even wider. On a table beside the tub was a big brass bowl: she'd be washing her hair, then, too. In the steaming water, among the usual cinnamon and liquorice sticks and cumin seeds, were slices of lemon.

I queried: 'Lemon?'

'It's good. Lightens your hair.' Her eyes sprang open. 'Not *your* hair,' she retracted. 'Lightens *light* hair.'

Yes: no good for me. Cloves and rosemary for me.

'Do you really have to go?' she asked.

I pulled up a stool, sat. 'Houses don't run themselves, do they.' I've an excellent steward – a legacy of Charles, who appointed well and inspired loyalty – but there's only so much he can do, or is willing to do. There's only so much that it's fair of me to expect him to take on. I do the household accounts. More than a hundred people look to me, ultimately, to keep them fed and clothed and educated. All those people needing to be encouraged, placated and sometimes, unfortunately, reprimanded: ladies and gentlemen, senior members of staff and the servants who work under them, and all their children. In kitchens and storehouses, chapel, gardens, laundry, the farm and stables. Permission to be given and funds found for orders: four or six hundred oranges this month, and four hundred or five hundred eggs? Each head of department will know his or her own requirements, but it's me who has to bring them together. We need barrels of soap for the laundry, but we also need soap for the kitchens and for our bedrooms. Wax for candles, of course, for the chandlery; but also for the laundresses, so that they can seal the edges of some of our clothes. We need bolts of fabric for me and the boys, and for our ladies and their children, and ushers and pages and maidservants; but we also need kitchen aprons and chapel robes, tablecloths, saddlecloths, blankets, curtains. And boots, the children have to be kept in boots: that's what always seems to catch me out, and – it seems to me – most often with my own children. How many times have we been ready to journey between London and Lincolnshire and I've glanced down to see holes in Harry's or Charlie's boots? And then we've had to delay for a new pair to be made. As lady of the household, I did all this when Charles was alive; I don't understand why it's been so much more tiring since he died. I said to Kate, 'You should come and see me, stay with me.'

She settled back in the bath, seeming to consider it. But she wouldn't. I knew it, somehow. Something had changed – everything had changed – and willowy, light-footed Kate was somehow more solid; she was unbudgeable. It was me who was going to have to do the running from now on. She surprised me by saying, 'If only you could just stay here for ever, you and the boys. I wish we all lived here, don't you?'

I shouldn't have been surprised, though. It's usual, isn't it: that desire to share a new-found happiness. To feel blessed and thereby magnanimous, keen to spread your blessings around. I'd been like that when I'd just had the boys: I'd wanted everyone to have children; I'd wanted so badly for Kate to have children. It took me years to calm down on that score.

Then she confided, 'It wasn't sudden, Thomas and I. It's not been sudden.'

I smiled at her: *if you wish; whatever you say*. No flash in the pan, was what she was understandably keen to imply.

But even if it *was* sudden, I wondered, why assume that I wouldn't understand? Me, of all people. Me, who knows all there is to know about sudden. Me, the girl who married Charles a mere three months after the death of his previous wife. Less sudden, yes, but still sudden, especially considering that the dead wife was the woman for whom he'd defied the king and risked the death penalty. Charles's elopement with the king's sister had been the love story of the century. And it really was; they did genuinely love each other. Then I came along, tripping along in the footsteps of everyone's favourite, fairytale princess. *That* was difficult, *that's* what difficult *means*. *That* was a scandal.

No, it's not the suddenness of it, I wanted to say as I smiled down at her: it's Thomas; *why Thomas*? But I couldn't say that, could I. Not then. Too late. It was done and dusted: she'd married him. And if she got wind of my distrust of him, she'd decide I should spend more time with him. So that I'd grow to like him, to love him. That was Kate all over: a plan of re-education for me. Well, I couldn't be bothered with that; that was to be avoided.

'I mean,' Kate said, 'he asked me to marry him before,' and clarified, 'before I married Henry.'

Well. This was new. 'But you were married to John.' Before Henry had come John, and there'd been very little time in between them.

'When John died.'

'What, he just' – I laughed – 'came up to you and asked you?' In passing? Because there couldn't have been time for much else.

She laughed with me – 'No!' – before turning contemplative. 'No, no. We talked about it a lot, at the time.' She smiled. 'He's a surprisingly devoted sort. I mean, you wouldn't think it of him, would you, but he waited for me.'

Well, either that, or she was one of his options, the one to which he returned when he couldn't get Elizabeth.

'We talked and talked . . . And I couldn't tell you, Cathy; it wouldn't have been fair on you. Henry was around by then, making his intentions clear. You remember that. I couldn't draw you into this mess. It was . . . frightening.' She winced: 'It was *miserable*. We could talk all we liked, Thomas and I, but there was no choice, really, was there. We all knew what Henry wanted, so in the end there was no choice.'

True: if Henry asked you to marry him, there was no saying no. However much he made it sound like a question – and he'd have been careful to do that; he had his pride – there was no saying no to a king, particularly when that king was Henry. All that we'd stood for, Kate and I, was nothing in the face of Henry because he wasn't a man but a king. And I suppose I'd assumed it hadn't mattered all that much because, yes, it'd be unpleasant and quite possibly dangerous for Kate, but if anyone – any woman – was up to it, she was. And, crucially, it wasn't going to be for long. She'd only have to be patient for a few years at most, taking what she could from the situation. Obviously it wasn't without its compensations, being queen. But I hadn't known that there was more to it, for her; that there was an actual loss involved. Not only had she had to take something on, but she'd had to leave something – someone – behind. Now, belatedly in on the secret, my heart throbbed for her. 'You should have told me,' I protested. 'Since when have I cared about "frightening"?' Thomas, forgotten; it didn't matter that it was Thomas. This was about Kate. 'I can't believe you didn't tell me. You should never have had to go through that alone.'

'Oh –' She waved a hand, dismissive, weary. 'I wasn't totally alone. Anne knew, of course. And because Anne knew, Will knew.'

Of course, of course: Anne, Will, her sister and brother. Family. A family which had then done very nicely from the royal marriage. As families always do. Don't misunderstand me, I like Anne, Kate's sister, very much; Will, too, but particularly Anne: we're good friends. There's no denying, though, that she and Will stood to do very well from Kate's marriage to Henry. They were hardly impartial advisors.

'I had to do it,' Kate was saying, 'and so I did do it, and I think I did it very well.'

No question of that. 'You did.' Her motto, I remembered: *To be useful in all I do*. Useful to her family in this case certainly.

I cut in: 'Does she – Anne – know now?' Of this marriage to Thomas.

Kate nodded, a by-the-by nod.

'And Will.' It wasn't a question, I already knew the answer, and indeed she didn't bother to confirm or deny it.

'I wish you'd told me.'

'I did,' she tried.

That was disingenuous of her; I gave her a look.

She relented a little. 'You're busy, Kate; you've the boys.'

I didn't relinquish that look.

'I couldn't have burdened you.'

'Oh –' Exasperation: words failed me.

'And you . . . you tend to talk me round.' She tried a smile.

'Yes, and perhaps that's *why* you should tell me what you're up to.'

I wasn't sure what had just been said; I wasn't sure, all of a sudden, where we were with this. Except that we were on uncertain ground.

'You scare people, you know, Cathy.' She was careful to make it sound good-humoured.

I rolled my eyes: *That's nonsense, that's ridiculous.* 'Everyone knows that's just me.' I speak my mind and I don't give an inch. 'The only people I frighten are the ones who deserve it,' I said. 'I don't frighten *you*.'

She smiled; her knowing smile, the mysterious, infuriating one that she favoured when declining to go on, when putting a stop to something. I found her towel, handed it to her. Listen: the truth is that no one ever scared Kate, even if it suited her on this occasion to think otherwise.

As best friends, Kate and I went back further than we could ever even know, to before we were born. Our mothers were very close friends. They came of age under the influence of the formidable queen Margaret Beaufort and the sparkling new Spanish one, and I'd often imagine their optimism as they came together over their books and in their debates and discussions, just as we, their daughters, were later doing. In our case, they were different books and ideas – our good catholic mothers would have turned in their graves if they knew – but they were books and ideas nonetheless. Excitement at the prospect that something of the world was understandable, if not open to change: that's what we shared with our mothers. The discovery that there was a better life to be lived. For women. I have a feeling that our mothers would have often said to each other, *Everything is different now; everything is possible.*

For women, was what they would have meant, because Margaret Beaufort and Catherine of Aragon were women who were serious about women. One of them had seen her generation of women run the estates while the men fought the Wars of the Roses; the other had witnessed her mother reign superbly in her own right.

It's what Kate and I were saying a generation later – *Everything's different now for women* – and we considered ourselves onto something new. But, then, women had had a setback, we'd come through difficult times and so we were, in a way, having to start all over again. What I recalled of Kate's mother Maud was an expression that implied she'd seen it all and was expecting worse, but I doubt she could have imagined just how bad the Anne Boleyn years would be. The locking away of one queen and then the execution of the next. No matter that Catherine was queen, the highest of all women in the land, or, moreover, that she was a good queen, then a fierce queen, fighting for her principles and the rights of her daughter. In the end, she was just a woman, meaning just a burden on a man, no longer pretty and not up to bearing a son. And then, in Anne Boleyn's world, at Anne Boleyn's court, there was room for only one woman, and no prizes for guessing whom. That was when most of us – women – slunk away into quiet lives, family lives. Then came Anne's arrest, and suddenly the woman who was above all other women was – officially – fickle, malicious, bewitching. No doubt about it: Kate and I became women at a time when women were seen as trouble.

Maud belonged, despite that heavy-weather expression of hers, to more optimistic times. It was my mother, the optimist, who lived on to face what was, for her, the end of the world: the Reformation. My mother was a foreigner. She'd come here with the Spanish queen-to-be, Catherine of Aragon, as chief hand-holder. She was Maria de Salinas in those days. Mary Salts to you. Married, Anglicised, she turned into Mary Willoughby. Maria de Salinas, the funny, clever Spaniard, was before my time, but nor did I ever really know the Mary Willoughby who had one of the king's ships named in her honour. Because that Mary was, by all accounts, carefree, a lover of life. Back in those days, the king had done more than name a ship after his favoured Spaniard: he found her a husband, a good one. And then she had me. And then everything went wrong: England went mad, in my mother's view, and she followed Catherine into exile, to various tumbledown, far-flung castles. She could have seen it as her duty, even if the hand-holding days had officially long passed, but it was so much more than that, and I'm not sure I have a word for it. 'Friendship' hardly does it justice: hardly explains leaving one's family, one's little girl, for ever, for a banished, tormented queen. Catherine died in my mother's arms and now my mother is buried alongside her. It was what she wanted, Catherine's tomb prised open for her when the time came. Two Spanish girls, Maria and Catalina, side by side in Peterborough.

Ten

It was summer when I next saw Kate. A couple of months had slipped by and suddenly it was June or July, I don't remember which. Strawberry season. She would have been married for six months or so and she looked better than I'd ever seen her – luminous – but there was desperation in her hug when she greeted me.

'What is it?' I was worried. 'What's the matter?'

'Oh, it's nothing,' the agitated tone making clear it was anything but. 'Really nothing.'

Thomas: that was my first thought. Here we go, honeymoon over. He's done something, shown his true colours. I tingled at the prospect of vindication. We were in the hall, surrounded by my boxes. The featherbed drivers were at work that morning, in the bedrooms, beating the mattresses, driving fresh air through all those feathers. So, I was temporarily displaced even before I'd properly arrived. One of my leather-covered wooden trunks doubled as a bench for us; we perched side by side. We were alone, Bella having been sent to pick flowers and herbs for my room.

'It's just . . .' Kate closed her eyes, hard, then opened them and stared at me, indignant. 'Anne Stanhope.' Ed Seymour's wife. 'Has Ed said anything to you?'

'Oh, he knows better than to mention her to me.' Not Thomas, then. Not this time. Oh, well.

She despaired, 'What *is* it with her?'

'What *isn't* it?' Loathsome woman. Snide. 'What's she done now?'

'She has my jewels, the queen's jewels. Not only is she keeping them from me – that would be bad enough – but she's actually going to *wear* them. She's claiming she's first lady of the realm.'

'Anne Stanhope?' I couldn't help but laugh. 'How's that?'

'Wife of the Lord Protector.'

'Oh, really,' was all I managed; it wasn't worth discussing. Kate was first lady of the realm, with the two princesses behind her, and then, if we were going to get down to detail, me: the Duchesses of Suffolk and of Norfolk, traditionally next behind royalty. Anne Stanhope was nobody.

Kate bit her lip. 'Well, he is first *man* of the realm, isn't he.'

'Well, he shouldn't be. Much as I like Ed, and much as I think it's no bad thing he's in control, it's not how Henry left it, is it.' Henry – dying – had stipulated a council of sixteen men, all equal, to oversee little Eddie in these years before he's old enough to rule alone. But they then agreed amongst themselves to promote Ed to Lord Protector. Not a bad choice, originally, those sixteen men. They're forward-looking enough, I've no complaints in that respect. But Kate should have been on that list with them. Everyone knew it. Even Henry himself knew it. She had run the country so well in his absence, and she was central to his children's lives. It was a surprise to Kate as well as to everyone else when Henry's order was made known. Nothing more than dowager queen: but what, quite, was that? No one seemed to know; there hadn't been one for generations. No doubt it was an unpleasant surprise for Thomas, who'd already proposed to her, who'd assumed he'd be getting a wife on the ruling council. I can guess, though, why Henry showered Kate with wealth in his will but no power. An extremely wealthy widow would be a prize. A dead Henry wouldn't be able to stop her falling prey personally to unscrupulous interests, but he could ensure England wouldn't fall with her.

'I'm dowager queen,' Kate was saying, 'I'm the only queen England has, for now. I was due to visit court a week or so ago and I asked Ed to make the jewels available for when I got there.'

I understood what that was about; she didn't need to spell it out. It would have been hard to go back to court as mere dowager queen: still the queen, but pensioned off. Especially hard, though, as one who was in disgrace for this hasty remarriage to a man-about-town. Those jewels would have helped; they would have reminded people who she was, who she'd been and who, officially, she still was. Reminded people what respect, officially, was due to her.

'Back comes this nonsense about Anne. And I know it's not *him* talking . . .'

'No,' I agreed. Ed famously doesn't stand up to his wife.

'. . . but my problem is that there's nowhere else to go with this. He's the ultimate authority, isn't he.'

'Yes and no. You could go to the king.'

She recoiled. 'He's just a child. I don't want to involve him.'

'He's a very grown-up child,' which was a polite way of putting it. Her view of Henry's son was one that I've never been able to share; I find him stiff, rather repulsive.

'But that's it. He takes everything very seriously; he'll take this so seriously. But because he *is* still a little boy, he'll be trying so hard to please everyone – Thomas and me because he loves us, and Ed because he's supposed to do as Ed says. He'll tie himself in knots.' She looked pained. She said, 'I can't bear to see him do that.'

Thomas would have no such scruples, was my bet. How much did Kate know of how Thomas behaved with the king? What I knew, I knew from Ed Seymour. I learned that Thomas was *paying* the boy to keep him on his side. Ed had complained to me that he was trying to limit the king's spending, to instil some financial sense into him, 'And then along comes "Uncle Thomas" behind my back, jangling his change and undermining me.' I'd asked if it was a lot of money. Not really, Ed had admitted, 'It's not much more than pocket money,' but that wasn't the point, he'd said, because any money looks a lot to a nine-year-old who's being taught to budget. 'And how does that make "Uncle Thomas" look to him?'

Like a saint, I'd answered.

He'd inclined his head. 'Exactly.'

Ed had also told me that before Thomas had married Kate, he'd turned up to see his nephew and got him on his own for a while. The boy had later reported their conversation, guilelessly, to his Uncle Ed. Thomas had appeared to confide in him: *I'm thinking of getting married; would you like me to get married? Your Uncle Thomas: settle down, get myself a nice wife. And then you can come and stay with us as often as you'd like. It would be nice, wouldn't it? So, who would you like me to marry, who would you choose for me?* Eddie had obliged, having several stabs at it: his sister, Mary, for example. Oh dear: not quite the answer Thomas had in mind. In the end, he'd had to prompt: *How about your wonderful stepmother?* Eddie enthused, *Oh, yes!* His two favourite grown-ups. All done, as far as Thomas was concerned: the king's permission. That's how he boasted of it later to his brother: 'I have the king's permission.'

I asked Kate: 'What does Thomas think of this business with the jewels?'

'Oh, he's furious.' Pleased with his indignation on her behalf.

An indignation that probably had a lot to do with an opportunity to take his brother to task and, into the bargain, gain some jewellery. 'What does he think you should do?'

'Go to Eddie.'

I bet he does.

But she wouldn't have it. 'This – these rivalries – it's all beyond Eddie, and the longer we can protect him from this kind of nonsense, the better. Honestly, you'd think we adults were the children. I hate what this – she – has turned me into. Scrabbling after some jewels. But they're England's jewels, for England's queens. They're in my safekeeping. I have a duty to keep them safe. If I let Anne Stanhope get hold of them, no one'll ever see them again. And did I mention that Anne has been saying that when I turn up at court, she'll have me carrying her train for her? And she's serious, Cathy, she's deadly serious.'

'She's mad,' I soothed. 'Very mad.'

'She calls me "Latimer's widow", you know.' John Latimer's widow, as she was before her queenship. Anne Stanhope was trying to make it seem as if Kate's queenship had never happened. 'She says Henry wasn't in his right mind when he married me. She says that I'm her husband's little brother's wife, and that's all I am.'

All you are. Lovely, willowy, wise Kate. Anne Stanhope was never, ever, a patch on her in any way whatsoever. To lighten the tone, I said, 'You got the handsome brother, though.'

And it worked, she laughed. And I laughed, to see her. So, there we both were, grinning away together and, for a moment, nothing else mattered. Two girls amusing themselves: we could still do that, could still be that.

Then Kate said, 'You know, I'm glad not to be at court. This Anne Stanhope business: I can go to court and tussle over her train, or I can just not go. That's how it seems to me now. And it's not as if I *need* to go, do I. Thomas and I don't need to go. We're happy here; really, really *happy*. I did my time there, and now my time's my own.'

I liked that; I was proud of her. Not for being happy with Thomas Seymour, but for kicking up her heels and suiting herself.

'When Sudeley's ready' – Thomas's latest acquisition in Gloucestershire, being renovated – 'we'll probably move there more or less permanently.'

That I liked rather less. 'Oh, Kate, that's such a long way.' A long way west.

'Good.' She laughed. 'The further, the better.' Then she realised what she'd said. 'Oh, I don't mean *from you.*' She laid a hand on my arm. 'I'm *including* you; *you're* coming with me. Well, for as much time as you can.'

Kate had finished telling me her woes and was ready to start getting dressed, so I nipped to check on Charlie. Harry wasn't with us; he was, by then, boarding at court, being schooled with the king. I wanted to see how my lonesome little Charlie was settling in. At twelve, he was becoming too old to be able to occupy himself with almost nothing – a stick and some long grass, a handful of stones and a stretch of water – but of course he was still years away from being resourceful, adaptable. My suspicion was that I'd find him hanging around, looking sorry for himself and getting in everyone's way.

I was told, though, that he was already with Thomas: in the gardens somewhere, was all the page knew. Three of Kate's greyhounds came with me, streaking ahead and then, from time to time, checking back. The gardens at Chelsea are stunning not merely because of the work that has gone into them – so many roses that the household distils its own rosewater – but also the imagination, and I don't mean summer houses, fountains, pools, because there's none of that showiness. It's the detail that's arresting, I thought, as I cut through an alleyway planted all over with thyme; it released its lovely, warm scent as I crushed it underfoot. It's a careful, old-fashioned garden. Rather like Kate was, in fact. It occurred to me that although Anne Stanhope is vicious, it wouldn't be hard for someone to be deeply envious of Kate. True, she'd never had the children she'd have loved to have, and she'd had to marry Henry in his final, dreadful years.

On the other hand, she had no children to fear for, she'd never been alone, she'd never had money worries and now never would. She was living a charmed life at Chelsea. It struck me that perhaps it would be easy to be as good as Kate if one were living her life.

Charlie was standing in the strawberry patch with one of his friends – another of the pages – and Thomas, who was declaiming to a huddle of giggling, basket-bristling kitchen maids. Spotting me, Charlie beamed; it wrenched my heart, that good-natured smile. You'd never know, to look at them – even to spend a few days with them – that my boys are so unalike. Harry seems so considered but actually he's everything, all things, and not least hot-headed: it's all there in Harry if you only know where to look or wait long enough. I don't mean that Charlie's any *less* – perhaps, indeed, he's *more* – but if you could cut him down the middle, he'd be the same all the way through: Charlie and more Charlie, like a perfect stone or a healthy tree trunk. Gem, oak, he stood there in that strawberry patch, my boy, turned into a sore thumb between that peacock of a man and girls with blushes like rose-infused cream. His body, I noticed, seemed to have grown too big for him – when had that happened? During the night? – so that he was all gangle. I reined in an urge to rush to him, grab him to me and hold on fast. Absently, he greeted the dogs.

'I mean it,' Thomas was laughing at the girls. 'Go. Go! Go and' – he gestured, suggesting a search for words – 'put your feet up.'

I had to shield my eyes to get a look at him.

'We'll *bring* you some,' he was saying. 'How's that: your own plateful, picked for you by Charlie's fair hands and my own; *served* to you.'

The notion was too much for them: hands fluttered to mouths, renewed giggling.

Thomas was going to pick strawberries? Dressed like that? I doubted I'd ever seen a deeper green – how could so much colour have been worked into that silk? – and gold thread ran like fire across it. Those leaves around his ankles could have been made from paper, by comparison. *Why* was Thomas going to pick strawberries? Pick better, could he, than those bob-kneed, flutter-handed, well-practised girls?

'So, *go*.' He swooped, snatched their baskets. 'Go!'

And they did, delighted, their honey-coloured dresses twirling around their legs.

Now, me: my turn. 'Cathy.' He was at a disadvantage, though, turned in my direction, his eyes screwed up against the sun.

'Thomas.'

He put the baskets down. 'Men's work, you know, strawberry-picking. No, don't laugh.' *He* did, openly, unafraid of showing those good teeth of his. 'Back-breaking work. But the boys and I' – mock-conspiratorial glance at the two boys – 'are here to do our best.' My son, on cue, grinned. At least he was still in the clothes he'd worn for travelling, not his best.

'Good for the soul,' Thomas declared, 'strawberry-picking. Don't you think? Couple of weeks a year: you need to act quick. I like that. Blink and you'd miss it, strawberry season. As if it's a secret.' A lazier smile this time. 'Reminds me, too, of being a boy: stealing them. I like that, too.'

I nodded at the plants at his feet. 'Except they're yours.' I addressed Charlie: 'I came to see where you were.' Charlie gave me a self-conscious shrug, *And here I am*. 'And there you are.' I turned to go, leaving him be. Clearly, he didn't want saving. Then again, I doubted he'd last long; I'd be seeing him indoors before half an hour was up.

Thomas said, 'Not for much longer he isn't,' and told Charlie and his friend, 'Cabbage leaves.'

The boys – unsurprisingly – looked blank.

I interceded: 'Cabbage leaves?'

'As many as you can get hold of – fistfuls; no mercy – before one of our gardener-girls chases you off.' Thomas indicated a far corner of the kitchen garden, then knelt to begin examining the plants. 'You've never tasted strawberries,' he said to neither of us in particular, 'if you haven't tasted strawberries that have been wrapped in cabbage leaves.'

Charlie dithered, unsure if this was a joke at his expense.

'Wrap them in cabbage leaves as soon as they're picked.' Thomas glanced up at me. 'Ever heard that?'

'Never.'

'French. It's what the French do. Or so I was told. By a Frenchwoman of my acquaintance.'

I did nothing or perhaps I did something – folded my arms, raised an eyebrow – but said nothing, because he, again, was the one who spoke: 'I've always wanted to try it.'

'Well, then,' I said to Charlie, who immediately loped off, friend following, delighted to be in on something.

Standing there, I realised how hot it was. There was no shade anywhere near. Sunlight slammed down. 'You have cabbages here,' I remarked. Not having the room in our kitchen garden, we have to have ours imported.

'We have pretty much everything here.' He didn't look

up, and he'd spoken faintly, his tone, it seemed to me, flat. So, I left him to it.

Incidentally, he was right about the strawberries. Or his Frenchwoman was.

Eleven

After those two or three strawberry-season days at Kate's, I didn't see Thomas again for the best part of a year. I saw as much of Kate as before, though, or perhaps even more. Thomas was often away at Sudeley, supervising the renovations, and Kate would write: come and stay; or, could she come to me? I was at my London house most of the time: near to my Harry. Whenever Kate and I met up that summer or autumn, she appeared unchanged, or certainly less changed than she'd been in those first months of her marriage. It seemed to me, if I considered it at all – and I don't think I did, I suspect I took it for granted – that I had my old Kate back.

She had a project that autumn which kept us busy. Her brother – divorced – liked Lizzie Brookes: that was how Kate put it when she first told me. And Kate liked Lizzie. Well, we both did.

No, she clarified, I mean he *really* likes her. This was new: this intrigued, knowing-eyed, matchmaking Kate. It would be so nice, she decided, if he could be happy.

There was nothing new in her wanting to make someone happy, but until now it had always been about books. To make someone happy had been to find them the best tutor. But now, matchmaking.

She had a point. Her brother had had romantic unhappiness in a spectacular fashion. The marriage that his mother had so carefully set up for him had gone bad; or, more accurately, had probably never been any good. Years into it, he discovered that his wife, Annie, had been having an affair. Wait: does that word – affair – do it justice? Put it this way: there was someone Annie loved, and that someone wasn't Will. Someone who'd got there first, or at least before the marriage ever really got started. Will had been busy, in those years of his marriage, being a Parr, being *the* Parr, the heir; as Useful In All He Did as his sister was. In his view, he was doing the right thing. The problem was that he was in all the right places, and home wasn't one of them. Two small children later, Annie upped and left.

Suddenly nothing was as Will had believed. His loving wife wasn't loving and wasn't his. His children weren't his: that was what he chose to believe. There'd be no Parr heir for whom all his hard work would pay off. And then there was the shame: never in short supply at court. Kate told me that Will shook, he babbled, his hands were freezing and his forehead burned. That was what she knew. What she didn't know to start with was that he requested an audience with Henry to remind him of the official penalty for an adulterous aristocratic wife. To plead for it. When Henry broke the news to Kate, he said, 'It *is* the penalty. Officially. That's what it *is*.' That was Henry all over: official when it suited him.

'But . . .' said Kate. Where should she start? *But* we're civilised, we've moved on. But there was Henry raising those hands of his as if to say, *My hands are tied.*

Kate knew what to do, of course. She knew not to argue with Henry. I'd never have been able to do that, but that's why it was she who was his wife. She could do one better, too: she could praise him and sound as if she meant it. *You're the most forward-thinking ruler that has ever been, and perhaps above all you're a man of conscience. Oh, and there's the small matter of you being a man who understands women – how many of those are there? – so you know how we can be, funny creatures that we are.* Something like that. It would have stuck in my throat but she was good, was Kate, she kept focused. In this case, on saving a woman's life.

Send her to me, was what she requested of Henry. For safekeeping. For now. Will's sick, she told him, but he'll get better . . . but not if he's responsible for his wife's death.

That's how she turned it around.

Don't – please – condemn him to that, she said. Send Annie to me.

Ah, yes, Kate and her strays: Henry would have liked that. He liked to have a compassionate wife. In his opinion, women should be compassionate. And he should, of course, have the best, the most compassionate woman.

So, it was Kate's doing, and she seemed to have done it easily: the immediate saving of one life, the far-sighted saving of the children's future so they didn't have to grow up motherless and the saving of her brother's sanity. I don't know that

I'd have been bothered about the latter. For a man who was pursuing the axe for the woman whom he'd married? Or indeed any woman, any person. But then I don't have a brother. I was – *am* – an only child. Out on a limb, from the beginning. Which is how I like it. I'm fond of Charles's earlier families – his daughters, their children – but glad not to be tied to them. Now that Charles is gone, my boys are the only family I have. Keeps it simple, I suppose, albeit fiercely so. Kate was like a sister to her many stepchildren. I was no more than a girl when my boys were born, but there has never been anything merely sisterly in what I feel towards them.

Kate pleaded well for her brother, and did it so that he didn't have to know, so that he could get on with recovering. Eventually we did have with us once again a good-natured, if emotionally bruised, Will: calming down and slowly turning back into an eligible bachelor.

In the meantime, though, Kate had wanted me over at her house. She wanted help with her reluctant house guest. Entertainment for her, or at least distraction. Although Kate didn't say as much, I knew her own ladies weren't up to it, being an unworldly bunch. No outsiders could do it because although everyone knew where Annie was, she had to be seen to have disappeared. No one else could visit. I wasn't included in that, never am; I do what I want. I didn't, though, want to do this. I'd never known Annie; we'd moved in different circles. So, it was a succession of strange afternoons and evenings that I spent at Kate's, sometimes playing cards or more often doing nothing at all. Annie clearly wasn't in the mood for fun and games, or indeed for anything. Kate and I exhausted ourselves coming up with chatter while avoiding mentioning anyone's name or anything that was happening to anyone, be it trouble or triumph, because we simply didn't know what might be sensitive for Annie. She probably didn't give a damn what we said. She'd sit well back in her chair, arms folded hard and high, making the barest of necessary responses. It was impossible for me to know what she was usually like, even how she'd usually look, this shadowed-eyed, unsmiling woman. What was obvious, though, was that she was furious: her sullenness was suppressed fury. Directed at everything and everyone, would be my guess. And whatever we did, and however we tried, Kate and I probably came into that, even if it was against Annie's better judgement, and I'd like to think it was. I'd like to think she was grateful to Kate and understood that we were on her side, but I suspect she couldn't help hating us. Well, we were ladies bountiful, weren't we. That's how it must have seemed to her. Everything was all right for us.

Whenever I think of her now, what I recall is the slow drumming of her heels against the legs of her chair, the very sound of desolation and defiance. I've been thinking of her a lot recently. You know what I think? I wonder whether perhaps her situation wasn't all that bad, in the end.

She was long gone by the autumn. She'd done her time at Kate's and had moved on to her new life – children in tow – with that lover of hers. And we were busy doing our best for Will. For Lizzie Brookes. We were at our best, perhaps, then, Kate and me. Girls together again. It was harmless fun. It was cosy. It was easy. Kate, being Useful; me, my views on love well known. Kate, convert. Me, old hand.

Old hand? I have to tell you: that's not how I felt, as I watched Will and Lizzie fall for each other. It had been so different for Charles and me. There'd been no mystery, for us. We did fall in love, yes, but only when we were married. Risking nothing. Not that our marriage was any less for it. On the contrary. But watching Will and Lizzie, I found myself wishing that I'd gone through what they had to endure. I was so very sure, then, that autumn, that I would never know what it is to have one's head turned and be held there, breath taken. Not to know quite what one was in for.

Twelve

It was a cosy, carefree autumn, that autumn; insular and frivolous, the autumn that was Kate's last. We met up as usual for the feast day of our namesake: St Catherine, on the twenty-fifth of November. Because we were outspoken on the need to rid religion of folklore, we had to keep it secret, this annual exception that we made. Which suited us fine. It was 'our day', and our 'feast' was exactly as we alone wanted it: steaming bowls of furmenty, the wheat-thickened, cinnamon-scented milk, chewy with dates and raisins; and our rich cream dowcet crusted with burned sugar. We sat at the fireside with our bowls in our laps, gossiping.

November became December and suddenly – or so it seemed to me – Kate had gone to Sudeley for Christmas: gone home for Christmas, gone to her new home. Sudeley was at last ready and she seemed to leave London without a backward glance. But Christmas for those of us who remained at or close to court was fun, as usual. My boys were particularly impressed, loved being in the thick of things, acting as if none of this – the feasts, masques, music – had ever happened before and had been contrived especially for their benefit. Full of it, standing tall, they seemed to be growing in front of my eyes and I saw them, for the first time, as stars of the rising generation. True, they'd been Knights of the Garter for almost a year, since the coronation, when Harry had walked behind Eddie, carrying the orb, but I'd never taken it seriously. They'd been my little boys, nominally in attendance on a nominal boy-king. Play-acting. Last Christmas, though, was a revelation: I saw them shaping up for their future as right-hand men to their monarch. Following in their father's footsteps.

Just after Christmas, I caught a bad cold and delayed my journey back to Lincolnshire. Three days on the road would have been quite beyond me. Taking to my bed for a few days, I missed a lot of the usual London New Year celebrations although I did manage to make an appearance for the gift-giving. My boys had been easy, this year, wanting money. And, despite the expense, I was particularly pleased with the cloth-of-tinsel doublets that I'd had made for the senior members of the household. Bella seemed delighted with her red silk purse. And her present to me was a little bag, too, this one for holding lavender: Holland linen, which she'd embroidered gorgeously. To Kate, I'd sent a length of that new, bobbin-made lace; and she'd sent me a beautiful gold brooch of a bee.

Still unwell, I missed the only event that had promised to liven up the lull after Epiphany: Kate's brother's marriage to Lizzie Brookes. Kate, too, missed it, for the same reason: she was ill. I'd assumed that her illness was similar to mine; there was a lot of it about. She felt slowed up, she wrote to me, and was sometimes sick. Well, the sickness I didn't have. She'd picked something up, she said, and couldn't shake it off. Her next letter mentioned she was no better. It's dreary, she complained: I'm bored and boring and poor Thomas must wonder what on earth he's married.

Ah, yes, poor Thomas. A third letter came with him on one of his trips to London but he didn't deliver it to me in person, sending it instead via one of his men. In it, among news of family and friends, were the words *I'm still wretched, a bit of a wreck.*

I didn't like the sound of that.

I'm coming, I wrote back. I was fine by then. *I need a good look at you*, I told her. Writing those words, I was remembering how well she'd looked when I'd last seen her. This was cruel, whatever it was, keeping her laid so low when she was at last ready to live life to the full. In her letters she'd been deliberately offhand, but I suspected she was worried. How could she not be?

Don't, came back the message. Don't come, don't worry. I'll be fine, I'll sleep this off. It's a bad time of year for getting better, that's all. And a look is definitely not a good idea. I warn you now, she declared: I look awful.

She knew I'd come. I'm coming, I replied. No arguments. I'll be no trouble, I'll keep myself to myself, but just let me see you. I need to see you.

And perhaps it's true that this was as much for my sake as for hers, and perhaps that's why she let me come. Everyone knows I'm no nurse. I'm hopeless with sickness, my own or anyone else's – even my boys', it hurts and shames me to say.

At times during the days before I set off to see Kate, I was frantic with worry about her; but at other times, I managed to reassure myself that it was a bad time of year and hardly anyone was fully well. Plague was around – Elizabeth and Jane's tutor, William, had died of it, Kate told me, during his trip home at Christmas – but there had been no cases anywhere near Sudeley and, anyway, whatever this indisposition of Kate's was, it clearly wasn't the plague. Come spring, I told myself in my good moments, she'll pick up. In the bad moments, though, I wondered: a day or two of sickness could be put down to bad food; and a week, well, it happens, particularly at this time of year. A couple of weeks of being unwell, even: yes. But this? This sickness for weeks with no let-up?

You see, when I was thirteen I'd had to stand by and watch Charles's previous wife sicken and die. Mary Rose: my sort-of-stepmother, the woman who'd taken me on. My own mother was away so much when I was a child, and my father was hopeless, and one of the ways in which he was hopeless was with money. So, when he was dead and I was nine, I was sold. Let's be frank: that's what it is when a girl becomes a ward, *she's sold*. A man pays to have a girl handed over to him with her inheritance, and he later gets the best possible deal when he marries her on to someone else. It was what Maud strove to avoid for Kate. Kate was independent until she was married, and the marriage was of her choice, or at least of her mother's choice and her mother had Kate's happiness at heart. I had no Maud championing me, no one had my happiness at heart and I became the Duke of Suffolk's ward, but, with that, my luck turned. Because what a place to be, to grow up: in the home of the king's adored brother-in-law, with his lovely wife Mary Rose and their children. My lonely years were over.

Mary Rose's illness seemed nothing much, at first. Tiredness. Summer stretched the days but she seemed unable to keep up, going to bed early, skipping a few social occasions that she'd have loved. She sounded breathless, too, full of sighs and exclamations where before she'd been lovably brisk, her habitual expression of impatience having been the pointed tapping of a fingernail. And her face began to look wrong to me: small, the features unused. That big, red laugh of a mouth and that clever gaze had gone slack, flat. Then came the sickness. Occasional, at first, but then relentless, monotonous. Soon, it was all she did: throw up. I was thirteen, I didn't want to hear it. It shames me to say it but it's the truth. Listen: I was thirteen. One day I noticed her face had changed again. There was no longer the flatness to it; on the contrary, she was all teeth, all jaw. And her hair, the amazing hair in which she'd taken so obvious a delight: that mane was now a clump, a kind of disfigurement.

Within a month or so, Mary Rose had slid into a state whereby everything was too much for her. Instead of a strutting redhead whose call to us – 'Girls!' – was accompanied by an arched eyebrow, we had a shuffling, wincing woman, pathetically grateful to us in anticipation of any small comforts we might be able to provide for her. Which we couldn't: we couldn't please her; she couldn't be pleased. It wasn't really to do with us; we were barely there for her by then; she tended by that stage to look through us.

Me, in particular. It shrinks fast, the world of a dying person: I understand that now; I've seen it happen now several times. But then, it was a shock. She had no spare energy for her thirteen-year-old ward; there was no room in her shrunken world for the tag-along, for the girl she'd once casually scooped up and taken under her wing.

I hated her for it; of course I did. And I hated her for her sickness which seemed to me not only disgusting but wilful. I longed to shake her out of it, to shake her back to herself. She'd been everything to me, she was all I had. My own mother had been too busy kneeling in front of a deposed queen to bother with me, but into her place strode Mary Rose. For five years, she'd listened to me, bolstered me, instructed and challenged me. And then, just as she had me desperate to be like her, she dropped it all, the striding and hair-tossing, the big-mouthed laughing, the passion for life. She dumped it all, as if it were nothing. I felt tricked. I took it as cruel.

Now I know better. If I could turn back time, I'd sit and read to her. I'd bring a single, lightly spiced, honey-baked fig. And if that didn't work, I'd clear away her untouched tray before it could sicken her. I realise, now, that she was frightened. I understand, now, that she couldn't possibly have been ready to go. My own mother died six years later and although her symptoms were much the same, she seemed less troubled, less pained. The difference, I suspect, was that she had what she needed: her child safely grown and happily married with healthy children of her own. Whereas no one could help Mary Rose because she knew that her son, too, would soon be dead. Her boy, her youngest. He was sliding down inside himself, becoming all shoulders; he was turning inside out, bony and blood-flushed. His eyes looked candlelit in broad daylight, and he was roped to a cough which allowed him no rest. How can it have been for Mary Rose to know that when the end came for him, she wouldn't be there to hold a cool hand to his forehead? Whenever I think of it, I find myself biting on my knuckles, as if I've stubbed something. The mercilessness of it. Her sunny-natured boy; her deliciously sly-boots, glinting-toothed boy; her tongue-tied, trying-hard boy: everything he'd ever been would soon be nothing. She was still – even in her illness – taking him a night light every evening: her boy, afraid of the dark, who would soon be sealed up in the family vault.

When she was dead, we took her to the abbey at St Edmondsbury. A long day's ride, there and back, on a long, midsummer day. I rode second in the procession, behind Frances and in front of Eleanor, in order of our ages as if I were their equal as a true daughter of Mary Rose. That was Charles's doing, and I was grateful to him.

Charles's choice for his own burial place was the church at our castle at Tattershall. But when the time came, Henry claimed him for St George's Chapel at Windsor, buried him there at his own expense. Then had requiem masses said for him at St Paul's and Westminster Abbey. Spectacular, then, in the end, Charles's dying, or so it must have seemed to everyone but us. Actually, it had been quick and quiet. I still don't know what I feel about all that pomp, about his being taken from us for his burial, but I hope it stays with the boys that their father was loved and valued by his king. And of course he was: loyal, fair and good-natured man that he was.

Thirteen

My preparations for my trip to Kate included explaining the situation to the boys. I didn't want to alarm them, but they had to understand that it was important for me to go and perhaps for me to stay a while. Charlie was to remain in London, I decided, close to Harry, with his tutor and, of course, enough staff to keep our Barbican house comfortable for him. I was mindful that none of us was at home at Grimsthorpe, and hadn't been, by then, for some time. Our absence felt, to me, a little like desertion. Which was ridiculous, because Grimsthorpe would – I knew – be running fine, albeit in its half-hearted winter way. The boys and I are, in a sense, superfluous there. Grimsthorpe's grounds might seem to be in hibernation, but that wouldn't be true of the house and outhouses. Baking, brewing and slaughtering would continue, our staff to be kept warm and fed. There were tens of horses to be tended to, exercised, shod. Chapel bells would, daily, be ringing. A busy, noisy world of its own, through summer and winter, work days and days of rest. If I'm honest, what was making me uneasy was that since Charles had died and Harry had been living at court, Grimsthorpe has no longer felt quite like home.

If Grimsthorpe had somehow come to seem an impossibly long way away, the distance was nothing compared to Sudeley's. Five or six days' riding, we were advised. I'd never been so far west. In fact, I'd barely ever been west. Suffolk born and bred, I've made my home in Lincolnshire and, of course, London. I could have been heading for the end of the earth, but I can't say I felt cowed. Winter does make travel difficult, dangerous, sometimes impossible, but its uncompromising nature appeals to me: it is so much itself. It'll never be mistaken for anything else, which can hardly be said of an English spring or summer. It has nothing of the unfolding and merging, the slackness of spring and summer, relish those two seasons though I do. I'm ready for winter every year. Come autumn, my stomach is pinched in anticipation, my nose twitching at the air's tartness, my fingers itching for the newly furred-over, berry-rich world. Autumn is tantalisingly brief; winter, just around the corner behind the darkening days.

And there are the clothes. Clothes in summer are no fun; they're a hindrance, perhaps particularly in England. My mother was never used to it, how we English don't dress for summer. 'You're the same colour all year, you English,' she'd say; 'England changes colour, but you don't.' But we do dress for winter. And that's another reason I welcome it: the chance to wear fur. My furrier had done a good job, last autumn, and I was ready for the worst that the winter could throw at me. I was swathed in sable, on that journey to Kate's, and started out in one of my new lettice caps, the white winter weasel fur pulled down over my ears.

I was prepared in other ways, too. My own doctor, Robert Keyns, was coming with me, in case I had any doubts when faced with Kate's. And I was taking my chaplain, Hugh, although I'd have no real need of him, knowing Kate's so well (John had been mine until she'd poached him, but what's a chaplain between friends?) Hugh was coming not for my sake but for Kate's: they were close friends. None of my ladies was accompanying me, such a journey at that time of year being too much to ask of them. But Bella, of course: she'd rise to the challenge. She's tougher than she looks, and young enough still to be excited by visits to other households. Doctor Keyns and Hugh were, of course, accompanied by their own travelling staff – a yeoman and groom each – who, added to the usual retinue, made us a crowd of thirty.

Sometimes it dragged us down, being such a multitude, trudging along, churning up the sodden ground; but at other times, it was the making of us, driving us on. The weather was bad and some days we had trouble covering even twenty miles. No snow, admittedly, but at least snow would have been something different. Instead, there was just wind and rain that didn't so much fall as whip at us. I chose to ride rather than be shut up in the coach. Inside, I'd have been sitting rigid, trying to keep my balance as the coach was heaved and wrenched through the mud. Riding, I kept busy along with everyone else and had the warmth of my horse.

We had an unscheduled stop one morning for a reshoeing, then, later the same day, a hunt in a village for something that would function as a pad to cover a sore under Hugh's saddle. Another day, at twilight, my steward halted us before our scheduled stop, just as we were about to pass a farmstead. He circled back to me and suggested I should dry off there and warm up. I glimpsed the main house through a bristle of bare trees. Wood smoke was billowing from the vent in a tatty thatch; below it, I could detect frankincense burning. A sick horse, then, in their stables; a horse with a cough. Not confidence-inspiring: the last thing we wanted was one of our horses down with an ailment. My steward was saying that he'd go and speak to someone in the farmhouse. I was uneasy. Of course it was an enticing prospect, a half-hour or hour at a fireside. But we'd managed so far; this would be the first time on this particular day that we'd made an extra stop. 'Shouldn't we press on?'

'Oh, we will,' he said, grimly. *Don't you worry.* 'But later.'

True: there was always later; unfortunately, there was always later. A break, though, might make it even harder. My chapped-faced companions were fidgeting, sniffing raucously; from the look and sound of them, they could have been treading water.

I asked, 'What about the rest of you?'

My steward claimed they'd be fine. 'We'll just rest up.'

'You'll freeze.'

'We'll keep busy. We've the horses to see to.'

So, that's how Bella and I came to be sitting around a fire in the middle of nowhere, being entertained – if that's the right word, and, upon reflection, it isn't – by the lady of the house. Anxious and apologetic, she wasn't easy company. There were disappointingly few distractions. Her husband was away on business for a day or two, she explained, their youngest son with him. The eldest was upstairs, asleep, ill: nothing much, she reassured us, just a mild fever and earache. I hoped she was telling the truth. Doctor Keyns went up to him, anyway. I felt I should send him up there, even though there was probably little he could do. If nothing else, he'd be a comforting presence for the child. For a doctor, he's unusually gifted in that respect. Having been up there for a while, he reappeared briefly to confirm that the fever was mild and to request a bowl of warm water.

The woman's daughter – eleven years old – sat with us, more composed than her mother, but cowed. The woman made moves to have a top table set for us but I was firm in my rebuttal and the table stayed bare, against the wall, across the room. What I didn't say was that I didn't want special treatment. Didn't want to have to act the guest. All I wanted was a fireside. I confided I'd love some potage, if the kitchen had any to spare. It did. The woman called behind a curtain for a servant to bring it and heat it over the fire. Bella and I were happy to sit on stools, our feet amid rushes, with our smoky, salty bowlfuls on our laps. The lady's array of pewter plate stayed unused across the room on the sideboard. Likewise, in its drawers, no doubt, the table linen with which she'd have liked to impress us. There was a suggestion in the woman's manner that we had snubbed her hospitality and although I understood – who else around here did she have, to impress? – I was unrepentant. I couldn't have cared less. I had enough to worry about. I wasn't there to make her feel better about herself, I was there to get dry.

I was under no illusions that this was a protestant household. Had the woman even heard of the changes? What would a person hear of change, I wondered, tucked under a thatch this far away from anywhere? The woman wore a heavy crucifix around her neck. I hate how the old religion so often has Jesus strung on crosses, dripping from them, utterly defeated. Catholics seem to forget that Jesus was a man. He had dust in his sandals. He was once alive. That's the point, isn't it? Jesus was once alive. And *so* alive. Passionate and inspired; clever and uncompromising. Expecting nothing but the best from people. Think of him rushing, livid, at the tables in the temple. He wasn't perfect – proud, demanding, sometimes dismissive – but he knew it. He was human, that's what he was. He was no stricken lamb.

And Mary, as the catholics have her: well, frankly, they can have her. Their doe-eyed Mary does nothing for me. There's nothing of motherhood that I recognise in that self-satisfied face, none of its fierceness and complexity.

That room in which Bella and I sat was comfortable enough – that sideboard, glazed windows, stools, and food to spare – but there was a serious lack of spirit in such a household, shadowed by superstition. What on earth would I have done if I'd been born into that? If I'd been trapped there or somewhere like that? In some respects, I've had a strange life – being a ward, then married so young – but at least I've lived it among open-minded, forward-thinking people. My sons, too: they're luckier than they know. Thinking of them as I sat there in that house, I had to resist the urge to rush upstairs and snatch that poor, ailing boy and take him and his cowed little sister with us. That's not the answer, I reminded myself. What needs to happen is change, and more and more of it: we need to push the changes into every far, cramped corner of this land. Kate and I, I reminded myself, that's what we're *for*, it's what we *do*, it's what we share above all, this belief in a better, *truer* life for everyone. Fortified, I thanked the lady of the household, said goodbye to the girl, and took Bella back outside with me to resume our journey.

Fourteen

I've never been so thrilled with the sight of any palace as I was with Sudeley, in the afternoon of our sixth day of riding. There it was, nestled in a bowl of hills, smoke pulsing from its many tall chimneys. Big and smart, that house, in golden stone. Our arrival was slickly managed by a teeming, newly liveried staff, and most of my entourage had taken up the invitation for a drink before I'd even dismounted. As my own horse was being led away, Kate's new Sudeley porter assured me that I'd be shown immediately to my room, where I'd find refreshments ready for me. I shook my head, asked him where Kate was. In her bedroom, he said, and I detected some uncertainty, as if he feared he were betraying a confidence.

'In bed?' By the clock in the courtyard it was a little after two in the afternoon.

Yes, he admitted.

That's where I'd go first, then, I told him. I swear he looked me up and down. Understandably so, I suppose: the bottom of my gown was sodden, and I appeared to be wearing an apron made of dampness. But I gave as good as I got – met and held his gaze – which was all it took.

'This way,' he allowed.

I went without my Doctor Keyns; I'd call for him later if I needed him. The porter led me down numerous hallways and up staircases, the floors and steps blond with rush matting, the matting jewelled with coloured light here and there beneath stained-glass windows. The little that I was seeing of Sudeley was impressive. Eventually, he indicated that we'd reached the door to Kate's suite of rooms. 'Thank you,' I said. He stood his ground. Protective, keen to do the job. Good, I was glad to see it. But in this case his efforts were misplaced. I quelled my weariness and something more, a dauntedness: was this how it was going to be, then, for me, here at Sudeley? New ground. Well, rise to it, I told myself. New ground needs new rules, that's all. Make it clear. He has to learn that it's me – me, in all the world – who has Kate's best interests at heart. I swished around him: one step, and he was barred from the door. He wouldn't be announcing my arrival; my arrival didn't need to be announced. I gave him a quick, sure smile: a further but unspoken *thank you*, a second dismissal. This time he conceded. I didn't care if he was on his way downstairs to whisper to other staff that I was difficult. It would only take one of Kate's old staff to put him right. And, anyway, I've been called worse.

I tapped on the door, heard nothing, and opened it to her favourite scent. Juniper: juniper burning in the grate. Clean, sharp, strong. Such a relief, that familiar fragrance and no sickroom fug. It was very Kate to have it smoking away, despite the circumstances. To get it organised. Whereas me, I have all manner of scents around my houses and sometimes none.

The room that swung into view as I opened the door was stunning. Emerald, gold, garnet, every inch of it gilded or painted or heaped with fabrics: over walls, window, floor, chairs. I called for Kate and from beyond one of the doors came her voice: 'You're here!' That door opened into her bedroom, which was even more sumptuous with its gigantic, curtained bed. And there, in the middle of it all, was Kate, pale, propped on a mound of pillows.

'You're *here*,' she said again.

Scattering the attending ladies – Marcella, Agnes, and one I didn't recognise – I laid my hand on her forehead. I'd known from the doorway that she wasn't dying; don't ask me how, but I'd known. She did, though, have a resigned look to her. She usually took such care with her appearance. Not having much to work with, she worked hard at it, going both for grandeur and detail. She didn't balk at expense, and she was meticulous, and the effect was exactly as she wanted: she was beautifully dressed, but there was nothing spectacular in her appearance. In a word: neatness. That's what she was: neat. Now, though, having been so long in bed, her body had the better of her. There was a grain to her skin, and sludge had collected in the corners of her eyes.

'No fever,' she said, matter-of-fact. 'And it's never a fever. I'm just . . .' But she dropped it and aimed instead for decisiveness. 'You know, this is ridiculous. I'm getting up.' Pungent warmth billowed from the bedclothes when she moved. 'I *can*,' she insisted. 'It's only that I never feel quite . . .' But she sank back into the pillows, slammed shut her eyes, whispered, 'I feel sick all the time, Cathy.'

I asked her if she needed to be handed a bowl. Somehow – motionless, wordless – she indicated no. It was more than helplessness: there was exasperation, too, which wasn't, I was sure, anything to do with my having offered her the bowl. I was puzzled. She clearly wasn't herself, and whatever was wrong wasn't in passing. Something had *happened*: that's what I felt. She was Kate, my old Kate, but also she wasn't. Something was preventing her being Kate: that was how I felt.

She was saying, 'If I move slowly . . .' but again didn't finish.

An idea occurred to me, but I dismissed it. Back it came, though, and there seemed no harm in checking, if only to lay it to rest. Lips to her ear, I asked, 'When did you last bleed?'

She closed her eyes as if I'd reminded her of something deeply disappointing. 'Months ago,' she whispered back. 'It's as if it's all stopped. I feel all . . . stopped up.'

Resolutely, I didn't look at the other women in the room. I didn't want to know if they'd heard; I just hoped they hadn't. This should stay private, for now. I stroked Kate's hair. 'Does anything hurt?'

'No, but everything's sore,' she confided. 'I feel sore and swollen all over. I need to get up, I need to get moving. I'd love to go riding.'

I shushed her. 'But you can't,' I said it for her, 'because you feel so sick.'

'I have good days and bad days.'

My idea was holding water. 'You might be pregnant.' I

listened to it, considered it: it made sense. But I didn't actually believe it. Kate? Mid-thirties, never-pregnant Kate? Composed Kate, laid low by a baby? It was unimaginable. She was childless, wasn't she? That's what Kate was; that's what she'd become.

She lamented, 'I've never been pregnant.' In her opinion, too, then, pregnancy was something that wouldn't be happening to her.

'But now,' I said, 'perhaps you are.' Back and forth it was going as we tried it out on each other. The sound of it. This strange but catchy tune.

'No. No, too late. I'm too old.' She couldn't hope for it; that's what I heard. Couldn't even hope. But the more she was dismissing it, the more it was making sense to me. I drew back and raised an eyebrow.

'I *am*. Too old. Aren't I?' There was a challenge in the look she gave me. 'I'm too old. For a woman who's never been pregnant. Because, I mean, why now?'

Well, there was an answer to that, wasn't there. *Thomas.* I had to raise that eyebrow again.

'No.' She wouldn't have it, or couldn't have it. Told herself, 'No.'

Kate, having a baby: she'd rise to it, wouldn't she, as she'd always risen to everything. She'd do it admirably, perfectly.

'You really think so? Do you really think I am?' Her hair rasped on the pillow as she turned towards me.

Well? *Did* I think so? Or had I, before she'd asked like that, wide-eyed, imploring? Yes, I did; I did think so. I was busy thinking something else, though, too: how I'd been a girl – fourteen, fifteen – when I'd had my babies. Kate would be a woman having a baby. She'd experience it differently.

She'd experience it, whereas it had simply happened to me and happened to me before I knew it. And now, for me, it was all over; long over. 'I think so,' I allowed. 'I think so, yes.'

A pause. Then, 'But, well, what do we do?'

Do? Do. She was bewildered, on the brink, teetering, a new life opening up for her. She sat up, managed it easily, freed from the fear that she was inexplicably sick and perhaps dying. For me, well, I was surprised to feel it as a weight: I was thinking, *So, we're back to babies.* Rather than something gone right, it seemed for a moment like something gone wrong.

I said, 'You stay here until you feel better,' because I couldn't think of what else to say. Start with the matter in hand: Kate, here, feeling sick.

'Do we tell anyone?' and, before I could answer, 'Thomas?'

Thomas: I'd forgotten about Thomas. He seemed an irrelevancy. 'Can you remember when you last bled?'

She went for, 'Early November, probably.'

I explained: 'Kate, we need the baby to move before we can be sure.' I was getting organised; I was getting my thoughts in order. There was nothing with which Doctor Keyns could help us – not yet, not unless there were problems.

'When would that be?' She was all eyes again.

I did my sums, took a guess: 'April?'

'But that's such a long time!'

'It is,' I agreed, remembering how it was.

'What will it feel like' – she pulled herself up sharp – 'If there *is* a baby?'

I had to think. 'A bubbling,' I tried. 'As if you've eaten something bad.'

She half laughed, half grimaced.

'But not,' I revised; and settled for, 'You'll know what I mean when it happens.'

'When it happens,' she echoed in a whisper, awed.

And we looked at each other. There we were, the two of us; the two of us and our little secret.

And then we were grinning, and then laughing, because – suddenly – how exhilarating: that there were still surprises to be had, great big, life-changing surprises.

Fifteen

And *she* was changed. She wanted to come down to dinner, was insistent. Flapping away those useless girls of hers, I refreshed, tidied and dressed her. Her helplessness and exasperation were clean gone now and my task was easy if we took it slowly. She was impatient with herself, dismissive of the sickness. 'Oh, it's only a bit of sickness! I have so much to *do*. I haven't even met Roger, the girls' new tutor, yet; can you believe that? And the cooks have been clamouring to see me for *weeks* but I haven't felt able even to *talk* about food. Well, I'm just going to *have* to, aren't I?' From time to time, though, she did have to stop and sit still on the edge of the bed, her feet listless among the angular ambers on her bedside oriental carpet. White and perfectly proportioned, those feet could have been a pair of shy creatures, or weathered from rock or shell. Motionless though she sometimes had to be, her eyes were alive again, had been blinked back into life, and her gaze flashed around us, drinking us down, making up for lost time. She chose a red gown. It was new; I'd never seen it before. She'd always favoured stately reds but this one was brighter, holly red, with golden embroidery – intricate flourishes, tiny rosettes – running across her shoulders and down her arms. Apart from there being perhaps as many as twenty yards of velvet in that gown, at perhaps almost twenty shillings a yard, there were weeks and weeks of needlecraft in it. I made an appreciative sound – lost for words – and she replied with a mere, 'Lucas de Lucca'. A dressmaker with whom we both had dealings. He'd never come up with something this grand for me. But then if he had, could I – *would* I – have dared afford it?

Clearly, a great deal of money had been and was still being spent at Sudeley. Some of it would have been necessary, of course: the place had been long neglected, apparently. But I was thinking back to the stables, to my arrival, my first impression: the new, crimson livery. A whole new livery. And not just *any* livery, either: those jackets were made of broadcloth and lined with flannel. They'd been edged with gold cord, too, and even the buttons were bigger and brighter than any I'd ever seen on any household staff anywhere else. As if the stables aren't already by far the most costly part of a household.

I hadn't been sure that the new red dress was right for Kate, couldn't imagine how she'd stand up to it, imagined she'd fade to nothing in it, but actually she wore it well; it brought out the best in her, lit her up. When she was dressed, I fastened her usual choker around her throat: a rope of gold-set rubies alternating with twinned pearls. And then there she stood, transformed, ready. Unlike me. While she went to prayers, I made do with a quick change into something serviceable.

We visitors had been well prepared for: dinner was spectacular. Kate did a good job of appearing to at least sample most of the dishes, but there were so many that even sampling alone would have been a tall order for someone in the best of health. Boiled beef, roast veal, rabbit, partridge and pigeon. Those at the tables lower down the room were enjoying a lot of fish; obviously there were remarkably well-stocked ponds at Sudeley. From the top table I could see my travelling companions, their relieved, appreciative faces. Flickering among them were the faces of the servers. Those boys were having a hard time of it, run off their feet, their fingers burned by steaming silverware. Could have been my boys there; could so easily have been Harry and Charlie, biding their time in a neighbouring household, learning the ropes and making connections, gathering favours before moving on up to court in someone's retinue and then, later, establishing themselves there. If we weren't who we are, if we weren't the Suffolks but were almost any other family, that's how it would have been for my boys.

I was of course sitting next to Kate. On my other side was Elizabeth. She seemed to be over the death of her tutor, was excitedly talking about his successor. Elizabeth is good at pleasantries – very good – but I'd been hoping for more interesting company. I was particularly keen to spend some time with Miles Coverdale. The Reverend Coverdale had arrived to live in Kate's own household. Forget the fabulous food, the lavish décor, and that red dress: under Kate's roof was the very best mind of our generation. Actually, on reflection, it was a blessing that it was Elizabeth next to me rather than Miles, because, amid the noise and bustle of the evening, conversation had to be minimal.

On Kate's other side was Thomas; she separated us. When she and I had arrived in the hall, Thomas – his jacket of cloth-of-gold – had taken her by the hand, laced his fingers with hers and squeezed. He did something similar with his smile, kept it to his eyes so that they sparkled full of it. All he said was, 'You.'

And she just smiled, an easier smile.

To me he said, 'You've already done her the world of good. I knew you would.'

Kate retired early; she wasn't long gone when Thomas came up behind me to ask if he could have a word. In private, was the implication. 'Library,' he suggested. 'Follow me,' and I did so, in silence, anxious not only as to what the problem might be, but also at the prospect of being alone with him, of there being no one else to fill any awkward silences. The library had been prepared for us, or he'd not long ago been in there: there were candles and a fire lit, and a jug of sweet, spiced wine stood with two glasses on a fire-side table. He offered me a drink, which I declined, having had enough. He poured himself a glass – his cuffs of lawn so fine as to be mere clouds around his wrists – and we took chairs on either side of the fire.

'So,' he began, 'I'm to be a father.' His face softened but stopped just above a smile, his eyes on mine as if for confirmation.

A jolt, a burn. 'She told you.' No longer our little secret, Kate's and mine. His smile said, *Of course she did.* Yes, of course. Of course she did. She was married to him; he was the father of the coming baby. I tended to forget all that.

'It's early days,' I warned. Had to. Men don't understand. Oh, they claim they do – make a show of it, frowning and nodding – but they don't.

'Yes.' He seemed keen to defer to me. 'Yes.' Then, 'You weren't scared, were you?'

'Scared?'

'When you had the boys.'

Very direct. Which took me by surprise. I'd been braced for silliness. Directness, though: I like it, I can respond to it. This was easy. I said, 'I was a child, Thomas.' Meaning that I hadn't known what it was to be scared. Hadn't known what there was to be scared of.

This he warmed to. 'You were, weren't you. It's funny to see you all together: you're so *friendly* with them; you could be their sister.'

'Oh' – don't worry – 'I'm very much their mother.' I added, 'Boys seem to need a mother so much more than girls do.'

A breezy, 'Boy or girl, mine will have the very best.'

'I don't doubt it.'

We both smiled, careful. Why, I was wondering, was I here? Was this it? Did he just want to talk to someone about impending fatherhood? 'You know, come to think of it, I was Elizabeth's age,' I said. His smile dissolved in his eyes; he was puzzled, so I had to explain. 'When I had the boys: Elizabeth's age, I was.' Incredible to think it. The same age as that girlish girl who was playing at being grown-up, trying it on for size. She'd rise to it, though, if she had to. 'And – you see? – Elizabeth's not scared, is she.'

'Of?'

'Of anything. Is she.'

He opened his mouth, then closed it.

'Comes later, doesn't it,' I said, 'being scared.'

'Oh, you're never scared,' he teased.

Gone, that directness. He was falling back on an idea of me, a simple one, the usual one. It bores me. I answered him back: 'Oh, yes, I am. I *am* scared, sometimes.'

'Not you,' he tried again, tiresomely.

'I'm scared for those I love.' Thank God, then, that there are so few of them.

'Scared of?'

I shrugged. 'Of what could happen to them.'

He lowered his eyes; he couldn't argue with that; there was so much that could happen. Then he said, 'But you'd fight for them.' For a moment, I thought he'd said 'pray': *You'd pray for them.*

Which is what anyone else would have said, piously. He was right, though: I'd fight; that's what I'd do. 'Yes,' I allowed. 'I'd fight for them. As long as there were a way to do it.'

'Have a drink.'

I shook my head. 'I'm exhausted.'

His smile broadened. 'All the more reason for a drink,' but there was no insistence, he'd already given up on me. He'd be content to sit alone, I knew, as I stood to go. It was something he'd been doing often, lately, I imagined, with Kate having been so sick. Suddenly tiredness welled up from somewhere deeper than the last few days and I could do nothing but stay where I was. My room was so far away in this huge house; I didn't even quite know where. Down shadowy, chilly corridors. If I ever managed to reach it, then there'd be the wearisome business of getting ready for bed. I was too tired even to acknowledge Bella; I wanted nothing but to stay where I was.

So, I sat back down again, which Thomas took as acquiescence. He brightened, reached for the jug of wine and a glass. He could do the talking. I didn't even have to listen; I could just drink.

'You know' – he handed me a ruby-filled glass of hippocras – 'I'd just accepted that I wouldn't be having children.' He said it casually; it was me who felt exposed by the revelation. He'd told me what I'd wanted to know but hadn't dared ask. He'd read my mind and hadn't spared me.

I was unsettled, and fended him off with a suitable platitude: 'Well, you've been pleasantly surprised.' Dutifully, we raised our glasses to his good fortune. As the hippocras twinkled in my mouth, I was thinking again, *Why, then, did you marry her?* Did he love Kate so very much that he'd been willing to forego the chance of an heir? I'd never come across a man from a wealthy family who hadn't at least one eye on the future of the family fortune. No one gave up on an heir for love. No one. True, he was impulsive, but there are other – better – ways to be impulsive than to marry the love of your life. He could have married sensibly – with an heir in mind – and then found other ways to enjoy life, couldn't he. Although not, of course, with Kate; she would never have been his mistress.

Again, he seemed to read my mind. 'All I wanted, in all my unmarried years, was to be happily married.' Gone was the lazy, confident smile; in its place, a tentative one, and I saw that he was offering me the truth. Not so far-fetched, either. Boys need mothers, men need wives. 'And I've known for years that Kate's the only one I could be happily married to. She's –' He shrugged. 'Well, you know what she is, all the things she is.'

'She's perfect.'

'Yes,' and we both laughed, as if it were a joke between us, her perfection. Or our being in the shadow of it: perhaps that was the joke. 'I've been lucky,' he said, and took a mouthful of wine. 'Very, very lucky. And now I'm even luckier.'

Because of the baby.

But suddenly he looked all at sea. 'Anyway,' he changed the subject, 'what do you think of Sudeley?'

Safer ground: we talked about the house, the building work, his plans and the difficulties of hiring good craftsmen. Then we couldn't avoid the subject of last year's poor harvest, the prospect of food shortages. We moved from that to my journey, and to other journeys that we'd both made, which led us to places we knew, and people. Nothing much, in the end, and it was easy – indeed, surprisingly pleasurable – to sit talking with him about nothing much. When the courtyard clock struck two, I was reminded that I should try to get some sleep, and made a move to go. He stayed, glass in hand. During the walk to my room, I revisited our conversation, dipping into pockets of it so far unexplored: other places, people we hadn't yet mentioned. Arriving, I signalled for a bleary Bella to settle back down on her mattress, and, still dressed, gave myself up to the big bed. As I melted into sleep, Thomas's voice was still with me, on me, in me, murmuring along with my blood.

Sixteen

The next day, I didn't – as I'd expected – sleep in, but woke in good time. I didn't get up, though, before savouring my surroundings. That's what the room demanded, glimmering beyond my bedposts, and I gave myself up to it. First, the ceiling: deep blue and lush with fat, gilded, sharp-pointed stars. If only the real sky were like that, rather than ruffled with cloud and smeared with chill, silvery dust. Then the walls: tapestries in which the thread was so rich and new that it gleamed, changing hue if I moved my head. The scenes were biblical but the scene-stealers were their gardens, trees resplendent with sun-rich fruits: oranges, lemons, pomegranates. Not for this room the usual English grassy hills and grey castles, the pale horses and feeble deer. And this was just a guest room.

I took my time in getting ready. There was no rush; I had nothing in particular to do that day, or any day I was here, being free of the responsibilities of running my own household. Bella took several gowns from their buckram bags before I made my choice. Sleeves, too: we had time to try pair after pair. Then, when I was as ready as I'd ever be, and had learned that Kate was still in her rooms, that's where I headed.

At Kate's bedroom door, I could hear voices, but not the respectful murmuring of servants or attendant ladies. It was busy in there. Something was going on.

Kate was dressed, but lying on her bed. Queen of this house. Beside her bed were those who could have been said to be her jesters: Elizabeth, Thomas and Mrs Ashley. No sign of Jane Grey. Elizabeth was sitting on a chair; Thomas was positioned behind her, plaiting her hair under Mrs Ashley's supervision and making a spectacle of his incompetence, feigning helplessness. Mrs Ashley was responding heartily to his little show: laughing, flushed, fingertips to her breastbone. Across the room, a cluster of attending ladies – Marcella, Agnes, Frankie – were agog and giggling. Quite an audience Thomas had. Elizabeth, though, held herself still, as required. She was good at it. A regal bearing, definitely: that long neck, the held-high chin.

Mrs Ashley was squealing, 'What are you *doing*?'

Thomas hissed, 'But this is what you're *telling* me to do!'

Elizabeth chimed in, 'Oh, Thomas!' Trying to be scathing, raising her glimmering, sketchy eyebrows.

Thomas protested, 'You've been doing this all your lives, you women.'

Elizabeth gave in to impatience and raised a hand to the back of her head, feeling her way.

'Uh-uh!' Thomas again. 'Stay *still*. Have a little faith. I'm nearly there. Don't *meddle*.'

Elizabeth dropped the hand back into her lap. '*Meddle*,' she repeated, mock-disdainful.

'We have to get you respectable,' he murmured, the show now of concentration. 'This' – he scooped up a heavy skein of her hair – 'has a life of its own. It's not to be trusted.' Then, 'Why do you women make life so difficult for yourselves?'

Elizabeth smirked, 'You just said it was easy for us.'

'For *you*, *yes*, practised as you all are. But it's all so complicated. Well, *isn't* it?'

Mrs Ashley trilled, 'Oh, Thomas . . .'

'I do *try*. At least I *try*. D'you want to try shaving me? Hmm?'

Elizabeth's eyes glinted, her mouth twitched. 'I have a *fairly* steady hand.'

Kate had been smiling that warm, full smile at me: *Come over here*, it said. She patted the bed, and I perched. She looked at Thomas, Elizabeth and Mrs Ashley, and then back to me, the look wry, knowing, amused.

'Yes,' I agreed, because I had to, was being asked to. Agreed to what precisely, though, I didn't know. I hated it, being sucked into Thomas and Elizabeth's audience just because I happened to be there. Hated having to watch – and, worse, applaud – a grown man behaving like a schoolboy. What had happened to the interestingly straightforward man I'd been talking with in the library, only a matter of hours ago? What on earth was he doing, behaving like this with Elizabeth? And what was Mrs Ashley thinking, letting him – worse, *encouraging* him to – behave like this? But that was just it: Mrs Ashley wasn't thinking at all, was she. I turned away, to Kate. 'You're dressed,' I said.

'I am.' She inclined her head, a tiny bowing. 'And that's how it's to be from now on, I've decided. No languishing.' She said it emphatically, as if chiding someone else, ribbing someone else.

Elizabeth's voice cut in: 'He might *want* you to stay there, in bed; that might be what he *wants*. To have you all to himself.'

I hadn't realised she could hear us amid Mrs Ashley and Thomas's high jinks. Or that she'd want to, that she'd try to. What was alarming, though, was that she seemed to be talking about Thomas: Thomas wanting Kate in bed. A horribly forward, inappropriate comment. I realised my mistake when she stretched towards Kate – confounding Thomas again ('Stay *still*!') – and laid a hand on Kate's stomach. They looked into each other's eyes, exchanged smiles. Kate placed a hand over Elizabeth's and, giving it something between a pat and a squeeze, held it there. *She knows*, I realised, shocked: Elizabeth knows about the pregnancy.

Thomas huffed, 'Right, I give up. I've done my best,' and Mrs Ashley took over with an exaggerated sigh, tied the two plaits up in an instant and then settled a hood over them. 'Done,' she announced to Elizabeth.

'Come on, then.' Elizabeth rose, echoing Mrs Ashley's sigh. 'Lessons. Jane'll be tapping her foot.'

Thomas said something about going hawking and suddenly they were all leaving. When the door had closed, and the three attending girls clearly weren't listening, having relapsed into chatter, I said, 'Elizabeth knows.' I kept my tone light – a mere remark, a passing observation – but it did indicate my surprise. Surprise, not dismay: I was careful with the distinction.

She gave me that irritatingly untroubled smile. 'Thomas told her.'

'Did he?' *When?* He'd only known himself since the previous evening. Did he rush to her room with the news this morning?

'He's so excited,' she continued, indulgently. 'And now so is she. It's touching. She's acting as if this baby's going to be her little brother or sister.'

'Acting' is the word, I thought. Elizabeth is forever acting.

Kate lamented, 'She's never had much of a family, has she. I mean, Mary . . .' She didn't finish, didn't have to: it went without saying that Mary wouldn't be an easy half-sister to have. I'd go further and say she's probably the worst possible half-sister to have, with that gravely wounded air and high-handed manner. 'And Eddie: well, Elizabeth and Eddie have always been so close, but nowadays that's hard.' Her face creased in concern. 'Being king has – inevitably – made him such a serious little boy.'

Such a repulsive little boy, in my opinion. The old king mightn't have been a breeze, but at least his life had colour and passion. This little king, though: thin-lipped, sanctimonious.

'And Elizabeth isn't serious,' Kate was saying. 'She's a hard worker – oh, a very hard worker – but she's not *serious*.' She looked searchingly at me. 'There is a difference, isn't there.'

I said nothing. Why were we talking about Elizabeth?

'She's a fun-lover, is Elizabeth.'

She strives for it, I thought. There's something off-putting about that. Something I don't trust.

Kate sighed and folded her arms across her chest. 'I do worry about her. She's only just settled here and there's been the loss of William' – her tutor – 'and now this big change coming . . . I don't want her to feel –'

Supplanted.

Elizabeth would be fine, I told her. A platitude, yes, but also the truth. Elizabeth would make something of the situation. Make something good of it for herself. That's what she does; that's what she's spent her life, so far, doing. Elizabeth is a survivor. She learns fast and works to keep people on her side. Has to. I understand it, having grown up with no real family of my own.

'So,' I kept it cheerful, 'who else knows?'

'Oh, if Elizabeth knows, Jane has to know: it's only fair. So, she knows, and has given us her blessing . . .'

'And Mrs Ashley seems to know.' No one had been whispering in her presence.

'Oh, Mrs Ashley.' She shrugged, dismissive. Then that look of concern, and it burned me. 'You shouldn't worry, Cathy. This isn't like you.'

It used to be me and Kate, then it was me and Kate and Thomas, then me and Kate and Thomas and a baby, and now . . . there were so many of them. All of them acting as if they were family. *What do these people know about family?* As if family is fun, as if fun is all that's needed. As if it were that easy. I was suddenly so tired of it, of them; so very tired, and I'd only been there a day.

I said, 'I miss the boys.' I hadn't meant to say it, it felt as if it wasn't what I'd meant to say, but as I did so it became the hard, inescapable truth. *You're losing your grip.* I was sitting there, poised, on the bed, but being silly about my boys; my boys, who – let's face it – had gone nowhere. It was me who'd upped and gone.

'You should have brought them,' Kate admonished, gently, her eyes seeking mine, and I felt her hand on mine, the confidence in it, the perfectly, instinctively judged weight of it. How did she do it? Parcel out her concern, yet give her all. She asked me, 'Why didn't you?'

Let her have the truth then: 'I didn't know what I'd find.'

'Oh – ' She winced, and there was the slightest recoil. 'I'm so, so sorry to have had you so worried.'

Wasn't that just so Kate? I couldn't help but smile. 'Listen,' I said, 'imagine my relief; it was worth it for that. You could look at it that way.'

And she laughed. 'To find out that, in fact, I'm blooming.'

Her queasiness had made her late for morning prayers, to which she was now going. I declined to join her – preferring to pray alone – and she didn't press me. Leaving the room, I almost bumped into Thomas, who was returning, had not yet gone hawking.

'Ah!'

I stopped, folded my arms. 'What?'

He looked puzzled. 'What?'

Me, too, now: confused, confounded.

He tried, 'I was just . . .' and indicated the door. *On my way to see Kate.*

Well, obviously. I made a definite sidestep, pointedly getting out of his way, and he smiled his thanks uncomfortably but didn't move off. We were at sixes and sevens. I took the opportunity, cut through all this nonsense: 'You told Elizabeth.' No preliminaries needed for Thomas, I sensed.

He widened his eyes, questioning: *Told her what?*

He knew full well what. 'About the baby.'

The same look: *And? Yes?*

'A little premature, don't you think?'

He exhaled, puffed it away. 'Elizabeth's a grown-up girl.'

I took him to mean she understood that there was a possibility of disappointment. He could also have meant she was discreet.

Then he broke, a little: 'I had to tell *some*one.'

'And that someone was Elizabeth?' Making it plain what I thought of her. I'd never have dared to do so to Kate, but I wasn't going to waste niceties on Thomas.

'She's family,' he said.

I was tired of this. 'She's not, though, is she.'

He made a show of considering this, head inclined. Allowing it. Then he dropped his head and threaded his hands together, contrite. I opened Kate's door for him. Interview over.

Seventeen

For weeks, Kate had told me, she'd been too sick to read. Like seasickness, was how she described it: she'd been quite unable to look down. Persuading herself that she was feeling better, she was keen to catch up. That's how she saw it: catching up. She was forever anxious she'd miss something. As I'd left her room, she'd indicated a pile of books. 'Look at these! Hugh brought them.' Hugh, my chaplain. 'Did he tell you about any of them?'

I glanced. 'That one, yes,' I said. 'Sounds good. But that one . . .' I wrinkled my nose. A recommendation from Hugh, but it hadn't appealed to me.

'I'm going to sit very still here for a while after prayers and read,' she told me, quietly jubilant.

'Good,' I said, 'because then you can tell me what they say.'

A joke, but I was also serious. It was how we worked.

Perhaps it was *why* we worked so well together. I'm not much of a reader, but I relish discussion, debate. Kate had an eye for details, but she'd hold fast to them, was afraid to peek beneath them or throw them up and see how they'd land. Whereas I love all that. So, it's not that I don't like ideas: give me some to work with, and I will. It's the books themselves that are the problem. Perhaps because I was never favoured – as Kate was – with an education. Reading books was easy for her, came as second nature, whereas I had make-do schooling and am forever having to translate what I read into words with which I'm comfortable. Perhaps it's more basic than that, though, too. The truth is, I'm no good at sitting still. This is how I see it: life is short and there's work to be done.

There was a fundamental difference in temperament between Kate and me. Think of Hugh, my chaplain: we shared Hugh Latimer as a great friend but I'm closer to him than Kate ever was, and I think I know why. There he was, an ardent Papist, dedicating his life to defending Catholicism, and then one morning he listened to a sermon and changed his mind. He heard what Thomas Bilney had to say, and it made perfect sense to him so he never looked back. Isn't that how it should be? I understand that. I *applaud* that. Kate, though, would have politely asked Bilney for a list of references in support of his argument so that she could go away and study them.

Having left Kate to her books, I headed off for a walk, avoiding the cultivated gardens in favour of the surrounding woods, the trees clotted with rooks' nests. The advantage of being a visitor: being unaccompanied, being unoccupied, able sometimes to slip away unnoticed. In the near distance, beyond some magnificent holly bushes, was a pond like a spillage of ink. And Thomas. Alone, too. As I saw him, he saw me. Saw, too, that I was about to try to shrink back unseen.

Caught out, I halted, and we both half laughed, half acknowledged it. He was chill-roughened: red eyes and nose. I joined him – had to, now – and there we stood, side by side at the edge of the water, its dull jade surface snagged by fussy ducks. Tightening my cloak around me, I enquired what he was doing.

'Same as you, probably.'

'Which is?'

'Being alone.' And then, hurriedly, 'Oh, I didn't mean –' *to be rude*. Apologetic smile. 'I just meant, getting out of the house.'

'It's a lovely house,' I countered. A humourless smile from him: he wasn't going to play along. Fair enough. 'Lovely gardens, though, as well,' I said.

'Thank you.'

The ducks, with their ratchedy chatter, sounded comically affronted.

'You must be very pleased with the gardens,' I added, for something more to say. He said nothing, probably not least because nothing needed to be said. '*I* am,' I said, and laughed, and cringed.

'Good,' he managed. 'That's good.'

'Well,' I said, 'I'll leave you to it,' but as I crunched back over fallen leaves, he called – 'Cathy!' – and said, 'You think I should be more cautious.' Referring, I presumed, to his telling Elizabeth about Kate's pregnancy. Before I could respond, he said, 'I'm no good at it,' and then, with a mere nod, was off, in the opposite direction.

I should have called after him, *No*. Because: *cautious? No*. I don't like anyone thinking of me as cautious, and particularly, I found, I didn't like it of him. I should have said, *It's nothing to do with caution, Thomas – life's too short for caution – but everything to do with knowing what you can get away with.*

Eighteen

I decided that I'd leave in a couple of days' time. Just as soon as we could get ourselves back on the road. I'd done my bit. Kate was fine; she'd be fine, left to Thomas. There was no more I could do. I'd be in the way. But then, that very night, something happened.

Two of Kate's ladies came for me, in the early hours; came bobbing with apology, pop-eyed in the darkness. One, I now knew to be Kate's usher's wife, Susan; the other was the useless Agnes. Behind them, lighting their way, was a man, a liveried servant, his torch billowing the stench of tallow. The ladies were a mess of cloaks and hastily tied hair. Ungowned and unjewelled, they looked as if they'd been used up by the previous day and as yet unreplenished. They were polite but kept to necessities; there were no niceties. 'She's in pain,' was what I heard. I asked my own Bella to stay. Nevertheless, we comprised quite a troop, hurrying wordless along the hallways under the dead-eyed stares of Kate's ancestors, our slippers whispering on the matting.

What – who – I saw first, in Kate's bedroom, was Thomas. *Thomas was there.* My first, sleep-slowed reaction was that he'd somehow broken into the room: this must be the moment between him doing so and someone coming to escort him from it. Because this was a place for women. Kate's ladies, though, were mere shadowy, peripheral presences. On the bed sat Thomas, white and gold: white nightgown and golden hair. Holding Kate's hand and stroking her hair, and talking, talking and talking. Some of it I could catch: *He's looking to us, so let's stay calm, for his sake; he wants to stay put, so let's make it easy for him; this is nothing but a bit of a clamour for attention from our little one.* I wanted to listen, just stand there and listen; I, too, wanted the reassurance of his words.

Kate was kneeling on her bed; kneeling down, folded up, as if to make as little of herself as possible. Perhaps to tighten herself, to hold fast. Her face was expressionless except for the faintest stain of a frown, and, if I hadn't known what was happening, I could have mistaken her pallor for anger. She looked up at me and there was nothing in the look. I had the sense that although she'd known I was on my way, it wasn't she who'd sent for me. That would have been Thomas, I realised, and he'd been right to do so even if there was nothing I could do.

I probably just said, 'Kate?'

'I think the baby's coming away,' she said to me. She'd spoken so flatly it was as if she'd been made to repeat it.

'Is it pain?' I took some steps towards her; I couldn't get closer because of Thomas. I stopped at a respectable distance. It made my heart clench to see her a prisoner of her pain.

'Blood, mostly,' she replied.

Blood. No mistaking blood, it's not like pain, it's so clear a signifier and yet there's no telling what it signifies. Both triumphant and sly, is blood.

She seemed to have to rouse herself for these minimal responses. I doubted she'd be telling me if I hadn't asked. I had to ask her how much blood.

'A cupful,' she guessed.

Admirably, Thomas didn't flinch.

I refrained from comment. 'And the pain?'

She shook her head.

'The pain,' I tried again. Not some polite enquiry about how she was feeling: I did need to know. I felt all their eyes on me: hers, Thomas's, the ladies'. Perhaps simply because I was the most recent arrival in the room, they were hoping I'd do something. There was no midwife, of course: a midwife hadn't yet been engaged, it was too early in this pregnancy for that. And no doctor – hers, or my marvellous Doctor Keyns – would be any good for this. This, a doctor would say, if it's happening, is natural.

She shook her head again. 'It's more a heaviness.'

'All the time?'

She nodded.

I hadn't got it right. 'So, it's constant?' I felt awful, having to push, to question. What I wanted to know was if the pain was cramps, but I didn't want to use the word, didn't want to say anything that could imply the possible loss of the baby although in fact she'd already raised it and indeed raised it first of all.

'It's just a feeling of heaviness,' was all she would say, and seemed sullen.

Dashed: that was the look of her. All expression dashed from her face. I'd never before seen her like this, and clearly she didn't like to be seen like this. Kate, I realised suddenly, was one for a brave face. I glanced around and there was Thomas, his eyes wide with expectation of something from me.

'It's probably nothing,' I said, uselessly. I wasn't lying; it was a kind of truth. I'd known pain and bleeding to happen to pregnant women and be of no consequence. But, then, we all knew of such cases. What mattered was whether Kate was just another such case. Nevertheless, I said to Kate, 'It happened to Brigid, and there was no problem. And Joanna. And Honor. You know that, don't you.' I'd felt I should say it.

She nodded, but her heart wasn't in it. I splayed my hands, a gesture of helplessness and perhaps of bowing out. There was nothing to be done, now, but make her comfortable and be reassuring, and Thomas had elected to do that.

Kate managed, 'You go back to bed, Cathy,' raising her head to say it. 'Get some sleep.' Then she said something to Susan about needing the closet.

Thomas stood up. '*I'll* take you back, Cathy.'

As soon as we were outside the room, I started again, felt obliged to. 'This' – indicating Kate's door – 'really means nothing –' It was distracting, disconcerting, that he was in his nightgown. It was *unnecessary*: had he really not had time to throw on some basic clothes? Would any other man of any other household appear like this in front of ladies?

He shook his head. 'I wish there was something I could do for her.'

Yes, well, we're all in that boat. Dutifully, I reassured him. 'You're doing it, Thomas. You're doing fine.'

Again, though, a shimmer of his hair in the candle glow. 'I always feel like this with her. I do so much want to make everything all right for her. Perfect for her. I do so much want her to be happy.'

'She *is* happy, Thomas.' I was weary. 'Not –' *now, of course.* 'Generally, though.' I started walking, and he, with the candle, had to join me, hurried to join me, releasing into the stone-coldness the fresh-bake scent of his warm skin. The glare of his nightgown, I averted my eyes from. Think of him as being like my boys, I told myself, as being no more than a boy. Because that's what he was like. He must be freezing, I realised, wearing just a nightgown, and I almost turned to check with him before stopping myself because he *wasn't* a boy, he could look after himself.

He said, 'I'm not up to it, am I.'

Now what? 'Up to what?'

'Being married.' He spoke conversationally. 'I really did think I could do it, but now I'm letting her down. I started too late. I don't have a clue.'

I didn't look at him, kept going. 'You seem to be doing fine.' Then, lax with tiredness, I couldn't resist: 'Maybe you try too hard.'

I sensed him look at me. 'I do, don't I.' He sounded surprised. 'Try too hard: yes, I do, don't I.'

I said nothing. I'd said enough.

'Whereas you,' he said, 'it'd be natural to you. You were married practically your whole life.'

'Yes, and I'm not now.'

'Yes' – *that was stupid of me* – 'I'm sorry.'

We walked the rest of the way in silence.

Back in bed, my thoughts turned to Charles. He'd never have had a crisis of confidence about being married. Or not when I knew him, but of course not, because by then he was well-practised. I didn't mind, in fact I'd liked it that he had a history. I was his third or fourth wife, depending on whether you counted the first marriage, and he didn't. Yes, he'd made mistakes, he'd not have pretended otherwise. Not that he could have pretended otherwise in the case of his first marriage, the disgrace being public. But that was back when he was no more than a boy, a silly boy. He lived it down and more than made up for it, and people had forgiven and forgotten.

When I came along, much later, I only knew about it second-hand, and knew very little. I still don't quite understand what happened. Nor, though, in a way, did Charles. Or that was the impression he wanted to give on the one occasion I persuaded him to talk about it. The story was that he'd been in love, was keen to marry, and she was pregnant. And then suddenly, somehow – *somehow?* – he was married to her aunt. The aunt did have land, which seemed to have something to do with the change of plans. She was a better prospect, quite a catch. But it was wrong, of course; wrong, and, as such, uncharacteristic of Charles. As always, if belatedly in this case, he did the right thing, had the marriage annulled and returned to Anne. His first love, his second wife. Perhaps they'd have stayed happy together if she hadn't died a couple of years later, giving birth to their second daughter.

His third wife was Mary Tudor and people think of her as Charles's great passion because, in not seeking permission to marry her, he defied her brother, the king. Ironically, it was the sheer audacity of the deed that saved him, so impressing Henry that – despite his initial, dreadful fury – he settled on crippling fines rather than the death sentence. Actually, Charles and Mary Rose's marriage had been long anticipated. Henry had promised Mary Rose that if she did as he ordered and married the old French king, she could, when widowed, marry the man of her choice. He'd have known, as everyone did, that the man of her choice was Charles. The permission was there, albeit tacit.

When the French king died, it was Charles whom Henry sent to fetch Mary Rose. And there, immediately, in France, they married. He said he did it because she begged him, terrified that her brother would go back on his word. 'I'd never seen a woman cry so much,' he told me, still a little dazed, all those years later, and he shrugged: what else could he have done? For a secular man, feet so firmly on the ground, Charles was deeply chivalrous. Mary Rose would have known full well that if she cried enough, he'd do what had to be done and marry her.

So, over the years, Charles had married for love, and for money. With me, coming last, it was both. Charles married me because I had lands to my name and because, when Mary Rose died, he no longer had a wife. My lands solved a big, persistent problem for him. Before me, despite his best efforts he'd only managed to accrue small, scattered estates. He'd been promoted fast and far above his station – by Henry, his friend, his king – and it was a job for him to keep up. He hadn't the necessary means to fund the life of a duke and had to work hard and cut corners. Which didn't always go unnoticed by others at court. Not that he cared: he wasn't proud, and he was always scrupulous in his dealings, which is more than could be said for most.

Love? Well, if Charles didn't, perhaps, understandably, at first love *me*, or not as a wife rather than a stepdaughter, he did love being married. In that sense, he married me for love. He was a man who enjoyed the company of women in a way I've rarely, if indeed ever, encountered since. Take Thomas, I thought as I lay there in my bed: Thomas gives the impression of liking women, but it's all show. Women provide an audience for him. That's what he likes. Charles had many genuine, abiding friendships with women, as well as with men. And with staff, as it happens, as well as equals. If sometimes his friendships got him into trouble – which, of course, he weathered without complaint – they more often did him well. Not for him the factions of courts. For a forward-thinking man, there was a quaintness to him: he was an old-fashioned courtier rather than a modern-day, ambitious councillor. Unfortunately, a tougher world awaits our sons.

I never envied any friend or acquaintance of mine her husband. As far as I was concerned, Charles was everything that a husband should be. Uneducated, admittedly, but true to himself. Slightly world-weary, perhaps, but all the warmer for it. I learned from Charles how to be married and I couldn't have had a better teacher. He'd made his mistakes and he'd done the right thing, he'd married for money and he'd married for love, he'd waited for years and then he'd acted impetuously at the risk of death. He'd had a brief, disastrous marriage, a long and happy marriage, and he'd had children, both boys and girls. By the time he got to me, he'd done it all.

Nineteen

I stayed on at Sudeley for just short of a week. Kate's bleeding persisted for a few days, but then, when it had stopped, I remained there for a few more days, just in case. She consulted her own doctor, didn't need to see mine. She was cheerful enough but didn't move far from her rooms and didn't do much. Her pile of books was never more than shuffled. She had no concentration for reading but talked often, instead, with Hugh. She was tired, of course, but it was more than that, this listlessness of hers. She was distracted, and any tentative confidence in her pregnancy had gone. She carried herself differently, I noticed. Well, much of the time she didn't carry herself at all. We sat around for hours on end, and she'd nap in the afternoons and then go off early to bed. I spent a lot of time with her and a lot of time without her; that's how I remember those days.

On two days, I travelled with her chaplain, John, and Hugh

to churches in nearby villages to see what had been done or still needed to be done. To see what, perhaps, we could do. To check, for instance, that there was not only a Bible in English but – often overlooked – that it was also made properly available to everyone. I've seen a lot of Bibles in cupboards. Mainly, though, of course, we were concerned what *shouldn't* be there: rood screen, icons, relics. Kate's motto might well have been To Be Useful In All I Do and I don't deny that she was, she was always very useful, always thinking about what needed to be done and how it could be done, but I'm *practical* and there's a difference. I don't mind getting my hands dirty. I'd happily strip a church with my own hands.

And that's what we did. Well, we took down some artefacts and removed them. And we arranged for a couple of walls to be whitewashed. That's all we did. But, then, that's all that needs to be done, in my opinion, to reform the church. Glorified housekeeping. Kate tended to overcomplicate it. For me, it's about clearing away the clutter. Getting to the truth.

I know what some people say, that we are ripping everything that's beautiful from our churches, but, believe me, they can't have been to many village churches such as those around Sudeley. Take those paintings: centuries-old patchy dragons, and gawky, blank-faced Adams and Eves. It's rubbish, most of it. I have nothing against beauty. On the contrary, I'm all for it. I'm hardly known for my austerity. The problem is when decoration is a distraction. I'll rephrase: it's not beauty that I have anything against, but the covering up of the truth.

Consider this. When I was a child, I revisited the little church where I'd been christened. The reason for our visit

I've forgotten, or more likely never knew. I accompanied my mother. The story of my christening, at that time, when I was six or seven, was fascinating to me, not that it was in fact much of a story. But it sounded like a story, it could be made to sound like one, and I had so few in my childhood. Or, more accurately, so few people around who would bother to tell me any. And, better still, this story was spun around me: me, who was no one at Parham Manor, or at most someone very small. The font at Ufford was beautiful. Carved with roses. I reached up and touched the roses which other hands had so long ago coaxed from stone and which more hands, ever since, had been smoothing back into it. I wonder if they've survived the changes. There was nothing complicated about those roses. They were just roses that weren't in fact roses. That was the extent of their deception.

It's heresy, I know, but I wonder, sometimes, if I need a church at all. I wonder if it's a church that I need, or simply somewhere quiet so that I can hear what's in my heart. God was a kind of king to my mother, a king of kings, so she needed guidance on how to approach Him. But for me, He's in my heart. Even as a child, I'd look at our priests and wonder: does God talk any louder and any clearer to those men than to me? Those book-dusty, shut-away men; those never-married men. What did they know about love? And it *is* love, it is *love*; that's what faith is. I'm convinced of that. It's not duty. Duty's too easy: you do your duty and it's done.

When I was a child, there were Masses at chapel all through the day. I should have been there every few hours, but there was no one to check up on me so of course I didn't go. I spent my days in the Parham gardens. And it didn't seem to matter. I didn't feel any further from God. Indeed, I felt nearer, out there, than whenever I was in the gloom of chapel, my throat clogged with incense. Left to my own devices in Parham's grounds, I chatted away to God. There was no one else to talk to. And when I was sent to the Suffolks, the habit stayed with me: when I was alone, I talked to God. And when I was married, I talked to Charles; but when I wasn't talking to Charles, I was talking to God. That's what silence was, for me. And solitude: that was what solitude was. Anything but.

And Jesus: Jesus was there, too, when I was young. Like a brother to me, an older brother away somewhere but nearby if I should need him, as if – like others' brothers – he were at court. He'd understand, if I should need him to. He'd be full of good humour, sometimes, and, other times, full of righteous indignation on my behalf. I'd learn everything from him. I admit it: whenever I *did* make it to chapel, my heart would give a little kick at the sight of him. He was my hero. We were on the same side, he and I; I knew it. So, you see, I had a lonely childhood, but I was never alone.

When Charles died, I carried on talking to him, under my breath. In my heart, you might say. Nothing special, usually: often not much more than what the boys and I had done that day. A few worries, perhaps. And it took me a long time to stop talking to Charles, perhaps a year or more. But when I did stop – it strikes me now – there was also no more talking to God. I don't know when exactly that had stopped, but – I now realise – there was no more of it. There was instead a silence and solitude so deadening that I never even knew, until now, that it was there.

Twenty

Naturally Kate's absence made no difference to the frantic pace of Sudeley evenings, with so many people to be fed and entertained. We had the distraction, that week, of a rather unusual travelling band of musicians. Nothing unusual in their stopping by, of course, and asking if we'd have them; what made them unusual was the music they chose to play. Spanish music. That's what they said it was when I enquired. Me, half-Spanish, having to ask. I took to it, which surprised me. Despite my mother, I'd always regarded myself as English through and through, as being utterly of this little kingdom of cynics with its unprepossessing landscape of standing water. But now the sound of the Spanish music, for me, was like being whispered to, whereas English songs suddenly sounded like a lot of bleating and complaint. That Spanish music, when I took it away with me to bed, humming it as best I could remember, brought to mind my mother as a girl stepping ashore here in England and taking a wry look around, while Maud, designated to meet her, stood straight-backed and ankle-deep in cold dew. The musicians stayed for a third evening because I was persuasive and tipped them more than I'd usually tip a band of players, which got me into some trouble with my steward, who would have to stretch what remained, when we departed, as tips for the Sudeley staff.

Even when Kate was with us for an evening, understandably she didn't dance. So, I had to do a lot of dancing that week, with Thomas. As did Elizabeth. Elizabeth, though, was keen. The difference in our enthusiasm could have been put down to my weariness from the day's riding to those villages in freezing rain, whereas Elizabeth had been cooped up by a fireside at her lessons and was raring to go. She was a confident dancer, for someone of her age. For anyone of any age. Her performance always went further, too, than fancy footwork. Sometime towards the end of each evening, when she was returning to the table from the dance floor, she'd loosen her hair and then affect not to notice the collective intake of breath as she shook that cloth of gold down her narrow back.

Once, she went further still, sitting in Thomas's lap. True, it was he who yanked her down but she didn't resist, not really, not more than for show. She sat there with his arms around her waist and his chin on her shoulder, and together, like that, they watched a whole dance. Why on earth would Thomas do that when there'd been rumours, only a year ago, of his interest in the girl? Mrs Ashley looked on, glazed, as if it were beyond her. When the dance ended, Elizabeth leaped up, pulling Thomas with her back to the dance floor.

Kate was with us only on the second evening of the musicians, which was when Thomas made an announcement.

He confided down the table, 'We had some news today from my brother.'

Kate clearly knew the news, because she wasn't included in the addressed audience and didn't look up. She continued tackling her roast apples, her spoon breaking through caramelised sugar and squelching into spiced dried fruits.

Thomas continued: 'There's going to be a Seymour baby' – he winced, theatrically – 'just before ours.'

A child of pallid Ed and the horrendous Anne Stanhope? Poor child, was my immediate reaction, when the very best that could happen was for it to take after Ed.

Amid the flutter at the news, Kate did look up, but still expressionless, to say, levelly, 'It's not a competition, Thomas.'

He looked about to turn contrite, but then glinted mischeviously and said, 'If that's what you think, you don't know me very well.'

And I laughed. I didn't mean to, but out it came, a single note, because I hadn't expected him to own up so readily or cheerfully to what was his glaring weakness. Kate's response to him was a roll of her eyes, with no hint of amusement or indulgence. Nor any of impatience or despair, either, though, to be fair. Just resigned.

Thomas's eyes I'd become rather interested in. Our dancing together had placed us in close confines whilst holding us at a formal distance, which had given me opportunities to scrutinise him. I'd look up into that perfect face and try to see where the perfection resided. To catch it out. A sham, it had to be. There couldn't be anything genuine about Thomas. His eyes intrigued me, not because they were beautiful but because they weren't. Other people look out from their eyes but Thomas's eyes themselves seemed to be doing the looking. His gaze slid over the surfaces, dispassionate. There was a flatness to it, which I now know I mistook for frankness. And frankness, as I say, I like, I respect and respond to.

On the last evening, during one dance, I found myself making a comment to him about his looks. 'Are you really forty?' Stupid of me to say it, because of course I'd have to go on to explain myself, I'd have to elaborate.

'I am.' He sounded amused and, indeed, expectant.

'You could be . . .' *So much younger* was what I'd meant, and we both knew it. I went for a simple, rounded. 'Ten years younger.'

'Thirty.' He considered. 'I'm glad I'm not.'

'No?'

He gave me a rueful smile. 'I wasn't very grown up at thirty.' Then more of a smile, 'You wouldn't have liked me at thirty.'

Oh, and I like you at forty, do I?

He said, 'You're not even thirty, yet, are you.'

I laughed it off. 'But I've had children.' No doubt I look older than my years. Certainly I feel it. Sometimes I feel twice my years.

The dance was ending, the languid applause beginning. Releasing my hand, he said, 'You know, Catherine, you have two tiny lines,' and he traced in the air at one side of my mouth. 'There' – the same flick of a fingertip at the other side – 'and there.'

This was unexpected – both the scrutiny, and his telling me.

And *Catherine*: how come the formal rendition of my name sounded so intimate?

Unprepared, I managed only something weakly sarcastic: *Oh, how attractive,* or some such phrase.

'Actually, they're . . .' But he stopped, inclined his head, seeming to think. 'They're very . . .' And then the slow smile, before he bowed and walked away.

That I remember. And something else, later. As we were parting from our last dance of the evening, he remarked to me, 'People think you're unapproachable, don't they.'

I said, 'Is that what *you* think?'

There was that same knowing smile, and all he said was, 'No, that's not what I think.'

Twenty-one

My next visit to Sudeley was planned for late March – me to Kate again, because she could hardly be expected to travel – and this time the boys were to accompany me. 'Bring them,' Kate had urged. 'They'll like Elizabeth, they're nearly the same age, they'll get on.' As if age has anything to do with it. The eight years between Kate and me hadn't stopped us being the best of friends.

Our friendship had grown, too, during difficult times. I'd begun coming back more regularly to court when Anne Boleyn had gone. Even so, the next queen, Jane Seymour, had been and gone before I was much around. And then I was asked to be one of the ladies-in-waiting for the next, Anne of Cleves, when she came from Flanders. Being foreign, she'd need the best of the English ladies, was the thinking. The request was flattering. And, anyway, Charles was keen for me to resume a role at court. So, that's how I came to be newly returned, hapless, during the Anne of Cleves débâcle. Kate was around, too, and that odd time – the setting aside of the newly arrived Anne and, in her place, the sudden, brief rise of the silly little Howard girl – was the unlikely backdrop to our intensifying friendship.

I remember one evening when Kate and I were sitting watching the two queens, the recently deposed one and the new one. There was Anne of Cleves, dumpy and fun, dancing away, drinking away, making the most of her unorthodox new position at court; and with her, her successor, the slip of a girl who was now queen, all a-giggle. Kate said to me, in an incredulous whisper, 'She's *your age*.' I could have been a generation older than that waif who was skidding around on the dance floor. That's how I felt. I was the mother of two growing children; I'd been married for five years. I felt that she could have been my daughter. If she'd been my daughter, though, of course, she wouldn't have been on her way back across the room to be pawed at by that varicosed lump. It was all too depressingly easy to see how it had happened. For almost twenty years she'd been just another of the Norfolk girls, one of the dispensable ones, a nonetity, so unimportant that no one had even bothered to make marriage plans for her. There'd been something to say for such a life, though: it had always been her own. Suddenly that was no longer the case and her tragedy was that she didn't realise it.

For all the spectacular nature of the girl-queen's fall, I don't think Kate and I spoke much about it, which isn't as strange as it might sound. What happened to Catherine Howard, after she'd done what she'd done, was as predictable as it was appalling. There was nothing to say. And if we never said to each other, as others said, *Why on earth did she do it? Why take such a risk?* it was, I suspect, because we could imagine very well why. She'd been doing as she was required to do, being married to that old man, being queen, and perhaps she assumed that she'd earned some pleasures of her own. And perhaps kissing some lovely-looking boy didn't seem all that bad and if it went further than kissing, well, it wasn't that different, was it. It was more of the same, in a way, and anyway it was inevitable, wasn't it, really, which made it sort of right or at least not so very wrong. And, actually, which *was* right? Submitting to a lecherous old man who'd abandoned his previous wives or had them killed, or kissing the young love of your life in an occasional stolen moment on someone's backstairs? I'm ashamed to say, though, that at the time of Catherine's disgrace what preoccupied me was that – according to her own testimony – those treason-implicated backstairs were Charles's and mine.

My March visit to Kate had us at Sudeley for the start of the new calendar year, 1548. The second new year of the year – second-best, simply official and needing none of the fuss of the first of January – but this one was celebrated in style at Sudeley. Any excuse at Sudeley. Several neighbouring families were invited for an evening of dining and dancing, and already staying were one of Kate's stepdaughters and family, plus two of Kate's goddaughters, and our friends the Cavendishes. The feast's centrepiece subtlety was of Sudeley itself: Sudeley, perfectly rendered in sugar paste and carried into the hall on a board on the shoulders of six men.

Late in the evening, when the immense meal had been cleared away, a troupe of acrobats had finished their performance and our own dancing had begun, Kate said into my ear, 'I need some air.' Stepping outside was lovely, like being doused in fresh, cool water. The sky was a mess of cloud lit by an almost full but somehow small, distant moon. Kate mimed fanning herself, before taking a deep, appreciative breath. 'You can smell that spring's here, can't you.' Then, almost as if announcing it, but also listening to how it sounded: 'Forty-eight.' Good is how it must have sounded to her, because she smiled. 'My year, I think,' she said, tentatively, adding, with a self-conscious little laugh, 'Big changes for me.' Then, cautiously: 'Whatever happens.' She wrapped her arms about herself. 'I can't believe that I . . . *have* all this.' She corrected, 'I don't mean –' and gestured vaguely: the house, the gardens. Sudeley. 'Even if everything goes wrong from now on: to think it's already been *this right* –'

Behind us, the hall door opened. Thomas. My spirits dipped: now we'd have to pay court to him. He claimed to be checking that we were all right. 'Of course,' Kate chided, but she reached for him, drew him to her. 'I needed some air.'

He pressed his lips to her forehead. 'Well, there's plenty of it out here.'

'Can you smell springtime?' she asked him.

'I can,' he humoured her.

'Are you happy, Thomas?' The same silky tone; she didn't doubt that he was.

'I am.'

I whispered, 'I'm off back inside now.'

Kate roused herself: 'No, *I'm* going; I'm hostess, after all. You two can stay here, if you like.'

The three of us, though, turned together to the door. Thomas reached to open it, then stepped back to let us through. Kate was ahead of me when he stepped up close behind me, lifted the veil of my hood and laid his lips to the back of my neck. Yes, there it was: the burn of his breath, in a place I hadn't even really known I had. I turned to find him already walking away into the gardens, blurring like the sweep of a torch. Kate was turning, too, holding open the door for me. My skin bore the faint dampness of Thomas's mouth. 'Actually,' I managed, backing into shadow, my blood shrill in my ears and scalding in my face, 'there's something I need to ask Thomas.'

She frowned, puzzled, squinted past me. 'Where is he?'

I glanced into the gardens.

'Oh,' she accepted, shrugged, and smiled, turning back: back to her guests.

And so there I was. Alone. Kate, gone, swallowed back into the hall; resuming, unthinking, unknowing.

Thomas, scarpered. Deed done.

And me, kissed by the husband of my pregnant best friend. *When she was there!*

Behind her back.

Behind *my* back.

Outrage clamoured inside me, beneath a prickling of disbelief that even Thomas would do this. Especially not with *me*, and not like *that*. But he had, hadn't he. It was done.

No. *Oh* no. A righteous rage fortified me. *I never liked you anyway, and now this!*

I've got you now.

I never shirk a confrontation. That, I knew, I could do.

He was already well ahead, and getting further away with every stride. Rushing along in his wake, I felt small but also brisk, strong, ready for this. Then he disappeared. I came to the arched breach in the yew hedge through which he must have gone, and halted. It was at least as deep as a castle wall. The inside was made of grotesque spans of bony branches, scythe-severed. I steeled myself, stepped in, and was suddenly slam up against someone. Him, of course, having stepped back in from the other side. I knew it instantly but still my intake of breath knifed my heart and my hands were at my breastbone as if to catch it. He said nothing, but then sighed: a slow exhalation. Mine – huge, in a rush – joined it. He placed a hand over my splayed, pressing pair and there we stood, for a moment, steadying each other.

When I was more composed, I looked up to begin saying what I'd planned to say, albeit with the forcefulness gone, but suddenly he was very close and there was a touch of his lips to mine. Just a touch, but then he didn't move away, didn't back off. His hand was still over my mine. My blood hammered in me, crazily clockwork, but the rest of me had stopped dead. What was happening was so utterly unexpected that I could do nothing but watch it unfold.

He did it again: that brush of his lips over mine, his breath hot with wine. That tiniest touch had somehow lit a wick in me, and I was ablaze. And now, invisible in the darkness, there was no Thomas: there was just a man who had kissed me, or half kissed me, or almost kissed me. So I did it back, put my lips up to his. And then his came to mine again, and again, and again, but each time you couldn't have called it so much as a kiss. Our hands, though: he had taken one of mine, laced his fingers with mine, and was gripping hard – hard enough, perhaps, even, to break them. I stood there, ready for the first snap. And then, suddenly, I didn't; I broke away. Walked away, telling myself it was nothing. It was a moment gone astray. A mistake. Only my heart knew differently, slamming itself against my breastbone.

Relieved to detect that he wasn't following me, I hurried back towards the hall to make my excuses and head for bed. Ending the day on which this had happened: that would be sufficient, it seemed to me in my confusion and panic. Yes, that would do the trick. Back inside the hall, I dodged dancers – including my own son, Harry, with Elizabeth – to reach Kate. Pleading a headache, I told her that I was retiring early. Concerned and disappointed, she dispensed a solemn little goodnight hug. Crossing the hall and talking to Kate, hugging her, I felt nothing, there was *no me* inside me. I could have been watching myself from up on one of the gilded beams. There she was, the Duchess of Suffolk, self-possessed, beyond reproach. I didn't tell Kate what had happened in the garden because next to nothing had happened, and I knew that it wouldn't be happening again.

Twenty-two

My heart knew differently, though, and remained insistent that night. Indignant, demanding. I seemed too big even for that immense bed. I felt different, yet also more me than ever before. I wasn't the woman I'd assumed I was, in control and rather cynical: not only, or perhaps even mostly, her. And you know what? I didn't mind.

And Thomas: he, too, was different from how I'd imagined. The Thomas of the yew arch, with those mere dabs of his lips onto mine, was reticent and tender. No use pretending otherwise, because I'd experienced it first-hand. There'd been nothing practised, it seemed to me, in what he'd done, in how he'd done it: not the actions of a philanderer. A surprise, it was, the tenderness, reticence, lack of confidence, and not an unpleasant one.

And Kate's marriage, of course: not so perfect after all.

That's how it all seemed to me, that first night, as I lay

there in my bed, thinking. I wondered what Thomas was thinking. Wondered if he was wondering what I was thinking. And had he planned this? That I dwelt on. And what was it that he was after? That, too, of course.

And Kate: oh, yes, rest assured, I did think of Kate. I made sure to. *Kate*, *Kate*, *Kate*, my oldest, my very best friend. But for all my summoning – *Kate, Kate, Kate* – she stayed stubbornly beyond reach, like an echo: distant, fading, unreal. And, anyway, Kate being Kate, whatever had happened in the garden – and something *had* happened, hadn't it – was nothing she'd ever understand.

The next morning, Thomas wasted no time in finding me, intercepting me not far from my room. Along he sauntered, accompanied by the usual adoring, fawning attendants, and asked me if he could have a word, which was for the benefit of those around us: a signal for them to retreat. Then we stepped away, back into the bay of a nearby window. All neatly done, but the situation was a mess and I had to have it cleared up. We stood side by side – had to, in the window casement – looking down onto the knot garden. Made for being looked down on, that little garden displayed its designs. One hyssop-hedged square of coal-dust and ground-up yellow tiles yielded an entwined K and T. And then Harry and Charlie: I saw them; there they were, below me, hurrying along with Elizabeth, shimmering in the diamonds of faintly green glass.

Thomas began, whispering: 'Last night: that was unforgivable of me and I apologise unreservedly. I was drunk and I should never have imposed myself on you like that. Thank you for having the presence of mind to get rid of me.'

When he'd finished this little speech, I had to make myself

look at him. There he was, very Thomas: lying, in the hope of getting away with it, whatever it was. Whatever it was, it hadn't been that he'd been drunk. I fought to contain my irritation, and simply said, 'Don't worry, I won't tell her.'

He looked at me: I mean, really looked; stopped in those slimy tracks of his, shut up and looked. He clearly didn't know what to think. *Good. You try it.* I left him to it. Continued on my way. The very picture, I knew, of cool and calm, but inside hounded by my heart.

Later that day, I did something that I didn't understand: went back to the yew arch. What I'd been expecting, I don't know, but of course there was nothing to see. Just the underside of some yew: roof and walls of thin, splayed branches. Up close, the minuscule leaves looked less dour than during winter: a dustier green, perhaps, and perhaps a tad plumper. I breathed in, deep, but the yew gave nothing away; there was only the warmth of foliage in general, and soil. It was nice to be enclosed, though: sheltered, greenery around me and dried mud beneath my shoes. Nice to be away from the relentless Sudeley chatter and Sudeley clamour: the slamming of shutters and scuffing of flagstones; the constant, careless hollering of servants in courtyards, and the dogs everywhere chipping away at any peace and quiet. The usual. Sudeley was no noisier than my own homes, but it wasn't my noise, the noise of my own servants, companions, children, dogs. Perhaps I'd returned to the scene in the hope that it would reveal to me why I'd done what I'd done. Or, indeed, *what* exactly I'd done. Acquiesced? Encouraged him? No clues, though. I coudn't make any sense of it.

I arrived back indoors to a flurry because pedlars were at the gatehouse. Some of the household's children had gathered

– the head cook's two infants, the steward's five, the doctor's daughter – and I contributed a coin to each child's funds, with the obligatory mock-serious warning to spend it wisely, which was a tall order, I knew, for a small person looking down into a big basket of dolls and puppets, and drums, whistles, tambourines. Kate was going down there with them, keen to witness their excitement.

'You know,' I called to her as she was leaving the room, 'I still have the best of my boys' toys' – a wooden castle, metal knights – 'you should have them, for the baby.' Then I realised and said more to myself than to her, 'I haven't asked: how the nursery's coming along?'

'Too early to see much,' she called back, 'but Thomas can tell you, he has it all under control.' She stepped aside and there he was, arrived beside her.

Seeing me, he shrank back. 'Yes,' he responded distractedly to her kiss, 'making myself busy, best I can.' Kate was moving off, behind the gaggle of children.

'Very impressive,' I said, flatly, for only him to hear.

'Don't,' he said, in exactly the same tone, and – thank God – followed her away.

With the children gone to the gatehouse, the house was relatively peaceful. Kate's stepdaughter's crowd had gone hunting, all of them except one of the sons who was in chapel, practising the organ. One of Kate's goddaughters, pregnant, was consulting the doctor about swollen legs; the other was visiting a neighbour with whom, on a previous visit, she'd struck up a friendship. While my boys played tennis Bess Cavendish and I were able to take a walk in the gardens, and have a proper conversation: houses, family, mutual acquaintances, the religious changes. I like Bess enormously. She'd taken on a lot, at twenty. Older than I was when I became a wife, stepmother, and lady of a household, but not *so* much so. We have a fair amount in common.

It was she who raised the subject of Kate and Thomas, as we strolled, remarking how well suited they seemed and who'd have thought it? I agreed: who, indeed. But she said no more on the subject. She herself was pregnant – the first of her own children – and she asked me if I'd be godmother. I was honoured, of course. I hope I do a good job for my godchildren; no one takes on the role of godparent lightly, and I'm no exception. Even better, she told me she'd be asking my Harry to be godfather. How he's growing up, she said, in a tone of admiration.

When I came back into the house, the children were dispersed, occupied. Kate was embroidering and, when I asked, held it up to show me.

'Oh, Kate, that's gorgeous!' Any embroidery I ever do shows the effort gone into it; hers could have been untouched by human hand, could have dropped off some passing angel.

'Frankie's design,' she demurred, 'she's the brains.'

Frankie Lassells dimpled, delighted.

'And you're the brawn,' I said.

Kate flexed her fingers. She turned serious, though, then, and came over to me.

'I worry it's too early,' she confided, steering me to a window. To start preparing for the baby, she meant. 'But they' – her ladies – 'wanted to get started.'

'Don't they always?' I remembered with horror how one's pregnancy becomes everyone else's business. Particularly hard on me, at fourteen.

She said, 'I mean, I haven't felt him move yet.' I heard the longing in her words, and the dread.

Please, God, I found myself thinking. *Please. Please let this baby move.*

'But you will,' I insisted. 'Give it another month. Now's too early, you know it is.' Oh, for the blissful ignorance of a fourteen-year-old: I hadn't known that babies *should* move. Second time around, though, of course, I did know. Which reminded me:

'Some barely do, you know. Charlie didn't much.'

Those big eyes of hers widened further. 'He didn't? I never knew that. You never said.'

'Didn't I?'

'Did you worry?'

I tried to remember. 'Well, I *noticed*. Don't know if I *worried*. I don't know if I knew to worry. I got used to it. Realised he was just different.' Different from Harry. 'And, I mean, he *is* different, isn't he?'

She was lightening up now; she'd been distracted. 'What are they up to, those boys of yours?'

Playing tennis, I told her. Or Harry was playing tennis, thrashing one of her pages, who was, it should be said, taking it valiantly. 'He would,' she said. 'He's a good boy.' Charlie had been holding a racket when I turned up, but was subjecting his partner – another page, Anthony – to close questioning about snails.

'Snails?' Kate wondered. 'Does Anthony know much about snails?'

'In Charlie's view – to judge from the intensity of the questioning – he knows all there is to know.'

'*Is* there much to know?'

'Again . . .'

'Well,' she shrugged, 'the things one doesn't know about one's nearest and dearest.'

'Or, indeed, it seems, about snails.'

She laughed. 'And are they getting on well with Elizabeth, your boys?'

'Think so.' I hadn't heard to the contrary. Harry had even deigned to dance with her, hadn't he.

'Told you,' she said. Then, 'I've never shown you this, have I?' beckoning for me to follow. In the adjoining room, her dressing room, she knelt at a chest, opened it and delved inside.

'What?' I wanted to know, but she gestured for me to wait, before coming up with an armful of ivory satin.

'Elizabeth's christening gown and cradle canopy.' Shimmering, they were; immaculate. Angel-wear, again. She held them for me to take, but I found myself stepping back as if I didn't dare. I'd never liked Anne Boleyn – who had? – and didn't feel any warmer towards her daughter, but to think of Anne and her ladies having laboured over this . . . To think of – to see evidence of – the mother love to which Elizabeth had been born. Which should have been hers. Which *was* once hers. To sense the hopes, the expectations that Anne must have had at that time. Not unreasonable ones. Just that she should be allowed to love her little girl. Anne's demise is spoken of as if it was her fate but – and this should never be forgotten – it was the doing of two men, Henry and his sidekick Cromwell. It's spoken of as what she deserved, but, frankly, her only sin was to be unlikeable. I was looking at the results of months of handiwork, the products of the rainy days and interminable evenings that are, inevitably, a feature of every woman's life, however powerful that woman. I was looking at the culmination of a lifetime of learning and practising needle skills: yes, even Anne Boleyn, who'd had her sights set so much higher than the next piece of embroidery. Suddenly I pitied Elizabeth for having had to make her way motherless in the world. What if it were my boys? Dependent on the goodwill of friends, on the survival of those friends. I wished I *could* like Elizabeth, and half envied Kate the easy affection she felt for her. I asked, 'How did you come by this?'

'It was just . . . *there*.' In one of the palaces, presumably; back when she was queen. 'I made sure it had a home, otherwise . . .' She'd taken it with her, rather than leave it to discolour and dampen at the bottom of some pile of blankets.

'Has she seen it?' Would I rather that she had or she hadn't? Equally poignant, both.

'She has,' but Kate knew to reassure me: 'It's nothing much to her yet. A curiosity, that's all. She might want to use it, though, when her time comes.'

Trust Kate to think ahead for her like that. Elizabeth couldn't possibly know what she had in Kate.

Twenty-three

My reason for going after Thomas, later that day, was that I felt there was more to be *said*. There *had* to be more to be said, hadn't there? To clear it up, put it behind us. I spotted him in the blossoming orchard with a man – presumably the fruiterer – and a couple of the usual attendants. Approaching them, I indicated that I'd like to speak with him; and then, when he'd finished with the fruiterer and sent the men ahead back to the house, I steeled myself to walk purposefully towards him. Once there, though, in front of him, I was lost for words and could only stand with my arms resolutely folded. He took a step towards me and, sighing, laid his head on mine. So, there we were, alone, forehead to forehead, shielded – just – from the house by trees. We kissed, then, in a small way. His tongue slid against mine. I didn't resist. It was as if he had exacted a promise. 'Come with me,' he whispered.

'Where?'

He led the way, which was how we ended up again in that tiny chamber of spiky leaves, where we kissed differently. None of the previous guardedness now. This was something we did now, rather than something we were merely trying.

Gift flashed into my mind: *You are – this is – a gift.* He cupped my face, laid his lips to the tip of my nose, then to each eyelid, then my forehead. On tiptoe, I took his mouth back down to mine. He slipped free, this time down my throat and across to a shoulder. Again, though, I took his mouth to mine and, celebrating my catch, pushed my tongue against his. His laugh was a kind of wince. 'Not just yet,' he said. Then, 'Could you meet me in the bower on the island?'

The green- and gold-painted pavilion, its columns feathery with honeysuckle, on an island in one of the fish ponds. In the furthest reaches of the garden.

My heart shrank. 'You've done this before, haven't you.'

'Never,' he said, calmly, as if he'd been expecting this from me. Then, 'Listen, I'm going to tell you something. There you were, back in the old days, the wife of the king's right-hand man: deeply respectable, except that everything you said and everything you did belied it. Do you have any idea how intoxicating that was for me? Nothing's changed,' he urged. 'That's still you.' And, 'I've never done this with anyone else. I've never wanted to. But, then, there never has been anyone like you, has there.'

I didn't listen to him; heard him, yes, but told myself not to believe him. I did say, though, 'The bower, then: when? How?'

'Late? Very late. And by moonlight; no lantern.'

'Tonight?' Again, 'But how?'

He considered. 'You don't sleep well, do you. You need a walk.'

'Alone? At that time of night?'

'Safest time,' he said. 'No one's around, are they? Well, not a walk, then; a sit on the back steps or something. Some air. You've only your own maidservant to give the slip.'

'Bella probably won't even wake.' Then, 'What about dogs, though?' I didn't want to be surprising a dog in the dark.

'All in at night here.'

'You're sure?'

'I'm sure. And I'll make double sure, I promise.'

'And what about *you*?'

'Me?'

'How will *you* get away?'

'Oh, me,' he laughed. 'I'm a law unto myself – didn't you know?'

If I stopped to think, I'd think *No*. I pressed onwards: 'What, then? Two o'clock?'

'Make it one.'

'Two would be safer,' I said.

'I don't think I can wait till two.' He laid his fingertips on my lips. 'One o'clock.'

So, you see? That's how it happens. It happens, *it's already happening*. Not *if* but how, where, when.

All that day, my boys came and went in crowds of boys, mud-splattered, mentioning people and places unknown to me; they could have been talking in code. Running wild, they were, albeit in their own well-mannered way. Good luck to them, I decided: they rarely have the chance. Elizabeth made a show of having declined their company. She and Jane seemed embarked upon some particularly demanding project for their new tutor, heads bowed over their books in an especially studious manner. Kate met with her steward to discuss a forthcoming distribution of alms in one of the villages, and then her choirmaster came along to make a case for the household needing a new harp. Next up was the wine merchant, passing through: a meeting with him and the keeper of the cellars. Then there was some business about pilfering from the laundry, before Kate nipped across the courtyard to call in on a servant who'd recently had twins, one of whom was so far surviving.

All day, I felt unable to take a whole breath, as if I were at odds with air itself. I watched Thomas with Kate, whenever they were together. Kate fussing in that unfussy way of hers, and Thomas humouring her. Like brother and sister, I decided: their obvious affection for each other laced with good-humoured impatience. Thomas saw to Kate's immediate, physical comforts, and attempted to entertain her. She made a show of keeping him in line, or trying to. That's how it'll go on, I felt, and on, and on, and I was glad I had no part in it.

I was half fascinated, though, because the Thomas whom I watched rearranging Kate's cushions wasn't the Thomas I now knew. *I know you*, was what I found myself thinking. *I know about you and you know about me.*

You, who kisses me for dear life.

I knew he didn't kiss Kate like that. Don't ask me how I knew; I just knew. Nor Elizabeth: that had indeed just been silliness, had been nothing; I knew that now, too.

Towards the end of the afternoon, I napped; or said I was going to nap. 'That's unlike you,' Kate worried, as I excused myself. 'Are we wearing you out?' I sent Bella from the room and lay on my gigantic bed, its hangings tied back, and stared across the room at the closed shutters, the thread of daylight in each seam. I let the sounds of the house wash over me, sounds which, up there in my room, were few, distant and indistinct. The brief growl of a door, here and there, closing into its frame. Sprinkles of footfalls: an overburdened floorboard, the chipping of leather soles at stone stairs. Not Kate's: she, I knew, had finally settled to some reading for an hour or two. Elizabeth and Jane, on the other hand, were having to leave their books for a dress fitting. Somewhere way below me, they were being encircled by strips of parchment into which new notches were being made to mark their growth (or, in tiny Jane's case, probably not). Elizabeth would be voicing opinions and suggestions – *that* red, *this* style of sleeve – to a ceaseless accompaniment from Mrs Ashley and a grudging, disapproving silence from Jane who favoured only black. No sound at all from outside the house: we might have been at sail, all of us, on a calm sea.

Hours later, I was back in that bed, now canopied, but listening hard. Quite what for, though, I don't think I knew. Silence, I suppose. A gap opening up in all the sounds of that house as it settled down for the night; a gap I could walk through into the gardens. And a deepening of Bella's breathing: that, too, of course. I lay there wondering how long past midnight it was, how close to the strike of one. Thinking that I should have agreed to leave my room at one, not arrive at the bower at one. I'd be late and he'd be gone, thinking I'd changed my mind. Even if I was on time, though, would he be there? Or would he have forgetten, or fallen asleep? Or had he never been serious? There'd been nothing from him all day to indicate otherwise; not so much as a catching of my eye. I lay there wondering if it was he who'd chosen the décor for my room, unknowing; unknowing that it would be me lying here looking at it one night, like this, in trepidation.

Eventually I took a chance on it being close to one and slipped from my bed, lit myself a candle. Pulled a cloak around me. For now, I kept the hood down on my shoulders. I knelt beside Bella, dodging her ale-musty breath. Hospitality was lavish in this household; we were all plied with more food and drink than we could comfortably manage. I regretted having to rouse her, but it had to be done; I couldn't risk her waking and finding me gone, raising the alarm. A squeeze of her shoulder did the trick, but she looked panicked as she opened her eyes.

'No –' I hushed her, 'I can't sleep. I'm slipping outside for some air. Don't worry about me. Yes?'

She frowned, perhaps confused, perhaps concerned.

I insisted: 'Yes?'

Her face relaxed.

'Good girl.' I patted her back down.

My own breathing was infuriatingly shaky. Luckily for me, she was too far gone to notice.

And then I was off on my own; gloriously on my own, almost as I'd been as a girl, the difference being that this was in darkness and someone was going to be alone *with* me. As I cut through the gardens, the house sank behind me, unseeing and insensible. My mind's eye flickered to my boys, sleeping safe and sound in there, sated with fresh air and adventures. They seemed both close by and far away, and it felt right, it all felt very right: them, there; and me, off on my own little adventure. When the darkness turned jagged with bats, I lost heart somewhat and cringed beneath my hood. Statues, too: they bothered me, seemed to be stepping from the foliage because suddenly there'd be one – marble glowing in moonshine – where I could have sworn there'd previously been nothing. Here and there were cats' eyes, scandalised or malevolent. What was gone from the gardens was the sound of the fountains. Somehow, they'd been switched off. Somewhere nearby was water, glistening and lifeless. My own silence I listened to in disbelief. How odd that, as I hurried frantically, I made no sound at all.

I was thinking, *I can't do this*. And then, *But I can, and no one will know.* I was thinking, *I have to find out.* Although what, I didn't know. As for Kate: this was nothing to Kate, was my view. What was this, compared to what she had with Thomas? She had that fabulous house behind me, full of their friends and relations. She had her pregnancy, their growing child. She had Thomas forever adjusting her pillows. Whereas this – this running through darkness, this meeting up – was something else.

Bess, too: I thought of Bess Cavendish, back there in the house. Bess, with whom only yesterday I'd imagined I had so much in common. The twenty-year-old newlywed who regarded Kate and Thomas as a good match. The rosy-cheeked mother-to-be of my unborn godchild. What would she make of this if she knew? She wouldn't, would she: she'd be unable to make anything of it. No one except Thomas would understand this.

I hesitated at the little bridge, reluctant to be marooned on the island if he wasn't already there. Fearful of being in the deeper darkness of the bower, listening for footsteps and having no route away except for the bridge over which those footsteps would be coming.

'Thomas?' I was halfway across.

'Here.' Inside, he was invisible to me. 'What kept you?' he joked.

I paused on the threshold, my eyes adjusting, Thomas's silhouette forming. 'What would Kate say if she knew about this?' I hadn't planned to say it, even to *think* it, but there it came, crashing in on us.

'Hey, hey, hey,' he whispered, admonished, taking my arm. 'She *won't* know about this, will she.'

'Over my dead body. I love her, Thomas,' I insisted, as if he were disputing it and I hated him for it. 'I love her.'

'Well, that we share,' he said. 'And now can we stop talking about Kate? Kate's inside, asleep.' The smells of the evening – smoke, drink – were around him like an echo. 'She's fine, she's happy, Cathy. Which is what matters.' Then, '*I* love her, remember? I *chose* her, she's my *wife*. This isn't about Kate; this has nothing to do with Kate.'

He was in his nightgown, I noticed with a jolt; I don't know what I'd expected. After all, I was in mine. So, there we were, both of us in our nightgowns like a married couple yet obviously not like any married couple. He lessened his grip on my arm and slid his hand down to mine, which could have been a kind of retreat except that he'd then turned my wrist and raised the underside to his lips. Kissing his way back up my arm to the crook of my elbow, he nosed into the sleeve of my gown. I inhaled the scent of his hair, found myself cradling his head. Then he was lower still, kneeling in front of me, pressing his face into my gown. I felt stranded, too tall, unsteady, and held onto his head. Now he was gathering up my gown – linen beating in the air – and up it came and down, covering him. So, he was gone from me, even as he came so much closer. His shrouded head was no head at all now but something strange. And his tongue was no longer the puppy of our previous kisses, rolling around, playful and unpredictable, but was sleek, strong and shocking in its precision. I stood my ground; had to. I was rooted, my feet – still shod – planted apart. He had me so still, straining in my stillness to be more and more still, straining for his touch but not daring to seek it. Nothing else mattered but the tip of his tongue. I was aware of the pleading in my stance and half ashamed by it, half thrilled. I was at his mercy, anticipating each lick as I would a pain: I was shrunk to it; there was nothing else to me.

Then he stopped, reappeared. 'Down,' I think he said, with a tug to my hand. My legs were shaking so much that I could barely bend them; I got to my knees as if I were clambering down into somewhere. And there we were, face to face in the darkness, and I detected his smile, a greeting.

'There's nothing on the floor,' I whispered.

'There's *me* on the floor. Get on top of me.'

My hands were on his shoulders so, when he lay down, he pulled me towards him. And there we were, together. Moments later, he gave a low, brief laugh of surprise at how easy it was. For me, there was a clarity as if I'd remembered something vital – the key, the answer – although actually I'd never known it.

Twenty-four

The next morning, my lips were sore, stubble-scoured. Anyone looking very closely would have seen the telltale blurring, but of course no one did.

'I've found us a room,' Thomas whispered to me, his mouth barely moving, his eyes carefully blank and looking elsewhere, nowhere. So, it was going to happen again. We were in Kate's room for a visit from the haberdasher. Thomas had chosen cambric for some new shirts, and Kate had bought lawn for their ruffs, fustian for lining some children's riding jackets, and five thousand pins. She had moved on to look at small items, taking the opportunity to stock up, and was now contemplating a goddaughter's forthcoming birthday. 'These, perhaps, d'you think?' she was asking Mrs Ashley, who was groaning with pleasure, stroking a pair of Spanish leather gloves which had slits in the fingers for showing off the wearer's rings. 'Lovely, aren't they? And then there's

Frankie: her birthday's next month, too, and I was wondering . . .' They sorted through pearl buttons and tortoise-shaped buttons fixed to cards, through spools of ribbon.

Thomas: I was breathing him in, taking him deep down. 'Where?'

'I'll show you. Go to the far gate of the knot garden. Immediately before supper.'

When the time came, I simply stepped back, and back, and drifted away as if I'd forgotten something, as if I had to attend to something. All day I'd worried about how I'd do it, but it was easy. A good time for it: the end of the day but the evening hadn't yet quite begun; a time when most of us withdraw, to finish up the business of the day and prepare for the evening. Dressing to be done, perhaps bathing. A walk, maybe, to wind down or wake up. In a big household, everyone assumes you're with someone else. Kate was at prayers with Jane Grey, Elizabeth and Mrs Ashley.

The area of the gardens stipulated by Thomas hadn't had any sun since the morning and then probably only obliquely. The air was sharp, and rather than return to my room and risk encountering Bella, I'd had to come as I was, cloakless. Thomas had been leaning back against a wall; he straightened up and came towards me with what seemed to be a genuine smile. 'You look lovely.' He was dazzlingly blond, boyish. My heart squeezed, but I said nothing.

'Come on.' He took me by the arm. Around the corner, we were into even deeper shade. We were near the fish ponds. The garden here was yew-heavy, yew-sombre, and doggedly topiaried as if to make something of nothing much. Making, though, for a rather peculiar landscape.

We reached a door and he took a key from the ring on

his belt. 'I have the only key, as far as I know.' In a household of this size, there'd always be a risk. 'This little room has its own staircase.'

An impressive find. 'What is it, this room?' I tried to sound businesslike; had no idea how else to be. We were climbing the narrow, spiral stone staircase, him leading the way.

'Just a room, a vacant one. Next staircase along is our doctor and his man and a couple of rooms for my men and theirs. It's all men over here; they're never here, they're all off' – he glanced down at me from the top step, laughed – 'doing whatever men do.'

What do men do? *This*, judging from Thomas. I felt guileless. *I won't, of course, do it: come to this room. I'm merely going to look around and imagine having such a life. Being such a person.*

But I was also thinking, *When do we begin?*

It was a room with a bed. A bedroom then, although no one's in particular. No, not a bedroom: a room with a bed. A room not much bigger than its bed, not least because the bed was huge, incongruous in this backstairs room. It was bare, stripped of its hangings and its mattress uncovered. The room, too: any hangings from the walls were gone; there was simply the shoulder-high panelling and, above it, plaster. The fireplace was swept, and there were no candles.

'What else is good about this room,' Thomas was saying, 'is that the bed's up.' Not dismantled, stacked away. I ran my fingertips down a post, over the ornately carved and gilded wood, but the gilt was fragile, brittle, coming away in flecks. 'I do like this one.' Thomas admired it. 'It was from my mother's old house.'

I recoiled, made a face.

'What?'

'Nothing.' *If you don't know, I'm not going to tell you.*

It took him a moment, but then he did know. 'Oh, honestly, Cathy! I'd like to think my mother would be happy for me. That *I'm* happy. Isn't that what you want for Harry and Charlie? That they live their lives to the full?' To my surprise, he was serious; he was looking searchingly at me, making it hard for me to avoid his gaze. I had to answer him, and properly, because he'd brought the boys into this and I didn't want their names taken in vain. It was dizzying, being here with him and then having to think seriously of my boys.

'What I want for both of my boys is that they're married to the right person.'

'And I'm not?' He was quick, bringing me up sharp.

He was indeed married to the right person, wasn't he. Problem was, *she* wasn't. I turned to the window, tried to open the shutters.

'And you were, weren't you,' he said, pleasantly disinterested, as if we were discussing the weather. 'You were married to the right person.'

I said, 'Please don't talk about Charles. Or the boys.' I didn't want anyone else brought into this room with us.

'I'm sorry,' he said, and did seem to be. 'You're absolutely right. And that's my point: it's different – *this* – from all that.'

This: what was it, *this*? A fragment of memory: his mouth on mine, and him pressed against me.

That was what it was, and I felt appalled and thrilled all at once.

I said, 'These' – shutters – 'won't open.'

'The view's important, is it?' He sounded amused, reached past me to give them a shove.

'Better not be,' I said, glancing out, 'because there isn't one.'

He went to laugh but fell short, gripped my shoulders instead. 'This isn't nothing, you know. Not for me. This is nowhere near nothing.' Then he did half laugh, at his own gibberish; then stopped and put his lips to mine just once. 'This is everything, really, isn't it,' he said softly to my mouth, 'when all's said and done?'

My body was immediately in agreement. My body was his. An actual pain it was, my ache for him.

'Supper,' I managed: a reminder that we'd be missed, very soon.

'You're right,' he said, and let me go, stood aside for me to lead the way back.

Twenty-five

You want me to say how hard it was, to cheat on my pregnant best friend. You don't want to hear how easy it was.

The first time in that room, Thomas and I were naked. I lay back on the bed and Thomas knelt between my knees to kiss my nipples, then my navel, before moving further down. His mouth turned so wet I could hardly feel it, couldn't feel enough of it. When he did finally push inside me, I held him by the hips, held him there, moved him there. *Just there.* I loved how little I needed of him.

I did need to look at him, though. To look and look and look. If anyone had asked why I did what I did, I'd have said, *Look at him*. Strenuous, it felt to me, my looking: a drinking down of him, which I was forever wanting to do better, harder, *more.* Whenever we were together, I'd be prompting him to turn, or I'd be holding him or positioning myself so that I could properly take in the sight of him. From the generous indentation on the crest of his lip, to the perfect, modest one-fingertip-sized indentation of his belly button. He'd laugh, sometimes, almost bashful, and perhaps half-heartedly dodge me, but actually he was the same: this was something we shared, that we never closed our eyes. His gaze was as bold and thorough on me as his hands. In those first few days I spent what felt like hours idling over Thomas, my eyes, fingertips and lips travelling the curves and textures of him. The striking flatness between his boyishly jutting hipbones. The springiness of the little fair hairs of his thighs. The silky skin in the fold between thigh and buttock, and the velvety skin right underneath him.

We never did have hours, though, of course, nor probably even so much as an hour. Yet each speck of time we had together sprung wide like level water. That dazzled me, that magic trick, and of course I went back and back for it.

I never worried that we'd be discovered. What we were doing had no place at Sudeley, so, while we were doing it, we were invisible. Nobody would be looking for this; nobody would see it. And as soon as we were back among others, there was indeed nothing to discover. It had happened, it had gone, we'd had what we needed of each other and, later, in company, barely glanced at each other. If Kate had confronted me, I'd probably have laughed, said, *Don't be absurd*, and believed myself because it *was* absurd.

And we *were* invisible in such a big household, particularly Kate's household: everyone so busy. Kate's time was taken up by those in need of her, and books and prayers. Her ladies were mere girls and stayed close to her. My boys were always off romping elsewhere, relishing the riches of Sudeley. Jane Grey had her nose in a book, and Mrs Ashley had her backside on a cushion. Elizabeth, though, I did fear. My first sight of her as a member of Kate's household: she'd been alone down by the river at Chelsea. As quick-footed as she was sharp-eyed, she could often, I noticed, give Mrs Ashley the slip. For all the strenuous appearance to the contrary, she didn't quite belong in the Sudeley household and I was forever half expecting to turn a corner and come across her.

Thomas didn't talk much to me when we were in our little room – which I liked: he, who with everyone else seemed never to stop – and his only talk was about where he wanted to take me. Down in the kitchens, deserted at night, up on one of the wide, scrubbed tables. Down further, in the wine cellar, wedged behind the barrels, the glow from our candle bouncing around the vaults. Out in the gardens, at the beebole wall, me perched on the rim of one of the hive-sized niches. Or in the maze.

'The maze?'

'They're being grown higher, that's what I've heard. New style. Higher than a person.'

That foxed me. 'You'd get lost.'

He grinned. 'I think that's the idea.' Then, a little more seriously, 'With a maze like that, at Sudeley, we'd be laughing, you and I.'

'But quietly.' I laid two fingertips to his lips.

'Chapel,' those lips said.

I took my hand away and sat up. 'Don't, Thomas. Please.' Even though I knew he wasn't serious.

He protested, wide-eyed, 'No one's ever there. Not like it used to be, in the old days.' Then he made it worse by adding, 'There's her walkway, too.' Kate's, he meant: the covered walkway from her apartment straight to chapel, that long, timber-built gallery.

I said, 'Did you do it there with her?'

That stopped him. He sat up. 'Good God, Cathy.' And then, as if to a recalcitrant child: 'Do you want to know how – where, when – Kate and I made love?' *Made love.* And past tense: no sex during pregnancy, of course. 'Do you? Because if you do, I'll tell you.' He would have, too. No, I said, chastened: no, I didn't want to know.

The second time in the room, we hadn't yet got quite naked, either of us, when he suggested, 'Lie on your front.' Him, still in his voluminous linen shirt; me, stripped of my gown and my petticoat but not my woollen stockings. I went to ease down a garter, slide a stocking down, but he laid a hand over mine and indicated with an sharp inclination of his head that I should turn over. I did so, and lay with my head on my folded arms. Behind me, he rummaged in the one chest that was in the room. 'Pillows,' he was saying. 'We need a pillow.' He came up with a bolster. 'Here.' Under my hips. I felt absurdly exposed and turned over, sat up, gathered myself. 'Trust me,' he said. So, I lay back down as he wanted, and he came to one side of me and kissed my shoulders. He kissed them at the very top, in the fold made by my raised arms, then on the blades themselves: a diligent single kiss to each blade. Then he inched his lips down my spine, giving me goosebumps, and into the small of my back, where he lingered. The rasp of his stubble, the tickle of a fop of hair.

Then nothing: he was gone. I lay there alone, exposed, unable to stop myself raising my lower half in blind search of him. Then he was there again, his mouth was there, but now at my stocking tops and then moving upwards. A steady, contemplative kiss to one buttock and then the other, and then, it seemed, everywhere at once.

I said, 'Is this what you do to all your servant girls?'

'I'm not interested in servant girls,' he replied. 'Never have been.'

I'd trusted him and he'd been right: being bared to him was glorious and I craved more, to be nothing more than my lower half. Then the kissing was over and there was the pressing of his thighs on mine. Carefully, he pushed inside me and immediately my rippling began. He laughed, and I was thinking, *How can this – so wonderful – be wrong? And what if I die without ever feeling this again?*

But, believe me, it was always just about to stop. That's how I understood it. There did always have to be one more time, because that would be the last one. There had to be a last time, and this – *this*, I'd think, thank God, finally – was it.

And yet I lived with an urge to shout. *It can't stop; can't you see?*

It would be against nature, to stop it; it would be a kind of death.

At times, it seemed reasonable to do what we did. The only person it would hurt would be Kate and she didn't know and never would.

Sometimes one of us would actually say to the other: *This will stop. One day soon this will stop.* Although once Thomas did say to me, 'This – you and me – it'll never stop.' That, too, was unimaginable, and dreadful. Unimaginable that it would stop, and unimaginable that it wouldn't.

The problem was that the time we spent together felt real, while everything else – the life that was supposed to be real – was sham, shadow. Our times together were like sunlight on water: diamond-bright and undeniable, but simultaneously nothing you could touch, let alone hold, and leaving no trace.

The problem, you see, was that we were getting away with it. Why, then, stop?

Only once did I come across someone as I hurried to our room; Harry, my own Harry. Alone, just standing by a yew hedge near the fish ponds, nowhere in particular, somewhere no one ever came. I turned a corner and there he was; I almost bumped into him. What on earth was he doing? Was he spying on me? If he was, he was doing it spectacularly badly. Which isn't his style. Chances were that he hadn't been expecting to see me and I was going to get away with it. This time, anyway: I resolved to be more careful, somehow, from now on. But what *was* he was doing, standing there? 'Harry?' I braved it and asked him, 'What are you doing?'

Such a big boy, now: a good head taller than me. '*Noth*ing!' He barely looked at me. 'What are *you* doing?'

The aggression in his question had me snapping back at him, 'Don't talk to me like that!' But then I did give him an answer, or of sorts: 'Walking. Thinking.' He didn't seem to hear me, so keen was he to scarper. For now – *for now* – I remained undiscovered.

Some days Thomas and I had almost no time at all, but still we did it. Knowingly, unapologetically, quick in the pursuit of something that seemed quite separate from ourselves. I had to have him inside me every day; a missed day was a missing day, the world crumpled. My blood was different in my veins now, luxuriously silty, peppered and precious. My body was a different body and knew what it needed.

There was a sense of *fit* between us: not merely physical, although definitely there was that. I didn't know how I lived the minutes when he wasn't inside me, when there was no glittery rub of him inside me. I crammed him into me, hauled him in. My urgency shocked and delighted me.

Me, cool and calculating Catherine.

Thomas never asked me how it had been for me with Charles; he knew better than to ask, and anyway he probably knew the answer. Charles had been scared. Of scaring me. I could guess what Thomas would say to that: *It would take a lot to scare you*. Seriously, though: I was fourteen, and almost immediately pregnant, then damaged, then pregnant again, damaged anew. That's how it started for Charles and me, and that's how it stayed. We never got over it. He was a nice man. I know what Thomas would have said to that: *And I'm not*. And, no, he wasn't.

Once he said, 'I want to be a good husband to Kate, and I think I can be, but at heart I'm yours. You know that, don't you.'

Once, and only once, he looked up at me and asked, 'Do you love me?'

I was shocked but replied unhesitatingly, 'Yes,' and heard it, and believed it.

Yes.

I adore you, adore you.

This is nothing to do with anyone else.

'Not even God?' I goaded him once when we were getting dressed.

'Oh, God understands,' he replied, as breezy as you like.

And, 'This is a sin,' I said, once.

His response was a deliberately weary sigh. 'And the day will come when we ask for forgiveness, and it'll be given.'

Persuasive, confidence like that.

'Not by Kate,' I said.

'We'll make sure we never have to *ask* Kate,' he said.

Kate. Oh, *Kate*: I loved her more than ever, I told myself. I ached to tell her what was happening. To tell her not as his wife – I didn't want to tell her that her husband was deceiving her – but as my best friend. Once or twice I even found myself turning around guileless to confide, *Kate? Guess what?* It was odd to me, though, in a way, that she didn't already know, that she couldn't detect what was happening. I felt it of everyone – that surely they could see it on me – but especially of her. She was my best friend; she knew everything about me. And now she didn't. She didn't know *this*. Something this big in my life, she didn't know. Well, she *should have*, I couldn't help but think. *If you don't know, Kate, it's because you're not looking.*

You could look at it this way: what Kate wanted of Thomas, she was getting. He hadn't stopped being attentive to her. Indeed – predictably – he was more attentive than ever. He loved her, I could see. He loved their life together: what they had, and what they were looking forward to. With her, for her, he was funny, and sympathetic. That was when they were together. But she had her own concerns, which took her from him. Her many concerns, from the state of reform to the children and staff of the household and of course – of course – her ever-progressing pregnancy.

Pregnancy. Preventing it: Thomas made something even of that, with me. Made a lot of it, keen to demonstrate his impeccable timing, his self-control; making a mess of me and then wiping me down with either my petticoat or his shirt.

Once, we didn't make it as far as the room, but did it against that little locked door: not even locked, but pressed hard shut by the weight of us. Struggling to raise and keep raised my buckram-stiffened petticoat. Later, going up those backstairs, I remembered Catherine Howard. People had died for doing this, I recalled; they had been hunted down. Up there in our room, I stood at the window and looked over the gardens towards the parkland with just one thought in my head: *Well, come and get me, if you dare.* I felt that reckless, and that invincible.

Only the dead could get close. Sometimes I'd hear my mother: *What on earth do you think you're doing?* But then I'd hear my reply: *I'm living my life.* I didn't really know what I meant by it, but it was always what I imagined saying and I believed it passionately. And Charles? Well, what could Charles have said to me? He'd left me, hadn't he, when he died.

To be honest, they both seemed very dead.

Twenty-six

Kate would be very pregnant, I knew, by the time of my next visit. That was how I thought of her, once I was back home: becoming very pregnant. Definitely pregnant, at around six, seven months: the bump a visible presence but not so ridiculous as to look unreal. Perfectly pregnant. That was from the outside looking on, but for Kate, too, surely, it would be the best phase, after the sickness and tiredness but before the incapacity. I was intrigued by the prospect of being able to gauge the physical change in her, to *see* her *different*. Here at last was something by which even she couldn't remain untouched. And for her, of course, the physical changes would be more profound than anything I'd see. Someone would be keeping constant company with her: someone who'd wake perhaps moments later than her – slow to stir, a tiny sleepyhead – but then be hard to settle at bedtime and need a murmured talking-to, a steadying hand.

A small, invisible person animated during conversations and comically excited by the first mouthful of every meal. More than a decade on, I still miss that intimacy. Perhaps I always will.

So there I was, looking forward to seeing Kate again, to spending time with her. I can't explain it, other than to say that I was two people, one snug inside the other. I was doing a balancing act, by necessity. This was my life now: this is what I did. It could be done.

Thomas and I had the briefest contact between my March and June visits to Sudeley: just one polite meeting, at my London house. Kate and I, though, were busy writing to each other as ever: a letter always on the go, a letter always on its week-long journey with a carrier. The difference now being that whenever I received one from her, I dreaded opening it, dreaded discovering that she knew. What would such a letter from her contain? I simply couldn't guess how she'd be, and that in itself was terrifying enough. Would she be cold, brief, requesting no further contact? Or a whirl of fury, recriminations and, perhaps even – who knows? – long-held resentments. The latter was unlikely, I felt, but, then, what did I know? I'd never known a pregnant Kate, had I, married to a man whom she'd very much wanted to marry. Oh, a disappointed Kate, yes, making clear her disappointment: her, I'd come across. I'd heard that rather patronising tone of hers. I'd heard it occasionally, directed at other people, but I didn't delude myself that I'd be getting away with a mere upbraiding.

Quill in hand, I still burned to confide in her, anticipating her advice and, yes, her admonishments. Longing for them, in fact. I wanted her to be my best friend, in other words.

I wondered how I'd explain myself, but never got further than, *Kate, just . . . just let me do this, let me have him for those minutes every day when you don't want him.* And, put like that, was it so unreasonable? *I want, I want . . .* I'd think hard but always only come up with, *I want the scent of him on my own skin.*

Whenever a letter came from her, I'd skim to see that it wasn't *that* letter, then take a breath and skim again for mention of Thomas. If she didn't mention him, or barely did so, I was uneasy. Were they drifting apart, or even arguing? Did she know, or nearly know? I was fearful of the undercurrents between them, of which I was sharply aware I knew nothing. If she did mention him, I'd expect to have some reaction, a jolt or flush, but in fact I never felt anything. Felt hollow. I'd be expecting, too, to feel some resentment of their daily life together; but then, whenever it was mentioned, it seemed unimportant. If I was interested at all, I wanted *his* account and felt impatient with her, with her words for getting in the way. Perhaps she no longer seemed a reliable witness because, to put it bluntly, she didn't even know something as basic as what her husband was up to.

Her letters contained household news, pregnancy news, and family news, which, a number of times, included mention of Thomas's disputes with his brother and his brother's wife over the leasing and sale of Seymour-family properties. The unresolved business of the queen's jewels still rankled. On a happier note, there would be something about a book she'd read, or a debate of which she'd heard or in which she was involved. There was always mention of the weather, and usually something – supposedly profound or funny – that Elizabeth had said. And about this time, there was trouble with one of her dogs, Damson: his misdemeanours figured, too, in most of those letters.

And there was nothing, nothing, nothing from Thomas. And no clue as to what that might mean. Or not mean. I couldn't write to him, and he knew it – or would have known it, had he thought about it, and I couldn't be sure that he had. I never did wonder what we might have written in those unwritten letters.

When we'd parted, he'd asked with some urgency, 'Will you come again soon?'

'Well,' I'd said, 'Kate does need me.' I didn't know why I'd said it, and, as perhaps I'd intended, he bridled.

'Well,' he said, 'there's that.'

We were standing at the foot of our little stone staircase.

'Are you coming to London?' I asked.

'I expect so.' Then, 'London's risky, Cathy. It's not . . . *here*.'

Here, which was also Kate's home. It would have been nice to be together somewhere else. There was Grimsthorpe, *my* non-London home, but we both knew he could never manufacture a reason to be there.

In the end, he arrived unannounced at my London house one evening in early May, ostensibly to be sociable as the husband of my best friend and to bring me news of her. It had been a long day – dogged rain and a collapsed roof in the stables, a skirmish between two footmen in which a knife was brandished, then news of the serious illness of Joanna's baby back at Grimsthorpe. We exchanged polite conversation for a half-hour or so. If we seemed ill at ease with each other, then that was only what our attendants would have expected, because we didn't really like each other, did we? Everyone knew that. And I began to wonder if they were right. I sat there, fire-flushed in my least flattering gown, my heart a wet sponge. He looked no better; in fact, he looked ridiculous, overdressed. I felt that I should be able to conjure the Thomas I'd known, but that vain imposter remained there across the room from me. What had happened in March seemed impossible, inexplicable. Had I been somehow hoodwinked? If so, by whom? Had it been him at fault or me? Had I imagined everything?

It was with dismay and relief that eventually I accompanied him down into the courtyard to see him off. There was nothing untoward in his taking my hand as he stood beside his horse; what was shocking was how hard he held it, which, of course, only he and I knew. There, with everyone around us, he gripped my hand and forced me to look up into his eyes, which, I realised, I'd so far avoided. And there, in those eyes, was that utter lack of compromise. What he said – all he said – was, 'When are you coming to Sudeley?' He'd lowered his voice just slightly; he could still have been heard by anyone if they'd chosen to listen and, of course, they'd have heard nothing but an innocent question.

I managed, 'Soon.'

He tightened his grip, both affirmation and threat. 'Soon,' he repeated, releasing me and swinging up onto his horse, sparking the commotion of hooves on cobbles. I was burning again, the wick relit.

Twenty-seven

When we arrived at Sudeley in June, Kate came to the draw-bridge to greet us. Even up close, her pregnancy barely showed beneath her stomacher, an extra panel of black satin. What was obviously bigger, though, and beyond the very best tailoring, was her newly broad face. In it the little nose and mouth looked smaller still and those eyes nothing much. Odd to see such a transformation. She was with Elizabeth and Jane. Jane was still no bigger than a six-year-old, but dressed as usual in adult black. Unsmiling, she seemed lost in thought. With Jane, I was beginning to understand, thinking took precedence over social niceties. Elizabeth, by contrast, was avid, and she glittered. In the late sunlight, her eyes were honey-coloured and her skin glowed like the flesh of a freshly bitten-into red apple.

I said something like, 'You all look so well!'

And Elizabeth enthused, 'Yes, doesn't she look fabulous?'

stepping backwards and then from side to side, arms open, as if showing off Kate but coincidentally making quite a display of herself.

Kate looked anything but fabulous when she came to find me minutes later in my room, where a bath was being prepared for me. With a touch to my arm, she said, 'Come for a walk.' She led me down the stairs and into her own garden at a brisk pace, her ladies lagging; she was clearly after some privacy for us. I was watching for Thomas, whom I'd not yet seen and of whom there'd been no mention; I didn't know whether or not I wanted us to come across him.

Stopping eventually at a bench – 'Here' – Kate acknowledged her breathlessness with splayed fingertips on her breastbone and a raised eyebrow. My turn to touch her arm, in concern. She smiled, shook her head. The bench was down a narrow path all of its own, and deep in an alcove; Marcella and Agnes remained at a distance, talking. We sat, and I waited. Once I'd have welcomed any confidence from her, but now I was wary.

She launched in with, 'Thomas is buying Jane's wardship.' Her hands were linked on her stomacher. I looked up again at her flat, pallid face. She appeared to be asking something of me. But I was struggling to understand. Thomas would have known how we – how *she*, his own wife – regarded the trade in wardships. Much of Kate's life had been and still was dedicated to circumventing it, first for herself and latterly for her various loved ones. And me, *me*: well, I'd *been* a ward, and if I'd been fine, that was only because I'd been lucky. And Thomas *knew* all that. Had he gone mad in my absence? I could only manage, 'What does he say?' Meaning, *How on earth does he explain himself?*

As if merely quoting, she replied, 'He says it's for the best.'

I gave no response because the answer made no sense to me, but she shrugged as if I'd said something.

So I said, 'I'll talk to him,' because that, at a guess, was what she was expecting from me: me, who never shied from confrontation. And suddenly I was desperate to do so. He'd let me down, coming up with such a scheme; he was letting *me* down.

But Kate blew away my offer with a sigh. 'Cathy,' she said, but then said nothing more. I was aware of my held breath. 'It's not *that*,' she tried, then tried again, 'It's not *just* that.' There was nothing to read in her clear, round eyes. 'He'd made two down payments before I discovered what he was up to.' She looked down at her hands, the eyes gone under colourless lashes. 'That's what bothers me: the secrecy. It's that,' she said again, but quieter, quite lost.

I had an excuse to go and find Thomas, and I adopted it wholeheartedly, powered by fury at him. I didn't care that I still hadn't had my bath and was unrefreshed after the day's hard ride. I found him in the hall with his master glazier, looking up at and discussing one of the immense windows. I've never known anyone keener on heraldic glass than Thomas. At Sudeley, any window big enough was set with elaborate rosettes of emerald, ruby and cat's-eye yellow, even if illuminating nothing but some corner of an obscure staircase. Quite whom they honoured was in most cases a mystery to me. It took me a while to realise that it wasn't me at fault, that they were in fact unreadable: a mishmash of motifs borrowed from faintly related families. Initially, that had seemed typical of Thomas, to me: pitiful, if not despicable, and I'd wondered how Kate could turn a blind eye to it.

And then I'd seen it differently, seen Thomas as loving the finer things in life and being playful, being irreverent, barefacedly making the most of his situation. Now, I didn't know, I just didn't know. There he was: less striking than I'd remembered but more . . . real. His hair was a shade darker than I'd remembered and a tad too long. His face had picked up touches of the sun. I wondered how bad I looked after my day of riding.

I'd halted pointedly at the door. Noticing me, he brought his discussion to an end, and, as soon as we were alone, strode towards me, smiling, arms outstretched: very Thomas. My blood eddied but I told myself to stand firm. He'd lost a tooth, I saw, a small bottom tooth; my heart snagged on its absence, the pain and trouble of it about which I'd known nothing. Grasping my own hands behind my back, I said what I'd come to say: 'You're buying Jane.'

He stopped mid-stride and his exaggerated sigh spoke of weariness at having to explain himself. I hated the implication, my bracketing with Kate: *Oh, you women!* He said, 'Frances and Henry are awful.' Her parents. 'You *know* that, Cathy. You'd rather they decided her fate?'

'*Buying* her,' I reiterated, carefully. 'Can't you just . . . be like Kate? Be . . . kind?' Be a mentor. Do your best.

'Well' – the slow smile – 'that's all very nice . . .' Meaning: unrealistic, ultimately useless.

I switched to, 'What does *Jane* think?'

He inclined his head and tried, 'Do we have to discuss this *now*?'

I pressed on: 'Yes.'

He spoke calmly: 'Jane thinks she could make an excellent Protestant queen, just as Kate was.'

'She's *ten*.'

'She won't always be ten. She's a very grown-up ten.'

I shook my head. 'This is about *your* future. You tried to marry a princess but were warned off, so you married an ex-queen, and now you'll go one better and *make* a queen, so you can be almost a *father* to a queen.'

He shrugged, feigned indifference. 'If that also happens to be true, are you going to deny it's a good idea?'

So, there it was. Take it or leave it, *This is who I am.*

I took it, had to. 'It's an unworkable idea: that's what it is, Thomas. Kate was last in line for an old king whom no one else, abroad, would ever marry. It's different for his son. Eddie won't need to settle for an English queen.'

'It *is* different,' he allowed, 'but not impossible. I'll just have to make sure it happens.'

I was scathing. 'And you think you can do that.'

He declined to rise to it. 'I think I can do that.' Then he tried again: 'Cathy, do we –'

'Yes,' I insisted, because I so badly wanted to insist on something. '*Yes*.'

And suddenly he was asking me, 'What did you think of Charles's motives when he married you?'

That floored me, but I didn't let him see. 'I understood them.'

'And they were . . . ?'

I wasn't having this. 'You know what they were.'

He nodded. 'The usual: land and heirs.'

I argued, 'He was a very nice man.'

'I'm sure he was.'

'No, I *mean* he was a *very* nice man.'

'*Cathy*, I'm sure he *was*.'

'Life goes on,' I blazed on in Charles's defence, 'and it's hard, at court.'

He spread his arms to indicate a truce, to make clear that – see? – we were on the same side.

A heartbeat's pause and I reined myself in. 'People were quick to suspect . . .' What? I didn't need too strong a word, because people had been, on the whole, forgiving of Charles. '. . . Insincerity.' No comparison to the general feeling about Thomas, which was much more damning. 'But just because he married me so quickly didn't mean he'd loved Mary Rose any less.'

'No.'

'Nor me,' I added quickly. 'Nor me any less, in time.'

'No.'

'It was just . . .' *Different.* And there I was, landed on familiar ground, on our ground, Thomas's and mine. There was no sense of homecoming, though. I changed the subject: 'You didn't tell Kate. You didn't tell her that you were buying Jane's wardship.'

'Well' – he seemed to be speaking over my head – 'I don't tell her everything, do I? I don't tell her anything that she won't like.'

That was a slap in the face. *Me*, he meant: *I* was what Kate wouldn't like. I shrugged – giving up on him – before I turned on my heel, and he let me go. Banging through the door, I almost bumped into Harry and Charlie, who were rushing in, breathing hard. 'What are you doing?' I barked at them, venting my fury before I could catch myself. They were still caked in mud, practically creaking with it, and they had no excuse for having not yet been near their baths.

Harry reared back, affronted, to glare at me. 'Finding

Thomas.' As if it was what they always did first at Sudeley. Perhaps it was.

I stepped aside, nothing to say.

Charlie hesitated – 'Mama?' – and I touched his arm as I strode away.

I felt hollow. Went into the formal garden and just stood there; had to just stand somewhere and the formal garden was as good a place as any. I hated myself and Thomas, and, if Kate knew what we'd done, she'd hate both of us, and there was nothing that could be done to make it better. What had happened could never be undone. I stood there for a while and then, because there was nothing else for it, picked myself up and went back to Kate.

'He says it's for the best,' was what I said as I approached her, and, embarrassed at my failure to have made a difference, laughed in a fashion.

She didn't. 'Oh, everything always is, with Thomas, isn't it.' She was making bedlinen with little Frankie Lassells and Agnes. I couldn't fathom exactly what she meant and didn't want to; I wanted to be off the subject, fast. But no: her eyes sparkled in a deliberate effort to make light. 'Did he say, "Trust me"?'

My heart lurched. I tried to look amused.

She laid the linen in her lap, winced with annoyance. 'My fingers are swollen.'

'Not long now,' I managed.

'This business of "for the best",' she said, getting to her feet, making it across to the fireplace, indicating for me to accompany her. 'He says the times demand it, the circumstances. And maybe he's right.' Absently, she tapped the stonework. 'Well, he *is* right. We *do* need an English queen.

We need a protestant queen and there's hardly an abundance of those abroad, is there? And in any case that's always so complicated, isn't it: going abroad. This . . . revolution of ours is so precarious, so precious: safest of all would be a home-grown queen.'

An English-educated – *Kate*-educated – queen: I saw that the future could be so very civilised. Protestant though Thomas was, however, the prospect of a good, protestant queen for England wasn't his motivation. He wanted Jane married to Eddie because then not only would he be uncle to the king but the new queen would be from his household, which would mean a lot of influence, a lot of favour. Or so he'd be hoping. Surely Kate could see that?

'And they're so well suited. Same age' – born within weeks of each other – 'and same ideas.' Well, yes, very keen on revolution, those two, convinced of it, famous for their conviction: a pair of serious little faces, books in their hands and heads bowed to Luther. But that was friendship. Being able to offer abroad the queenship of England gave Eddie a bargaining power too great to pass over in favour of choosing a like-minded spouse. However regrettable it was – and it was – that little boy's life wasn't his own. As king, a lifetime of conjugal fireside chats would almost certainly be an unaffordable luxury for him. Kate wasn't being practical. 'What's depressing,' she said, 'is that we still need to resort to the old ways.' The buying of a wardship. 'It doesn't feel right.'

What wasn't right was Thomas's self-interest. I didn't want to think about it.

Suddenly Kate smiled, grabbed my hand and pressed it to her stomacher. Raised her eyebrows: *You feel him?* A weird flexing. 'Always so restless,' she said, wryly. 'Like his father.' I took my hand away, and she resumed: 'It's depressing to see Jane *bought*, handed over. To see her *knowing* that. *Any* girl, but particularly one as proud and self-contained as Jane. And of course I know she'll be safe; she couldn't *be* safer, with Thomas and me, and it's immeasurably better than her being with Frances and Henry. I *know* that, and, more importantly, *she* knows that. But it's the principle, isn't it. Thomas can't understand why anyone would allow a principle to get in the way, as he sees it. I don't know what he thinks principles are for.' She sighed. 'But, then, an awful lot of people would say "told you so".'

Not knowing what to say, I said, 'He just wasn't the obvious choice for you, that's all.'

'But you understand, don't you,' she said, immediately, and there was no plea in it; it was statement pure and simple. 'You understand what it is about him.'

I floated through the moment, determined to feel nothing, to clean myself out of feeling and then start from scratch. As if I barely knew him.

Before I could respond, though, she said, 'Everyone else is so deferential, so false,' and then laughed, 'I mean, except you, of course.'

I made sure to echo the laugh.

'Thomas is *true*, isn't he. True to himself. He gets into scrapes, yes, which doesn't make him the easiest of husbands, but I've never had cause to doubt his devotion to me, and how many wives can say that?'

Nothing from me. Not even a heartbeat.

'Everyone's so cautious, but Thomas is . . . Well, he's silly, sometimes, I know, but he's *alive* in a way that nobody else is, he's . . .'

Reckless. I looked away, down at the floor, wanting to cry without quite knowing for whom.

She said, 'Anyway, I did choose him, I did marry him, and' – she patted her belly – 'it worked, didn't it.'

And then we did laugh, both of us, relieved; I managed it, managed to catch her up and laugh along with her.

She turned serious again, though. 'I *know* he didn't tell me because he knew I wouldn't like it. The problem is, he's good at that; he's always doing it.'

'He is?' My smile, again, felt fixed.

'You know, Cathy, however it might look to the contrary, he's not an easy man to live with. All that fun with everyone in his household, yes. But with everyone else . . .' she whispered, 'it's the opposite, he's at war. At *war*. I'm only now uncovering the extent of it. Tenants . . .' Her tone suggested she was embarking on a list, but she abandoned it. 'He's even in trouble at home now.'

My heart flipped. I said nothing. *Wait*.

Barely audibly, she confided, 'Mrs Ashley thinks he's overfamiliar with Elizabeth.' She flicked her eyes skywards. 'That was what she said: "Overfamiliar". I said to her, "But he's overfamiliar with everyone, isn't he, really; that's what he *is*. That's Thomas."'

Keep looking into her eyes: receptive, loyal. *And wait for details.*

'I mean, she has a point in that Elizabeth isn't everyone, she's royal and Thomas could get into a lot of trouble for barging into her bedroom and playing these tickling games –'

'Tickling games?'

'Oh, *you* know; you know how they are. Like father and daughter, it seems to me, and I love to see it.' Mildly affronted, she added, 'And Mrs Ashley and I have always agreed that we don't want Elizabeth growing up as if she's in a nunnery.'

I asked, 'What *are* these "tickling games"?' I wondered how I looked – what was she seeing on my face? – not least because I had no idea how I felt. Thomas teasing Elizabeth was nothing, I knew very well; but still I didn't like it, even if I didn't quite know why. And, anyway, it was dangerous, and what was dangerous for him was dangerous for his family, for Kate and the baby.

'Tickling.' Kate shrugged. 'Reaching under the bedclothes and . . .' But she stopped.

'Tickling,' I had to say it for her. And then I almost laughed: *Thomas, really, honestly, you do push it, don't you.* Oh, this was easy: I didn't need to have any feelings whatsoever about this; this was a purely practical consideration. 'Kate,' I stressed, 'he probably does need to be more careful, doesn't he?' Surely there was no denying it.

She did, though; she did deny it, in a way. Folding her arms, frowning, looking at the floor, she said, 'Well, I'm not going to mention it to him, because it would make it worse. If he's told he can't do something, he does it all the more.'

Breathe, Cathy.

She looked at me. 'He means no harm,' she said, making clear that she was finished, that the subject was closed.

Twenty-eight

For almost a week, I avoided Thomas: avoided being alone with him, even for a moment; avoided even catching his eye. *Decided*, is how it seemed to me, those first few days at Sudeley in June, without me – or indeed him – having had to decide it. Somehow, it had finished and I accepted the end, was thankful, glad, relieved. What had happened with Thomas had been a madness; it was as if I'd been ill. This, now, was another new life, my second within months: no simple going back, I knew, to where I'd once been. No, this would need living through; I would need to find a way through. Going to chapel, praying hard and listening harder to Miles Coverdale's sermons, I told myself that I could do better than before, could learn from this.

There would never be anything I could do to make it up to Kate: I was under no illusions about that. The best I could do for her would be to forget that it ever happened:

the closest I could come to making it never have happened.

I ached, but that was to be expected, wasn't it? A real, physical ache. I paid it no heed. Stopped up my yearning. The ache, I knew, was for Thomas's unflinching focus on me, as palpable as his touch upon my skin.

It wasn't hard to avoid him, because he in turn gave me a wide berth. So wide that he was away on business for two days at a neighbouring landowner's, before spending a day at home in conference with his treasurer. On that occasion he was free by suppertime but nevertheless declined to join us – 'I think I'll say no, ladies, if you don't mind; it's been a long day.' I'd heard him when he'd arrived back from his trip saying to Kate that life would be easier if they had the royal jewellery back from his brother and sister-in-law. She'd replied, 'But you wouldn't be *selling* it, would you.' He'd changed the subject. I couldn't tell if she'd been puzzled by what he'd said or had understood full well what he'd let slip, and was reminding him that it wasn't his to sell.

Yet it also *was* hard, somehow, to keep my distance from Thomas; it must have been, because I was exhausted. Perhaps it was the resolve that it took. No help was the lack of distractions at Sudeley. I'd come with very few of my own household and – as usual, because of the distance – none of my ladies. A visit from Kate's brother and his new wife Lizzie had been anticipated, but, due to some political crisis of what seemed to me a spectacularly uninteresting nature, he'd had to stay at court. John Pankhurst – Kate's chaplain, my ex-chaplain – was laid up in bed with his habitual fever and sickness. Susan, the usher's wife, was visiting her ailing mother. The rest of Kate's ladies were a dead loss. The girls' new tutor, Roger, was usually good for conversation, but he was preoccupied with some financial crisis of his brother's and always in his room writing letters. Twittery Mrs Ashley was best avoided in my view. As for my boys, and Elizabeth and Jane, I didn't really know where they were; all I knew was that they weren't around. The only visitor to Sudeley that week was the bonesetter, for Charlie's little friend, Anthony, who'd fallen from a tree and broken an ankle.

Kate's advanced pregnancy meant that she didn't do much, but it shouldn't have meant that she was any poorer company for me. That was down to the midwife, who was already in residence. Her name was Mary Odell, and she was a very nice woman. That was the problem: I don't tend to get on with very nice people. I wish I did, but I don't; it just doesn't happen; perhaps it's that I can't quite take them seriously. Whereas Kate, of course, does. So there Kate was, in her element, often keeping company with the cheerful Mary Odell and assuming – not unreasonably – that I was happy to do likewise.

Mary was probably in her forties, a tall, brisk blonde, papery-skinned, chapped-knuckled. My own first midwife, the meaty-armed Mrs Arkwright, had scowled through my pregnancy, barely ever giving me a second glance. It had all been about the heir, to her. Her job, as she saw it, was safe delivery of the heir. Actually, that *was* her job, and she was unsurpassed at it. Charles had appointed her on her reputation. 'But she was the very best around,' he'd claimed, dismayed and contrite, when I said a year later that I didn't want her for my second pregnancy. Actually, I didn't *say* it, I *cried* it, and he was mortified: why on earth hadn't I said at the time? I had to tell him: how would I have known? What had I known about midwives and how they could be, how they were supposed to be? I'd been fourteen, fifteen, at the time, motherless, sisterless. I hadn't known that Mrs Arkwright could have been said to be limited in her view that there was no point to me other than to reproduce. I hadn't known until Kate had come along to tell me.

Kate. When Harry was six weeks old, I'd arrived reluctantly for a stay at court. I don't remember the circumstances, just my reluctance and how court was suddenly incomprehensible to me, from the hours everyone kept to the conversations they considered called for. I was seized by questions which no one else even recognised as questions, usually answering only with a knowing and unhelpful 'Ha!', giving the impression that having a baby was a business simultaneously odd and predictable and thus unworthy of consideration. Harry was having none of this, bawling at them, all of them, roaring his impatience. He didn't belong to the world of court or to any world that wasn't his own, his Harry-world. And where he was, I was, too, dragged along in his wake. I was a foot soldier and the sole one because this business of having a baby seemed too confounding to entrust to anyone not intimately involved. Harry's nurses, my ladies and even my husband retreated from me, puzzled and a little piqued. Harry and I were left alone in our suite, or so it felt, to muddle through the days and nights.

Then came Kate's tentative knock at the door, a diffident 'Hello, you,' to me, then a gutsy 'Helloooo, you,' to Harry. *At last*, I saw him think. For me: well, I was rather more thrown. I hadn't seen Kate since I was a girl. At a loss, I indicated the side of my bed. Immediately – but delicately – she sat. I don't remember what we went on to talk about, only that she conversed with me as if I were an adult when everyone else was treating me as a child, whilst somehow also allowing me to be a child when the general expectation had been for me to be an adult. Whatever she did, however she did it, she got it right, and from the off. As she did with Harry, too. Harry, whom everyone else had *regarded* – exclaimed about, discussed – if they'd bothered with him at all, so that he had glared and tried to fight his corner, exhausting and frustrating himself with useless thrusts of his arms and legs. Kate talked to him and he waved at her, reached for her, his rosebud mouth open in imitation and invitation.

Kate continued to come by whenever, as far as I could tell, she didn't have to do anything else in particular. She never asked me how I was, in the way that other people did, the way that made me cry. She let me be. But she also didn't, getting me up and out, eventually, and without any of the chiding that others had considered necessary. Together, we took Harry to see trees, horses, and, one evening, the moon. When I finally did appear in hall, it was beside Kate and I walked tall, with Harry.

When I knew I was pregnant again, Kate came to Grimsthorpe to help me choose my midwife, which is how I ended up with the incomparable old Betty Bright, regrettably now long since dead.

And now, thirteen years later, I remembered all this as if it were yesterday and I wanted to be for Kate as she had been for me. But I knew it couldn't happen. I'd known it from the start of her pregnancy, not simply from meeting the capable Mary Odell. True, Kate might run into difficulties, of course she might, and help of a practical nature, I was ready to give. But I would never be able to do for her as she'd done for me. There was no call for it.

I began to make a habit of taking walks, long walks, alone, way beyond the gardens. The air was blood-warm, the sky squint-inducingly luminous despite the cover of pleated cloud. Massive trees glowered on the horizon as if they were thunderclouds, and underfoot the grasses of the pathways were extravagantly noisy. Barley was being grown: up close, feathery plaits; stretching into the distance, expanses of pale gold stippled with the faintest green. Once, I spotted a small, delicately striped snail on a hedgerow leaf and found myself actually speaking aloud to it: *Do you like this* – the sun on our backs – *as much as I do?* Even though I knew, really, that it couldn't; it would be swooning in its shell, longing for shade. It *ought* to, though, is perhaps what I meant. Because how unthinkable that anyone – anything – didn't love this: the freedom out here. But most of the time, there was nothing in me at all. Nothing *to* me. I was opened up to the vast sky, looking around and around.

During Thomas's first supper back with us, he'd no sooner sat down than he announced, 'We have a decision to make.' He sounded pleased; looked it, too, glancing around us, clearly enjoying our attention and being about to throw us something of a test. I couldn't have cared less. 'What are we going to do,' he asked, 'about St John the Baptist's day? Celebrate it or not?'

Kate followed suit: snapped to attention and looked bright-eyed at the youngsters around the table. Wearily I watched them Being A Family.

The feast day of St John the Baptist, Midsummer Day. Coming up, I suddenly realised, in a few days' time. Midsummer: three months since the start of the new calendar year. Since the start of . . . Three months *already*, or *only* three months? I didn't know; I felt too tired to know the answer. Could have been either.

'Celebrate it.' Elizabeth was unhesitating, unequivocal. 'All depends on whether you see it as St John's or Midsummer.' Everyone knew this; she was merely stating the obvious to get the discussion going. St John the Baptist's was a feast day, a catholic celebration. Not, then, something for this household. Midsummer, though, was exactly the kind of celebration this household would relish: open house; an all-night party.

'Well, which *do* we see it as?' Kate's question sounded genuine; she was sincerely interested.

'Midsummer, of course,' breezed Elizabeth, 'because then we can celebrate it.'

Thomas laughed.

My Harry cleared his throat. 'The Lord Protector' – he glanced at Thomas, perhaps nervous at mentioning Thomas's brother – 'is allowing it in London.'

'So I'd heard,' Thomas remarked.

Charlie piped up, 'That's because everyone was so upset at Corpus Christi being banned.' My London-based boys, with their London-based concerns. I couldn't help but smile.

'Well, that was Corpus Christi,' said Elizabeth. 'That *had* to go; you don't get more catholic than Corpus Christi, do you. This, though, is different.'

Kate ventured, 'And perhaps people can only take so much change at one time.' Then she made the mistake of trying to include little Jane Grey: 'What do you think, Jane?'

Jane said, 'People should take however much change they have to take.'

My boys turned to the food on their plates. No such luxury for the adults, who had to respond.

Thomas frowned, making a show of thinking, and Kate, likewise, inclined her head.

Elizabeth, though, rounded on her. 'There's no *harm* in it. If we say it's non-religious for us, then it *is* non-religious for us. And, I mean, it *is* for me, I can assure you. And I'm sure that's the same for everyone here.' She added in conclusion, 'I want to celebrate Midsummer.'

Jane was scandalised. 'You act as if it doesn't matter. It *does* matter.' I was amazed: until this, I'd never heard her speak this way. She switched to Kate, helpless. 'What about leading by example? Isn't that always what you say we should do?'

Kate was obviously – visibly – torn between her girls.

Thomas cut in with, 'What do you think, Cathy?' It was the first time he'd addressed me openly and in an instant he'd directed everyone's eyes to me. I recoiled, resentful, and anyway quite unable to work up enthusiasm for the discussion. Whereas usually – *before* – I'd have been preoccupied by the very same issues. I went for, 'Whatever Ed has decided on is good enough for me.' And meant it. Ed Seymour could do the thinking on this one. It was what he was paid to do, and he was paid to do it because he was good at it.

Elizabeth chipped in, sarcastically, 'You, of the strong opinions.'

I turned to her and said, 'That *is* my opinion, and it's a strong one.'

Thomas broke the pause: 'With all due respect to the dissenters' – as if there were more than one – 'I decree that we in this household celebrate Midsummer's Day,' and emphasised, with a look at Jane Grey, '*Midsummer's* Day.'

Elizabeth whooped, and my boys – predictably – looked pleased. Jane's face registered nothing.

Twenty-nine

Elizabeth's a protestant, of course, but not as Jane is. No one can doubt Elizabeth's protestant pedigree: born to the pair who led the break from Rome, born *because of* the break from Rome. She's grown up protestant through and through: she's not one for a bended knee, and she *is* one for asking questions. I'll give her that. And now she was being brought up by Kate, whom people were calling the Protestant Queen. How different Elizabeth is in every possible way from her elder, catholic half-sister. They even *move* differently: Mary making stately swishes of her skirts; Elizabeth half skipping, always looking as if she's just been let out of somewhere. And those skirts themselves: Mary's are bruise purple, leaf green and a brick red that wouldn't flatter anyone, let alone her, whereas Elizabeth favours crimson, flame and gold.

Protestantism is in Elizabeth's blood but it's there

unthinkingly, of no great importance to her. What is of great importance is what other people think of her. No taking after her mother in that. Strange, at first thought, that it was Kate and not Anne Boleyn who was the Protestant Queen. But even though Anne Boleyn's protestantism was strong and deep, it was secondary to her ambitions; it wasn't what she was *about*. Her aim in life was to marry the king. She and the other queens – Jane Seymour, Anne of Cleves – just happened to be protestant. For Kate, it wasn't that she was a queen and she was protestant but that she made her queenship about protestantism, something that she worked hard for others to have.

I've always believed that a woman can in principle learn and think as well as a man. Maybe it's because I never had a brother: I was never second-best. You could call that luck. What was unlucky, though, was that I never had the education that a brother of mine might have had. Oh, my mother had excellent intentions but circumstances overtook her and then my education was no longer in her hands. In any case, I doubt her heart would have been in it, by then. Her heart had followed Queen Catherine into banishment, where their own spectacular cleverness had ended up counting for nothing. They had just become middle-aged women from a forgotten country, required to live on meagre supplies in disused castles.

Me, meanwhile: I was in Charles's hands. And Charles – open-minded and generous though he was – was a pragmatist. Education for its own sake wasn't a priority. And anyway circumstances overtook me again and instead of having lessons at fourteen, fifteen, I was having children. Charles was never against education for his wife, he'd never have stopped me learning, and in fact he'd probably wanted me to do it, but it just never happened.

So, I didn't have much of an education, but I've always been sure that if I *had*, I'd have been as clever as most men. My lack of education is what's at fault, not my being a woman.

Take Hugh: my dear chaplain, my brilliant friend Hugh Latimer. He has all the time in the world to think, in his suite of rooms at marvellous Cambridge. Cambridge, where my boys will soon be going. Perhaps Hugh is better able to turn his attention to Heaven because he has fewer ties here on earth. No household to run. And I'll do all I can to keep it that way for him. Why not? People need to do our thinking, just as people need to do our farming, and it might as well be those who are good at it, who have a passion for it. And anyway it's what I can *do*, looking after Hugh, taking him in. It's what *I'm* good at. As was publishing Kate. People listened to Kate; that was what *she's* good at. You can preach all you like, but it's useless if no one's listening. So I published Kate: *The Lamentation of a Sinner*. Persuaded her brother to write an introduction, and had the book printed and sold. And, oh, did it sell. I'm a doer, a fixer, sometimes a funder.

But that, I was beginning to suspect, was not good enough for Jane Grey. In Jane's view, I've learned, the world is carelessly and shamelessly askew. Kept tilted by a few, while the rest blunder around like cattle. We all disgust her, is my suspicion. Even me? Enlightened me? Oh, me especially, is my guess. *Because* I'm enlightened, I've eighteen years on her, but England remains only reluctantly protestant. She must wonder what I've been doing. Tell me, though, what is it that Jane has been so busy doing. Gliding around, theological texts in hand, stern-faced and pure of heart. If she isn't going to go out and dismantle churches in the name of her revolution (and it's hard to imagine her spending her days kneeling on flagstones, packing icons into caskets), if it really is – for her – about hearts and minds, then she needs to learn to speak hers. As it is, no one can hear her. No one would *want* to hear her, with her face like that.

But why does it matter to me what Jane Grey might think of me? It surprises me that it does. Perhaps it's that I feel judged and found wanting, and I'm unused to that.

My boys are big-hearted but keen-eyed and I trust their judgements of their peers. They've never taken to Jane. Only a day or so before that discussion about whether to celebrate Midsummer, Charlie had tried to tell me something. 'Mama? You know Jane?'

'I do know Jane, yes.' I was irritable, and distracted. You see? Thomas took me not only from my best friend, but also from my sons.

'Well,' Charlie confided, 'I don't really like being left with her.'

I probably said something like, *Don't you? Oh dear.* Or, *Nor would I, to be honest.* I should have listened to what Charlie was saying; I should have listened to what was being said. If I had I might have averted disaster.

Left with her. Left.

Thirty

That evening of the discussion about Midsummer, Thomas's last words to me, as I was at the door of Kate's room on my way back to my own, were, 'Come for a walk with me tomorrow.' Spoken across everybody. I dithered, taken aback. He boomed, 'Kate tells me you've been going for walks by yourself because she' – and he indicated her belly – 'can only waddle. Well, I'm here now.' I found I was looking to Kate. Nothing from her, though, but a benign smile. 'A lot's happening in the gardens,' he continued. 'I've much to show you.'

Charlie looked up anxiously from the cushions at Thomas's feet. 'But we'll still be riding tomorrow, won't we?'

Thomas nudged him with his foot, in a kind of reproach. 'Of course we will.'

Closing the door behind me, it was Charlie I felt for. Thomas no doubt would find time for him, but I was pained to see my son at his mercy. That casual prod with his shoe. I kept composed along the hallways and up the stairs, but back in my room, preparing for bed, my composure began to unravel. I was sharp in my unlacings and whipped off my layers, crushing linens and silks. Sensing Bella's concern, I did calm down. But all I could think was: *Funny*, was it? Was this how it would be now, what we'd done? A little joke between us?

I did go for that walk with him, though, the following day. He persuaded me by cajoling me, making it public again. 'That walk, Cathy.'

Kate: 'Yes, do: go.' She was preoccupied. There seemed to be some problem with Jane: Jane looked clingy; Kate, motherly.

I said, 'Charlie?' *You coming?* Harry was nowhere to be seen. Charlie said he had to see to a litter of puppies: some Thomas-instigated task, I guessed, from which he wasn't about to be deflected. I looked around, helpless. I'd have even welcomed Elizabeth's company, but where was she on the one occasion I wanted her? Thomas was already explaining where he'd be taking me, what we'd be seeing. A new this, a new that.

Outside, high-spirited house martins more than compensated for our lack of conversation. We set off under a pewter sky, the tang of rain in the air. As we walked, I couldn't bring myself even to look at Thomas. He tolerated it, saying nothing. We didn't seem to be going anywhere in particular. Eventually, I said, 'Kate's cross with you.' Pathetic, not least because she wasn't. But I wanted her to be. I wanted him to be in trouble.

'Oh, Kate's *always* cross with me,' he said, cheerfully and incredulously, as if I'd missed something fundamental. His confidence was audible, his belief that she wouldn't get much more cross, that it would always be more of the same. Possibly, he was right. If she ever discovered what we'd done, quite possibly she'd be different with Thomas from how she'd be with me. Thomas was her husband and the father of her coming child. Thomas might be almost forgiven, or at least tolerated. Not me, though, of course. 'Anyway, she isn't,' he countered. 'Midsummer was her idea.'

I shook my head. 'Jane's wardship.'

'Oh, that.' Dismissed. Good-naturedly, he said, '*You're* cross with me.' Then, when I went to contradict him, 'Don't –' *lie to me*. Still good-naturedly.

So, I told him the truth, or as close as I could get to it. 'I don't know *what* I am with you, Thomas.'

'You know, I've never wavered in how I feel about *you*.'

I wasn't having that. 'You didn't *like* me.' I was remembering how suspicious of me he'd looked when I'd first turned up to witness their newly wedded bliss at Chelsea.

He laughed. '*You* didn't like *me*. Oh, don't worry, I'm used to it. What I was doing was keeping out of your way. As I am now.' Still cheerful. 'Making life easier for you.' Suddenly, he spoke more seriously, lowering his voice to confide, 'Cathy, I have no wish to make life difficult for you.'

I didn't respond.

'And, anyway, even way back,' he began again, 'when you were Charles's ever-so-respectable wife: remember what I told you about that? How it was so clear that in fact you weren't? Well, *that* I liked.' He laughed.

He'd seen only half the picture, only seen what he'd wanted to see. Whatever I'd said and whatever I'd done, back in those days, was said and done with Charles. Neither of us was really all that respectable. The Suffolks, we were, England's foremost couple after the king and queen, yet we hosted people considered to be heretics; we welcomed them to live in our household and promoted them wherever possible at court. Even *I* wonder now, looking back: how did we get away with it? My guess is, by never lying about what we were up to. Never hiding it. Never flaunting it, either, though. We simply stood our ground and did what we felt had to be done. People trusted Charles. My being married to him had enabled me to be who I was.

I changed the subject. 'Your Midsummer celebrations are all very well for now, but something tells me there won't be many parties when Jane's queen.'

'Oh, we'll just pretend we haven't heard her, and carry on as usual.'

I smiled, couldn't help myself: the image of the Sudeley household partying while Jane stood grim-faced in the background, squeaking her condemnation, trying to make herself heard. 'Harder to pretend that of Eddie, though.' Not much more vocal power to the little king, but even at ten years old he's learned how to make people listen. 'You couple her up with him, and any party-goers have a problem.' I was relaxing a little now. This – politics – felt safe, even enjoyable.

Thomas complained, 'Eddie's a good child, he's just in the wrong hands.'

'Your brother's hands.' I snatched up a sprig of rosemary: verdant, oily, astringent. 'What do you have against your brother?'

'What do you have *for* him?'

'Oh, well, now, let's see: he's trustworthy, clever. Diplomatic.'

Thomas kicked a fragment of tile. 'He's *boring*.'

It was predictable. Something Harry might have said. I felt weary. Wished even, suddenly, that my companion here was Thomas's brother rather than Thomas. He'd be droning on about taxation or something, but I'd have the sun on my back and I'd be looking at flowers with nothing required of me but to enthuse over them.

Thomas said, 'I don't think my brother knows anything of life, *any*thing.'

'And you do.'

He didn't rise to it. 'You know I do. And I know *you* do.' He took my hand; I withdrew it. He took it again and raised it so we could both see it. 'You think the world is a better place if I don't do this?'

'For your wife,' I said, 'yes.' And, anyway, it was never just a held hand, was it.

He seemed amused. 'Kate's fine, Cathy. She has everything she wants. Certainly she has everything that she wants of me. I love her; I love her more than I can say. You know that.'

We'd been through all this; this was old ground. Back then, it had worked, had been persuasive. But now . . .

I took my hand back again.

'This isn't you,' he lamented.

A spark of panic, because I felt somehow exposed, as if he'd threatened to tell Kate. I wanted so much to say, *You don't know me*. But he did, didn't he; he *did* know me. Heavy-hearted, I walked beside him in silence. We'd done an almost circular route when we reached the mulberry tree.

'There won't be any fruit for some years,' Thomas said,

matter-of-fact, looking into the branches, as if conversing with one of his gardeners.

For something to say, I told him, 'The berries are so fragile; at Thomas More's, we had to stand beneath and' – I didn't know quite how to explain it – 'drink them down.' Off the branches, I meant. Put our mouths up to berries that would have disintegrated at a touch.

'Did you?' was all Thomas said, with a studied indifference to the old world, to those who were powerful before the Seymours. The studied indifference of the newcomer, the latecomer.

Thomas More: felt like a lifetime ago to me. Being welcome in the More household: a lifetime ago. Charles and I were newly married, then. Catholic, because we knew no other way to be. In those days, the old days, there *was* no other way to be.

Odd that Kate and I should have had an exchange on that very subject only the following day. It was the closest we ever came to having a row. She'd spent a couple of hours reading before going as usual to prayers. When I turned up, later, to accompany her down to dinner, she patted her pile of books and remarked, 'What would our mothers have made of all this.' Not an actual question. Nor was her smile a smile, but a kind of wince. I was perplexed. Our mothers? What did our mothers have to do with anything? And anyway, what did it matter? Our mothers were gone.

What I said, though, was, 'They'd have been proud of us.' Because we were our mothers' daughters, as they had been theirs. Doing as they had done, continuing what theirs had begun. Acquainting ourselves with the latest books. Coming up with questions. Taking no one's word for anything.

Our mothers. More than a turn of phrase, no mere reference to our mother's generation. Kate, I knew, did mean our actual mothers, Maria and Maud. Never mind what our mothers would have made of us: what, I always wonder, did they make of each other when they met? That I would love to have seen. In breezed Maria, from Spain at the heartfelt request of her girlhood friend, the new queen. Maria: not merely fluent in English but witty in it, too. More than ready for some of England's rumoured irreverence. And there to greet her, if it could have been called that, was Maud, as English as a downpour. Long-faced, sharp-tongued, narrowed-eyed. Understimate Maud at your peril, though. Remember: she was the driving force behind the royal school, where everything was discussed, debated, either demolished or defended. With the exception of the church. Because no one, yet, in England, had gone that far. No one had any idea, yet, that anyone could go that far.

That was left to us. Our generation. It took time, but the time has come and here we are – my generation – doing what has to be done. That's the only difference, I said to Kate, between our mothers and us. We are bringing the church down to earth, back to the people, which our mothers never did. But if they were young women now, if they were clever young women now, this is what they'd be doing: reading the books that we're reading, having the debates that we're having.

Kate didn't see it that way. She said, 'They were *catholic*,' and stared at me, wide-eyed, as if I'd missed something glaringly obvious and she had to confront me with it. Which was ridiculous, of course, and I laughed. Yes, I told her, I do happen to know that, I was aware of that. But listen, I said: they'd *had* to be catholic. Because there was nothing else to be. There was no other way to think. And now – thank God, *thank God* – there is. *There is.* So – a smile from me now, and it was a proper one, no wincing or laughing – they'd have been proud of us.

'You really believe that,' she said, the clear implication being that I couldn't possibly.

'Funnily enough,' I said, 'I do, and you know why? Because it's the truth.'

'Oh, Cathy,' she sighed, sounding disappointed. She'd spoken quietly, or perhaps it was that her voice had sounded quiet because – I now realised – mine had been raised. She turned around and said to the window, 'We're destroying everything they cared about. What they lived for. I'm not saying that's wrong – I'm as certain as you are that it's right – but are you telling me that you don't ever, just for an instant, just sometimes, think how very sad they'd have been?' She turned back for my answer, a pleading in that turn. I shook my head. There was a silence before she said, wistfully, 'You can't say it, can you.'

This was absurd; I stood my ground. 'Why should I? Because it would make you feel better if I did?'

'No,' she sounded weary, 'because it's the truth.'

'I don't lie,' I warned her.

'No, you just don't always tell the truth.'

We stood staring at each other. She was the one, in time, to look away. 'So,' she said, 'anyway, it really doesn't bother you.'

'No,' I said. 'Absolutely not,' and took a step towards her, before I could stop myself, but only one, because it would be best, I judged, for me to leave. As I did, I said, 'Because I'm not sentimental, Kate.'

Thirty-one

Midsummer morning, my curtains and shutters opened to flawless weather, the sky a pale, airy blue. On my way over to Kate's rooms, I came across her and Thomas standing at a window in one of the hallways, the two of them in the green-gold glimmer of the glass. Her strange but beautiful shape: a bowing of her; the shy upward reach of her belly. I retraced my last step back onto the stairs, but too late. Turning, she was radiant in a gown of apricot over a honey kirtle. 'Cathy,' she enthused, 'what a day!'

Thomas smirked. 'Looks like God's for a party after all.'

Kate flashed him an amused glance and laid a hand briefly on his arm. That easy affection, the lightness of her touch, had my heart flick shut but still the thought came barging through: *I've loved that man, hard and frantic.*

To my relief, they were about to go their separate ways. When Thomas was gone, I fell into step with Kate, and checked with her, 'Do you need me around today?' Because I had plans. Quite apart from the three-month anniversary that I wanted to forget, to erase, to not be an anniversary, was the awkwardness of being in a household not my own during its frenetic preparations for a celebration. I'd be superfluous, which, feeling as I currently did, was something best avoided. I'd been at a loose end too much lately, and look where it had got me. Kate answered me that everything was under control and the only tasks that she'd set herself were the garland-making and trying to stop the children becoming overexcited. I'd already given some thought to my boys' day, and asked her if she could spare her choirmaster for a couple of hours for lessons, and she was happy to oblige.

'And you?' she asked.

'A ride,' I chanced. A long ride, a day's riding: that was the plan. Riding put her out of my sight and me beyond her reach. And I wanted to turn my back on Sudeley for a while before it clamoured for my attention, that evening.

She encouraged me to take whomever I needed from the stables, but I chose a small party of men I barely knew – none of my own staff – and then, riding, kept any exchanges to the purely practical. I rode up and over that crest of a day and came back down none the wiser, but it had been what I'd wanted to do and I'd done it.

I arrived back late in the afternoon and Sudeley had been hotting up in my absence, the air pungent with roasting meats. On my way up to my room I saw that trestle tables had been erected in the formal garden, their tablecloths dazzling among the muted green-blues of the lavender, rosemary and yew. Staff were staking the paths with torches and setting down lanterns, all of course as yet unlit, around the bases of statues. When Bella began preparing me a bath, I left her to it. Kate's rooms were where I went, but she wasn't there. (I wondered – was forever wondering, couldn't stop wondering – where Thomas was.) Her ladies said she was in chapel, at prayers; she'd spent the morning writing letters and meeting with a couple of local clergymen, then had enjoyed an afternoon in the gardens, collecting armfuls of flowers and foliage for the house. The ladies' talk turned to the evening's musicians – who was best and why, and when they'd be playing – and the food, principally the Sudeley pastry cook's legendary hot strawberry and almond pies. I had to interrupt to check up on my boys: had they been keeping themselves out of trouble? Oh, yes, absolutely, came back the assurance. I don't know why I asked really, because, of course, my boys could easily pull the wool over these ladies' eyes, were they so inclined.

Later, bathed and dressed, I returned to Kate's rooms, wary as ever of coming across Thomas on the way, trying to listen ahead, around corners. Hallway windows were open into the early evening, open onto that slow evaporation of colour and clamour from the gardens. I'd like to have savoured it, to have settled on a window-seat and given myself up to the wisps of conversations from people walking along the pathways below. More distant was the piping of children's voices. A couple of musicians tuning up, too: that insistent, exploratory plucking of one string at a time.

No Thomas on the way, nor in Kate's rooms. I was both relieved and disarmed, standing there at the end of Kate's bed with a feeling to which I was becoming accustomed, a sensation of no feeling. The sense of a feeling postponed. Kate, on the contrary, looked brimful, reclining against her pillows with one bare foot in Agnes's lap. Agnes's long fingers were pressing at the ankle. A tall, fair pair, they made, Kate and Agnes. Unbothered and capable. Kate was in a gown I'd never seen before: the pale gold velvet stamped with a small, square pattern and sewn all over with pearls. She shone, she looked so perfect that she could have been a painting. In a chair beside the bed, Elizabeth lounged; on a cushion at her feet was Mrs Ashley, unpicking a kirtle – one of Elizabeth's, I recognised – perhaps for the re-use of the material or perhaps for the turning of a panel, the hiding of a stain. Kate made polite enquiries about my ride, before conversation moved on to preparations for the evening.

'Elizabeth can't decide what to wear,' Kate said in an exaggerated tone of warning, giving me an amused look.

'Clothes,' I suggested. On cue, Elizabeth tutted and rolled her eyes. She never has any difficulty making any decision about anything; the fuss was simply for attention.

'Easy for you to say.' Kate smiled at me. 'You're another one.'

'Another what?'

'Someone who'd look good in anything. In a sack.' She looked me up and down. 'Although a sack's not what we have here, is it. It's absolutely gorgeous, Cathy. Is it Lucas?' From Lucas de Lucca, she meant. She made a twirling motion with one hand, but I don't twirl for anyone.

I said, 'You don't look so bad yourself.'

'Oh, but the effort this took us!' She patted Agnes's hand. 'To get me looking even half decent. Half *human*, in fact. Anyway, it's only us this evening, only Sudeley people; it's not as if we're at court. I've told Elizabeth she shouldn't worry. And she'll look stunning, anyway, whatever she ends up wearing.' Mrs Ashley looked up, distractedly, complacently, in a dutiful kind of seconding. Elizabeth rolled her eyes again, but this time happily. 'Nevertheless –' Kate sighed, extracting herself from Agnes, Agnes relinquishing her, 'it seems my presence is required in her room.'

'It is,' insisted Elizabeth.

Kate stood. 'You're lucky to have the choice. Whereas me' – hands patting the bump – 'I'm a bit restricted.' That glimmering gown of hers: she wasn't hard done by. I dismissed her complaint with a laugh and she inclined her head, accepting it, then the head tipped towards the door. 'Is this' – Elizabeth's dress choice – 'something you'd like to get involved in?' Mischievous, knowing the answer. I said I'd go and find my boys, asked where they were. Building the bonfire, Elizabeth said, as she left.

The stack of wood was at the front of the house; I'd seen it as I'd ridden back, but hadn't seen the boys. This time, after I'd skirted the maze, there they were. 'Found you.'

Harry said, 'Where is everybody?' As if they should already have been there. We were hours from darkness.

'*I'm* here.' I opened my arms, partly a display of affection, partly a display of my attire. He barely looked at me.

'Yes, thank you, a lovely day,' I said, sarcastically. 'And you?'

Charlie said, 'We've been building the bonfire,' his enthusiasm tentative in front of his brother.

'So I see.' I made a show of examining it. 'It's amazing.'

'Well,' he folded his arms, 'it *will* be.' Businesslike.

'No bones, I hope.'

Harry grumbled, 'It's no good without the bones.'

We'd discussed this. No bones, he'd been told. They'd all been told. Yes, we could celebrate Midsummer, but no, there'd be no bones. That disgusting tradition of burning bones on the John the Baptist bonfire: the rolling black smoke, the stench.

'There are no bones,' Charlie assured me, quietly.

'Good. We don't want that stink.'

'But that' – Harry drew himself up to patronise me – 'is the point of it.' *Out with the old*.

'Well, the point of this one can be to have a nice evening around a nice bonfire.' What was happening to me? I was turning into my mother. 'Is it far enough from the tithe barn?'

Charlie said, 'Mr Billings says so.' Presumably a groundsman. 'Thomas put me in charge,' he added.

And how had Harry taken that? I wondered. The answer was in Harry's sneer: *child's play*, said his expression. I checked again: 'You're sure it's safe?'

'Very. Thomas said to keep asking Mr Billings and I did.'

'Good.' And a good choice from Thomas, if unintentional: I was happier with my fate in Charlie's hands, at this time, than Harry's. Ready to move off, I finished with, 'How did you find the choirmaster this morning?'

'All right.' Charlie, noncommittal. Then, artless, 'Harry's written a song.'

'Charlie!' Harry took a swipe at him; he ducked.

'*Harry!*' I was livid at the aggression towards his brother. Charlie looked stung, though probably more by my intervention than by Harry's reprimand. If I hadn't been there, he'd have doubtless shrugged it off. But I *was* there; I couldn't stand by and let it go. 'Apologise to Charlie!'

'Leave me alone. Both of you.'

He stalked off; we watched him go. Turning to shrug at

Charlie, I saw that he looked sheepish. There was more to this than I'd appreciated. 'What? What was it about the song?'

Gravely, he confided, 'It was lovey-dovey.'

Which, of course, at the time, ignorant of what was happening, I found touching and amusing.

Thirty-two

All evening, that vast bonfire was compelling, tearing into its wood and hurling smoke, but by eleven o'clock a small crowd of us had retreated, exhausted, to Kate's private garden at the back of the house. Despite the many benches, we'd somehow ended up sitting where we'd been standing, on the steps. There we were, among clouds of fleabane growing from between the tiles, the tiny flowers as perfect as if concocted by a confectioner in sugar. The sky was Madonna-blue, silvered with stars and hung with a fat, buttery moon.

Elizabeth was leaning back against Kate's kirtle. She'd spent the evening dancing, and cajoling everyone else to join her. Rigorous, as usual, in her pursuit of a good time for all. Quite something to watch. Watch was all I'd done, my excuse being my long day's ride. Harry, though, to my surprise, had fallen in with her, thrown himself into it. His exuberance had drawn some admiring but baffled attention ('Just look at that young chap!' I overheard from a manor tenant). The spectacle was endearing to me, too, but also unnerving: I was aware of a helplessness in him, even as I didn't understand it. Now he was lying face down on some grass, head on folded arms, glancing up from time to time. Not, I feared, very soberly.

Charlie had sat out the dances, as had Jane. The two of them were now side by side on a step, spooning up sticky cherry pie from a shared plate: Jane, huge-eyed, unblinking; Charlie, frowning, intent.

Thomas was elsewhere. I'd last seen him playing cards with his men in the formal garden and presumably he was still doing so. Occasionally we could hear something of the games: a groan of dismay, a yell of triumph.

I didn't want to think about Thomas.

Suddenly Kate put her hands to her bump. 'He's hiccuping.'

'All that gooseberry fool,' I said. That cheek-twingeingly sharp gooseberry fool which had been my favourite pudding of the evening.

Elizabeth swivelled, her rose garland moonlit. 'Can I feel?' Kate guided her hand. 'Hiccuping?' Elizabeth wondered, head cocked as if listening for something. 'Really?'

'Uh-huh.'

I said, 'Charlie used to do it all the time.' Actually, it was Harry who used to do it, but I suspected he'd object to my saying so. Charlie's frown deepened; Jane sneaked a hand up over a smile.

Elizabeth gave a little start. 'There he is!'

Harry looked up, eyes heavy-lidded, and Elizabeth met him with a slow smile. As if pacified, he folded himself back down.

When Elizabeth's hand was back in her own lap, Kate turned to me, eyes shining: 'Odd to think, isn't it, that next year – everything being well – there'll be someone else enjoying all this with us.' She added, 'Not that he's not enjoying it now, in his own little way. He knows something's going on. He knows he's in good company.' Her hand was on mine, briefly. 'Loving company,' she said.

Listen: I went to find Thomas because, on that beautiful evening, with Kate holding my hand, it seemed to me that all the damage that could ever be done had already been done. Whatever I did now made no difference. That's the only way I can explain it.

I made my excuses, such as they were, none being required on a long evening of everyone coming and going. I didn't have far to go: through the gate of Kate's garden and all of fifty paces or so to where the card game was under way. I stayed at a distance, perched on a step. When he noticed, he came over, no one else as much as glancing up because the game was in full swing. He sat beside me. 'What is it?' He could see there was a problem and assumed it was with Kate. I didn't reply – couldn't put it into words – but shook my head, *Not Kate.* Then lowered my head into my hands. He laid a hand on my arm. *I'm lost, I'm lost,* was all I could think, desperate and furious. Yet even as I was thinking it, there was in my core a stirring, there was *life.*

We did nothing that night. Didn't even talk about it. It was enough for me to have come to him; it would have been too much to do any more.

The next day, it began again. 'Not our old room,' Thomas said. We were all leaving chapel; he'd fallen into step with me and slowed me up. 'Not unless it's Eleanor you're keen on' – Marcella's sister, staying – 'because that's who you'll find there.' For that, he got the most deeply disapproving look I could dredge up. Bad enough in the first place that he'd intercepted me on the way out of chapel.

Suddenly, Elizabeth was there, sweeping alongside Thomas. 'Thomas?'

Emphatically: 'Yes, Elizabeth.'

'Would you talk to the new Master of the Horse for me? About Cristobal?' One of her horses.

Kate heard; twisted around, called back, 'Don't worry, I've already done it. Didn't I say?'

Elizabeth skipped ahead of us. 'Oh. Thank you.'

'And it's fine, Elizabeth: fine.'

I couldn't help but feel that Elizabeth had fabricated a reason for interrupting us. Thomas spoke hurriedly now. 'The only other room is on the servants' side.'

To cover up our whispering, I called ahead to Kate, 'Are you sure you don't need one of our stables?' We'd had a conversation earlier about the stabling arrangements for my own horses.

Again, she twisted, called: 'No. Really, Cathy, we're fine.'

Thomas continued, 'Herb garden, stairs on your left.' Then, 'Usual time.' Some time in the hour before supper: the earlier, of course, the better.

I didn't like the prospect of being on the servants' side of the house: so many more people, even if they were supposed to be busy elsewhere. When the time came, I stood in the stairwell – pressed back against the wall, hiding from anyone who might come into the little walled garden – because he hadn't been able to tell me which room, and these stairs led up to a lot of rooms. What I could see, from where I stood, was rosemary, symbol of fidelity in marriage. What I was thinking was, *Why am I doing this? Cowering here, waiting for this man.*

And then along he came, and I knew. *Excitement*. It's the only word for that blooming of my heart under my breast-bone. He sauntered down the path, glinting in the sunlight, beautifully clothed. Beautiful naked, too, I recalled: the penny-flat nipples and, down from his navel, the line of fur. 'I can't do this,' I told him, when he reached me. He froze, wide-eyed, as if looking for a way to be helpful. 'I can't come here,' I explained, 'it's too risky.'

'But you *are* here.' He smiled.

Remind me, 'What is it that I'm supposed to be doing here?'

A shrug. 'Looking for someone?' His fingertips were tracing the shape of one breast beneath the bodice of my kirtle.

I batted his hand away. '*Who?*' Who on earth would I be looking for? These servants weren't mine.

He peered up the stairs as if for inspiration. 'Dominic. The farrier's boy.'

It made no sense to me. 'But why would I want to find *him*?'

'You *don't* want to find him. You want to be *looking* for him, not *finding* him. Trust me: if there's someone you want to look for but never find, Dominic's your little man.' Twisted logic. He started up the stairs, whispering, 'My falconer's our neighbour.'

'Oh, good,' I hissed, sarcastically. 'A hawk-eyed falconer.'

Smiling, he shook his head. 'Best kind. He's not in the least interested in humans.'

Our new room: on bare boards lay a narrow, straw-stuffed

mattress. 'Reduced circumstances.' Thomas sounded cheerful. I, too, liked it; liked it better than that previous gloomy room of ours, dominated by his mother's old bed. Here, limewashed walls glowed with late-afternoon sunshine. Even as I was taking it in, he was unpinning me, casually. My petticoat slid from my shoulders but there was no chest over which to drape it, so I stepped out of it, left it where it was, comically half standing.

Later, the warm sunshine made us slower than usual to get up and leave. I was lying on top of him; there was no room on the mattress to lie side by side. We hadn't spoken much – what was there to say? – but then he said, dreamily, 'Kate tells me you were to marry the son.'

I didn't follow, raised my head.

He gazed fondly back at me. 'Charles's son.'

'Why did she say that?'

He frowned, puzzled. 'Isn't it true?'

I sat up. 'It's true, but why did she say it?'

He shrugged with his mouth. 'Just in conversation.'

'You have conversations about me?'

He tucked his hands behind his head, and smiled. 'Yes, we have conversations about you. You think I should refuse? When she starts talking about you, I should say, "Oh, sorry, Kate, I really can't discuss Cathy"? That would look good.' Then, 'You two have conversations about *me*.'

'Less often than you think.' *Less often than you'd like.* I glanced around for my shift. 'Anyway, Kate doesn't know everything about me.'

'Clearly not,' he said, and I hated him for it, which he must have sensed because he shut up. I put on my shift and stockings. Then he started again: 'So, were you?'

'Was I what?'

Belatedly, he sat up and began to cast around for his clothes. 'Supposed to marry the son.'

'Does it matter?' I stepped into my petticoat.

'You tell me.'

'There's nothing to tell.' I was amazed that he didn't know, but then, of course, my little scandal was before the Seymours' time, was done and dusted before they came on the scene. I was well and truly respectable by the time they arrived. 'I was supposed to be marrying him but he died.'

'How long before?'

'Before what?' And a prompt, 'Thomas . . .' *repin me, please.*

He rose, stepped beside me, got to it. 'Before you married Charles.'

I was going to have to go through it all. 'He died *after*.'

'How did that happen?'

His interest sounded genuine, but puzzled me. 'Why are you pursuing this?'

His turn to be foxed. 'I don't know really. Just trying to find the heart of you, I suppose.'

That's not your domain. 'Why are you so interested in whether I have a heart?'

'Not *if*. I never said *if*, did I.'

If I gave him what he wanted, I suspected, he'd let me be. 'I was engaged to Charles's son,' and I stressed, '*by* others.'

'Yes, well, by Charles, I imagine,' said Thomas.

'Yes, by Charles,' I allowed.

'And then Charles changed his mind, and married you himself.' He'd finished repinning me and now I had to turn to the tricky business of my hair, of tidying it, of making the most of a bad job, mirror-less and maid-less.

Thank goodness for hoods. He'd resumed dressing himself. 'And you' – he spoke downwards, absorbed in those eyelets – 'you, who'd been this boy's stepsister and his soon-to-be wife: there you were, suddenly his stepmother.'

'Stranger things have happened, Thomas, as you well know.'

He wasn't deflected. 'What was he like, this boy?'

What was he *like*? 'Oh, Thomas, it was a long, long time ago.' A glance from him suggested that he wasn't keen to settle for that. He'd have to, though. It was the truth. 'Nice,' I said: what more could I say? He was a nice boy. He was just a boy. I tried to explain, 'I didn't really notice what he "was like"; he was just always there.' Or not, come to think of it. He was always off somewhere, doing whatever he did: climbing trees, swimming, making pets of voles. Sandy-haired, straw-haired, endearingly unkempt regardless of what anyone tried to do for him. We got on well, considering he was a year younger than me and a year makes a difference at that age. He'd show me his pets, for which he couldn't do enough, and make a fuss of my dog. Often I was invited along with him: we rode together most afternoons. He treated me as an equal, which his sisters, friendly though they were to me, never quite did. He'd have made a good husband, is my guess, and been a worthy successor to Charles: generous, kind, no airs and graces. Strange to think that if he'd survived – Mary Rose's boy, the baby of her family – my own sons would never have existed. Not simply strange, but unthinkable.

My little husband-to-be was Charles's second Harry. My own, just a year later, was – is – Charles's third, and the survivor. Third time lucky. The heir and then the successor. When second Harry was no longer around, that's when I noticed him. Noticed him missing. Missed him. Charles had sent for me to come to his study and when I'd settled in the huge chair there, he said, slowly, 'I wonder, Cathy, whether we – you and I – shouldn't get married.' He looked concerned.

I said, 'But who will marry Harry?' My innocence now makes me wince. I feel for Charles, too, in retrospect, having to face the unworldly little girl that was me.

He took a moment to answer. 'You know, Cathy, he's very, very ill.'

I'd known he was ill; everyone knew; he hadn't been well for a while. Not riding much. Good days and bad days. Bad nights, sometimes, with Mary Rose comforting him when she was strong enough to make her way to his room. But *very, very ill*: that was something else; that was what Mary Rose had been, and look what had just happened to her. *Harry?* Tree-climbing, bareback-riding Harry? *Twelve*-year-old Harry? Charles's expression was telling me, *Yes, Harry*.

Charles wouldn't have wanted to hurt his son but he was a pragmatist. A gentle, wise pragmatist but a pragmatist all the same. So, we married. Harry went off to court, on one of his good days, presumably one of his last, and never came home again. I never saw him again. Never went riding with him again.

Harry had been just like me, we'd been two of a kind, kicking around the estate, almost the same age and with the same future, but suddenly – he'd been made no one. Me, too, in a way: I'd been taken from who I was. Fourteen and pregnant, I was no longer the girl I had been, no longer the girl I should have stayed until I'd been ready to let her go. To think, now: Harry was around the age of my own boys when it all happened to him. He lost his mother and then, within months, his sisters were married off according to plan but the plan for his own future was cancelled and his wife-to-be became his stepmother. He would have felt so ill, too; worse and worse every day, and with no mother to comfort him. And me? Standing there in front of Thomas, I remembered how – newly married, then pregnant – I'd been mad with loneliness and no one, *no one* had known. That was what had done it: my being so desperate but not even Charles knowing it; not even Kate, until later, until too late. That was what changed me. That was what made me what I am.

Thirty-three

Thomas had told me that he wouldn't be around the following afternoon. A local friend would be visiting and they'd be playing tennis. Last thing, he suggested: come to our secret room at night, before bedtime. Impossible, I argued, and in retrospect I should have argued harder. You'll find a way, he told me: you did, before. He'd wait, he told me, until I managed it; he'd wait, however long it took.

That evening I was on my way back to my own room, ostensibly turning in for the night, annoyingly joined by Agnes and Marcella, when Harry stepped out from behind a staircase. This was dizzying, because, as far as I'd known, he was still in the hall with his friends and his brother. Somehow he'd managed to follow me and then get ahead. He stood his ground, serious-faced, his gaze flicking warily to the two ladies. He asked, 'Can we talk?' Even this, from him, sounded like a challenge, albeit reined in. I indicated to the ladies that they should go ahead. Still that look from Harry, though: a refusal to yield. Whatever he wanted to say, he wanted greater privacy for it than allowed by a hallway. So, where to? 'The library,' I decided. It would be warm enough despite the lack of a fire, but of course we'd need lights.' We'll need the candles lit,' I called to the departing Marcella, who said she'd send someone.

Harry and I walked together and waited in awkward silence at the door to the dark library. My assumption was that he was in trouble. A dispute with a friend, perhaps, or he'd offended someone or broken something here. Once the man with the taper had been and we were settled in the library, Harry said, 'I need your advice,' before revising, 'I need your *help*,' his chin tilted in defiance. I kept my expression clear and spread my hands: *It's yours to take.* My heart was heavy, though, because I held no great hope that this uneasy concord of ours wouldn't collapse in the blink of an eye.

'I don't know how to start.' He gave an exasperated, humourless laugh, but then, suddenly: 'I'm in love with Elizabeth.' My heart dropped like a shot bird. *In love with*: grown-up words from my boy, hanging on him like fancy dress, incongruous and pitiful and endearing at the same time. And *Elizabeth*. Elizabeth! As if she'd give him a second glance. *Damn* Elizabeth.

'As is Elizabeth with me,' he added, and everything changed, lurched, my reaction going in two directions at once: *This – with Elizabeth – is actually already happening*; and, *She's second in line to the throne, so this can't happen, can't be happening, can't have happened*. I got a hold on my nerve and held on hard while asking, 'She said so?' and trying to look pleased. I needed information from him.

'Yes.' He, too, looked pleased, enormously so. He looked very handsome, grinning away, and I glimpsed him through her eyes. Fear was washing through me, but I steadied myself to ask, 'When did this happen?'

'Oh' – as if chronology and facts were charming irrelevancies – 'I suppose it's always been happening for me ever since we first met. First sight,' he claimed, proudly; then, 'No, not sight, to be honest, although of course she is –' and he halted, bashful.

Beautiful.

Was she? Was it beauty that she had, or something more complex? More dangerous.

'I suppose it happened the first time I heard her speak, although I don't remember what she said, doesn't matter what she said.' He leaned forward, and urged, 'It's just that she thinks like I do.' As if that were a miracle. As if no one else ever had or ever will do. I felt so very tired. He was glowing, and there I was in that glow, reflecting it, having to reflect it, feeling it burn on my face. There we sat, smiling at each other.

'And Elizabeth?' I probed. 'You've talked together about how you both feel?'

'And written,' he enthused, to my utter dread. 'We've been writing, all along.'

There are letters, there is evidence. I wanted to scream at him, *We all know it's treason to make such an approach to anyone in line, and we all know the sentence for treason.* I should have guessed, though, shouldn't I, that he'd be capable of this. He's forever been running before he could walk. Think of him as a baby, his readiness for a world which wasn't yet interested in him and required him to bide his time. Remember his offended stare, his disbelief, his rage.

'So,' my son was continuing, cheerfully, 'where do we go from here? What happens now?'

Nowhere. Nothing. I'd have to get him out of danger. I'd have to make this . . . unhappen somehow. Make it not have happened. Make it something else. 'Well,' I was buying time, 'you're both very young.' Not that Council would care. Old enough, in their eyes, to do damage. Old enough to be made an example of. Old enough to kneel at a block. Oh, the faint downiness of his nape when he was a toddler: a surprise, a little secret, little joke, that golden mist with its own grain. His perfect, God-made nape, the softest part of him and also the strongest. And now someone – some nobody – would quite possibly require him to bare that nape and slam down onto it a butchering blade. As if my son were nothing. To make him nothing and to make nothing of all that has gone into him: my ever-vigilant love; the love that he has drunk from me; his to take, gladly given and relentlessly taken.

'We're the age you were when you married,' he came back quickly, keenly; keen to claim this affinity.

'Not by choice,' I had to remind him.

He wasn't to be deflected. 'It worked for you, though, didn't it.'

I didn't know, any more; I really didn't know.

'And,' Harry continued, 'how would it be any different if I was older? I'm lucky it's happened early. You always said I'd know when I met the right person.'

Did I?

'You always said I should follow my heart.'

'Yes.' I said that?

He was getting wind of my resistance. 'That's what you brought us up to believe,' he reminded me.

I felt that I was watching myself, and I watched with sadness and despair to see where this was going. Our first chance for a truce for so long was probably about to be our last because I'd have to try to save him and he didn't want to be saved and would rage against me for it.

Memories, suddenly. Harry, aged three, toddling past chapel, from which was coming the sound of choir practice, the scorching voices of the boys at the top and everywhere below them voices striking bell-like on each note, and so many of those notes, massed and mad-turning. And Harry looking up at me, trying to express himself with his few words: 'It's not a man speaking in there, it's a man crying. It's sad, that music. It's scary-sad.' And at around the same age, Harry playing with a toy cart, flattening himself to the floor the better to appreciate the revolutions of its chunky wheels. I'd seen then that he was impressively long, no longer a baby, as I'd assumed, but a boy, and a boy, to judge from his expression, with serious concerns. Six, seven: a boy whose climbing of trees was both as certain and as carefree as the singing of a song. Nine or so: a boy whose steadying hand on the muzzle of a skittish horse had exactly the right balance of authority and reassurance, a hand that worked its own small wonder. And last summer, a young man who plunged in after a slipped child, a servant's child, hauled her from the river and pounded the fluid from her lungs, forcing his own air down her in long, luxurious breaths while everyone else, including me, was still only just letting go of an initial sharp intake. Oh, believe you me, no one, *but no one*, was going to make nothing of this boy, turn this boy into nothing.

I said to Harry, 'It's just that it's complicated, you know, this situation with Elizabeth.'

'That's why I'm here.' For him, we were conspirators now, heads together, rather than him opening up to me and me failing him.

'It's Council's decision,' I was thinking aloud, 'who Elizabeth marries. Her being second in line.'

'I know.' He was impatient.

I confronted him with hard fact: 'It's treason, Harry, to' – how to put this? – 'have anything romantic to do with her.'

This, though, he dismissed. 'I'm the Duke of Suffolk. There's no one in England higher in rank. I'm the son of her father's oldest friend. And I'm *his* son's right-hand man. So, as long as no one's looking abroad for a husband for her . . .' He gave me a questioning look, as if he expected me to know. Which I didn't. Having been rather preoccupied of late. He continued, 'You have friends on the Council, they're all your friends. The Lord Protector himself, he's one of your best friends.'

Thomas's brother. It seemed ages ago, when I'd had the ear of Ed. Another world, one that I'd left for an involvement with his brother. That world beckoned now; made its presence felt, loud and clear; was real again. Harry will go on to be brilliant: an excellent husband and father, and a far-sighted, humane influence on the king. He has to do so much, and will do it gloriously. He is truly God's gift. No one is going to go against God to put a stop to him. I asked him, 'Who knows about this?'

'No one.'

'*No* one?' *Think*. 'Mrs Ashley?'

He half laughed, dismissive, '*Oh*, no.'

I recalled Mrs Ashley's thinking on the matter of Elizabeth's conduct: Thomas, overfamiliar. Thomas, red herring, in fact, it now seemed.

Harry urged, 'You can do this for me, I know you can.'

I stood up. 'Oh, I'm sure I can help you,' I said, 'but first, I have to ask: do you have Elizabeth's letters to you, here at Sudeley?' He said he did. 'I need all the letters,' I said, 'yours to her and hers to you,' and raised a hand to silence the inevitable objection. I didn't want to read them: that was the last thing I wanted to do. 'Council will need to be shown that this comes from her as much as from you,' I lied, as I began extinguishing our candles. And now for the truth: 'I really, really need to have that evidence, Harry.'

I could go to Thomas now: I was alone. I wasn't going to stay there, though. Not now; not after this. I needed to think. But I had to tell him that I wasn't coming, rather than simply fail to turn up. I couldn't risk him coming looking for me. He'd already be there, in our little room, was my guess. Not long after I'd gone, he'd have made his own excuses for leaving the hall, probably hinting at joining staff in the kitchens for card games. He had little need to lay false trails, to go to his room and pretend to go to bed; he was less answerable to his own attendants than I was to Kate's. I departed from Harry in the direction of my room, before switching route. Outside, the full moon lit my way, and then, sure enough, there was the suggestion of candlelight in our little window.

Inside, Thomas was sitting on the mattress. 'What is it?' he asked, smile vanishing, as soon as I entered the room.

Having just come from Harry, I was full of it. Back pressed to the door, I gave him the gist of what Harry had confided. I had no concerns about Thomas keeping this secret: he was already sworn to secrecy, with me, albeit on a different matter. He looked unsurprised, though. 'You knew?'

He seemed to have to consider how to answer. 'Well, he *had* sort of *half* broached the subject with me.'

'When?' Fury flared inside me. 'You didn't say!'

'To you?' He laughed it off. 'You bet I didn't.' Then, offering his hand, 'Come here.'

'No!' Instinct backed me harder into the door.

'It was just the other day,' he added, as if that made it better. As if, perhaps, given more time, he might have reconsidered and told me, tipped me off that my son was risking his life.

What I had to know was, 'Have you said anything to anyone?' and again, before he'd even had a chance to reply, '*Thomas? Think*: to *any*one?'

'No!' He acted affronted: 'Why would I betray Harry's trust? And, anyway, I didn't *know*; he'd *half* broached it, I said.'

'Do you think *anyone* knows?'

'No.' Confident.

'No?'

'No. Harry trusts me. He was coming to me first.'

I raged at him, albeit in a whisper, 'I can't believe you didn't tell me. This is *treason*, Thomas.' He tutted. 'It's *treason*,' I insisted. Typical, typical Thomas, blind to danger.

'They're *children*,' he hissed back.

'They're *fourteen*,' I said. 'Elizabeth could easily have a baby. Council will go to any length to make sure that doesn't happen until they want it to happen. And Harry . . .' Old enough, as far as Council is concerned, to be a threat. And to Council, they're much more than children. She's their precious second in line, and he's heir to a family so close to the throne to need an occasional pruning back.

Thomas said, 'Telling them "no" isn't going to work,' and – *how dare he?* – gave me a look to imply that I, more than most, should appreciate the lure of the forbidden. 'And, anyway,' he shrugged, 'who knows? Elizabeth's going to have to marry someone soon, isn't she.'

Not my son, she isn't. She's dangerous, we don't want the complication of having her in the family even if Council were to permit it. '*You* . . .' I despaired, furious. His ceaseless ambition, for himself and anyone connected to him: his unrealistic, *stupid* ambitions. I came close, now, to the edge of the mattress, better to impress upon him: 'This is about Harry, my boy, my son . . .'

'And Elizabeth.' His eyes, on mine, didn't flinch.

'I don't care about Elizabeth.'

'No,' he said, quietly, 'I know you don't.' Then, 'But, look, Cathy, who's to know? We're *here*,' he reminded me, 'at *Sudeley*. We're all friends here. Days away from . . .' He flapped a hand: anyone who matters, Council. Then his hand was on my wrist. 'We're *safe.*' A slow smile: 'Now, come here.'

'No.' I extracted myself, stood up. 'I can't. I need to think.' It was more than that, though. I couldn't bear to have anything to do with someone who could be reckless with my son's life.

Thomas seemed to accept my leaving, and, indeed, made a move to accompany me. When I objected – this was a bad time, people would still be around and returning to their rooms – he countered that there was nothing that couldn't be explained away about the two of us walking together. Moreover, he said, it was more credible that we'd bumped into each other and been talking together for a while than that I'd been walking alone around Sudeley for no reason at close to midnight. And so he came with me to the staircase most convenient for my room. He knew better than to talk on the way, and certainly not on the subject of Harry and Elizabeth. We met no one, kept to the shadows and kept moving. Perhaps our success made him overconfident, or perhaps he was trying to appease my obvious fury, but at the door to my staircase he overstepped the mark and kissed me goodnight, although the kiss itself was nothing but a pointedly respectful and cautious touch of his lips to mine.

Thirty-four

In the morning, I was woken from a belated sleep by Kate. There she was, leaning over me as best she could, her hand on my shoulder. There, in my room, at my bedside, with no attendants. I was sitting up in a flash: 'What?'

She shook her head – *Nothing* – but there was no smile. 'It's just that . . . you're in bed so late. It's not like you.'

'What time is it?'

'Eight.'

Not late, then. 'I didn't sleep well,' I mumbled, a propos of nothing. Nothing was making sense.

'Nor me,' said quickly and quietly. Then, 'Can you come to my study when you're up?'

So, something *was* the matter. My stomach clenched. She said no more and left. I dressed slowly, shrugging off Bella's attempts to help, desperate to be alone. *Kate knows*, I kept telling myself; told myself and told myself – *Think, Cathy, think* – but still couldn't believe it. *How* did she know? How could she *possibly* know? And *what – exactly* – did she know? I had a sensation of her hands already around my throat; my own hands were there again and again, to check, to plead.

Kate was alone in her study when I got there; she was pacing but indicated that I should sit. I didn't want to give myself up to the chair, but nor did I want to risk my legs giving way. Doing as I was told, sitting down, I felt trapped. The room was overly draped, caked in paint and gilt, the air laden with beeswax and motes. Kate looked as she had never before looked: as if she were sick with madness. Her huge, raw eyes darted, unseeing. I had no idea what was about to come my way – nothing would have surprised me, and anything would have – or *how* it was about to come; no idea how I might try to defend myself, what I could perhaps try to deny. *So, this is the end*: it was happening, at last, and of course it was. How had I ever assumed otherwise? I was going to be cast out, in disgrace. And when, really, anyway, had it ever been any different? Me, who'd been picked up for a while by a duke. That's all it had been, my life, the good life that I'd had. I'd never been up to it; I'd made a good show of it but I'd never, really, been up to it, and she knew it. *So, this is where it ends, for me.* And for me, I didn't care: *Let it come.* My boys, though . . . No, I didn't think of the boys, didn't dare. Whatever was about to happen to me I deserved, but the boys, my perfect Suffolk boys, who should have been facing their perfect futures . . .

Kate paused, leaned on the back of her chair, widened her already wide eyes and exclaimed, 'It's *Thomas*, isn't it!' Rushing on in a goading, sarcastic, fake-jocular tone, 'You know, you're going to have to help me with this one, Cathy; you're really going to have to help me. I'm quite sure we can find a way to deal with this, you and me; there must be a way we can deal with it.'

Me, woman of words: I had no idea what to say; there were no words inside me, none. Blood thumped in my ears, and I was trembling, shaking, quaking. How visibly? I was ridiculous, nothing but a bundle of passions and grievances. And her: unrecognisable, too, this frayed, laid-low woman. Witty and daring was how I was supposed to have been; and Kate, clear-sighted and composed. But now look at us. What I'd done had destroyed both of us.

She said, 'I saw Thomas kissing someone last night,' and, having said it, she was suddenly a picture of calm. It was me, now, who was obliged to react. *Someone*: she'd said *someone*, kissing *someone*. When I said nothing – desperate for clarification, elaboration – she continued, 'At one of the doors at the back. Midnight. I just happened to look out and there he was.' A correction: 'There *they* were. Kissing.' She broke her stillness, stepped to the window.

What had it looked like, that one, brief, reluctantly received touch of his lips to mine? There had been no passion in it. Anger burned away my breath: it had so nearly been all right but now, because of one, pointless, momentary mistake by Thomas, it wasn't. Had she already been to Thomas with this? If so, what had he said?

'Of course, it wouldn't surprise most people, would it, but, well, you know' – and she turned back to me, impassioned – 'I really did think it was something I'd never have to worry about, with him. Oh, a lot *else*, yes. But not *that*. He's always been so very, very loving to me. I really did think –' But there she stopped. When she spoke again, it was to tell me what I needed to know: 'I haven't yet spoken to Thomas.'

Just me and her, then, so far. I made myself ask, 'Who was it? The woman.' Subdued, my question sounded oddly nonchalant. If she'd replied, *Well, it was you, wasn't it*, or, *It was you, as you well know*, what would I have said? Perhaps I'd have said, *Oh,* that *kissing, you mean. Oh,* that. And then perhaps, *Oh, no, no,* that *was just . . .*

She frowned. 'Who was the woman? I don't know,' as if this was of not much more than passing interest, or certainly not her main concern. 'I couldn't see.'

Careful, Cathy. Perhaps she was springing me a trap. Again cautiously, I asked, 'But how could you not see?'

'It was dark.' She was exasperated, genuinely: she really hadn't seen. 'I'm not bothered who she was, to tell you the truth; I'm bothered that it was *Thomas.*'

A spark of hope had hit my heart and taken my breath away: *she really didn't know who the woman was!*

'She's not staff, though,' she said, and my heart flattened.

'Not staff?' I needed to know precisely what she'd seen.

She shook her head. 'Oh, you know how you know: dress, demeanour . . . The stairs she was going up, too: this side of the house, not servants' stairs. Whoever she was, she was one of us.'

Us. I looked down at my hands, tried to think. 'So, how did you know it was Thomas?'

This, she considered risible. 'Oh, I know.' *I know my own husband.* Then, more reasonably, 'I just knew, Cathy. It was Thomas.' She knew him enough to recognise him in darkness, across a garden, merged with someone else's silhouette.

I asked her what she was going to do.

'Speak to Thomas.'

What on earth would he say? He was quite likely not to lie but to tell something close to the truth. That's the problem with him, I realised: he's not so much a liar as a man who believes his own nonsense. 'Perhaps it was nothing,' I suggested. 'Nothing much.' A kiss, I meant her to understand: one kiss, a momentary silliness of his.

Sceptical, she said, 'Yes, that's probably what he'll tell me. But –' She inclined her head, absently tapped the glass in the window; she was thinking. 'There was considerable familiarity in it,' she decided.

Panic battered my heart, because there was to be no escape. But then: *familiarity.* The word had sparked an idea and there it was, bright and insistent. *Elizabeth.* It was Elizabeth who'd been overfamiliar with Thomas. And now this, the kissing: Kate might believe it of her.

But no.

No, I couldn't.

Could I?

'You don't think it was Elizabeth, do you?' I only put it to her as an idea; didn't claim it *was* Elizabeth. Wouldn't have dared. I'd still been wondering whether to say anything at all as I'd somehow gone ahead and voiced it, and it sounded properly tentative.

She looked blank. 'Elizabeth?'

What had I done?

'Well,' I flailed, 'Mrs Ashley . . .' but I didn't say it. Kate, too, said nothing and I feared that this was something else that was about to go against me; she might be about to throw at me, *What* are *you? What kind of woman* are *you, to suggest such a thing?* When she did finally speak, though, what she said was, 'My stepdaughter. My fourteen-year-old stepdaughter.'

There had been a shift; Thomas was, now, accused. The accusation was out of my hands and had a life of its own. This was complicated, and could easily be exposed as nonsense. I almost said, 'It might *not* have been Elizabeth.' I could still have said it, could have checked the momentum and brought some sense to the matter.

Kate said, 'Second in line,' and, full of wonder, 'He couldn't do any worse, could he.'

She seemed to require a reply, so I had to say, 'Probably not, no.'

'Did he not think what this – whatever it is, just a few kisses or whatever it is – could do to her?'

Her? *Her?* Oh, believe me, she gets what she deserves.

'She's fourteen, Cathy,' Kate despaired.

Fourteen, just as I was when –

Kate said, 'Don't, Cathy.' She sounded sad. 'Don't be angry.'

Was I? *Why* was I? Unclenching my fists, I glimpsed a scattering of fingernail marks in each palm.

'It's for *me* to be angry,' she said, 'if I can work myself up to it. I'm not sure I have the energy. Problem is, I'm getting so used to stupidity from Thomas and having to deal with the consequences.'

As if this were just another of his ill-judged plans.

The way I saw it: even if he hadn't done what I'd said he'd done, he could have, might have, probably would have. And what *had* he done? Far, far worse than I'd led her to believe. He'd had sex again and again with his pregnant wife's best friend. 'But *this*,' I insisted. 'How *could* he? And *her*?'

Kate spoke wearily. 'Oh, I doubt Elizabeth had much to do with it. Thomas can be very persuasive.'

Had I been persuaded? Yes and no. I didn't know, I didn't

know the truth of it. And Kate, what about her? Had she been persuaded to marry him? Were we two women who'd let ourselves be persuaded? Is that what had happened to us?

She should rest, I insisted, and think through her approach before confronting either Elizabeth or Thomas. The truth was, I had to get to him before she did. At the door, though, opening it and glancing back, I stopped in my tracks. Because there was something odd in the way that Kate was looking at me. Sneaking a look: that was what she was doing. Moments later, I'd decide that it was as if she didn't know me. At the time, I came up with no more than an instinctive, 'What?'

'Nothing,' she replied too quickly, adding a similarly quick, utterly unconvincing smile. Then, 'Nothing. Nothing!' and laughing, as if giving herself a shake. Only when I was on the other side of the door did I wonder: had she been looking at me as if perhaps I fitted the shape of the woman whom she'd glimpsed with Thomas? That wasn't it, was it? There in the hallway, hands pressed flat onto the full skirt of my gown, I wondered how distinctive an outline I'd make in semi-darkness. *Not* distinctive, I told myself: I might well be in other ways – certainly I'd hope to be – but not in my appearance, my size and shape. But, then . . . that look, that look of hers . . . Appraising, and quizzical.

I shook off that sickening doubt by rushing around Sudeley to ask after Thomas's whereabouts, all the time making sure to appear calm. Eventually, I learned that he was in chapel.

Chapel, of all places.

Nevertheless, it had to be done. I knocked at the door to his box but didn't wait for the invitation to enter. My hope was that I'd find him alone; it was possible that he'd go unattended. Inside, he was indeed kneeling alone and didn't seem to resent my intrusion, even welcomed it, looking around at me with a smile.

Ridiculously, I whispered, 'What are you doing here?' Someone might be below us in the chapel; we could well be overheard.

He took no offence at my pointless question, smiling and shrugging as if to say, *Just the usual*. 'But what are *you* doing here?' His question, on the contrary, was joshing, affectionate.

I knelt alongside him. 'Kate saw you kiss someone last night. Outside, down by the backstairs.'

The smile plummeted, his eyes widening. 'You,' he breathed, as if it was this which was news to him: that it was me.

I shook my head. 'She doesn't know it was me.' Because she didn't, did she? *Dress . . . demeanour . . .* Mine didn't differ from any of her ladies', from Elizabeth's . . .

'She told you this?'

'Just now.'

He looked away, unfocused, then back. 'How was she?'

A bit late to be concerned. 'Fine.' My whisper was sharp. 'She thinks it was Elizabeth.'

I could see that he'd been about to query, *Fine?* But now it was, 'Elizabeth?' And again, but to himself, '*Elizabeth?*' He was amazed. 'Why would she think that?'

'Because Mrs Ashley once said she was worried –'

'Oh, that . . .' He dismissed it, frowning.

'You knew?'

He barely answered. 'Kate mentioned it, but –' It occurred to him: 'What did *you* say?'

I looked him hard in the eyes. 'That it seemed likely to me.'

He reeled, almost laughing at the absurdity. '*What?*'

'Listen, Thomas,' I urged, 'you can say it was nothing. I don't care what you say. You can say it was a moment that got out of hand, a one-off. You can say Elizabeth was keen for some kissing practice and twisted your arm. Or she was upset about something and you were comforting her and it went a bit too far. Say whatever you like. Say you were drunk. Both of you. Whatever you like. But say it was Elizabeth.'

He shuffled back on his knees to make some distance between us, to be able to see me better.

He was incredulous. 'I will *not* say it was Elizabeth!'

I didn't waver, kept calm and delivered the threat as I'd planned. 'If you don't, I'll tell her it was me, and I'll tell her it was no one-off.'

This he found even less believable. 'You wouldn't dare.'

'Think, Thomas, think: which is she more likely to forgive you? Going momentarily too far with an excitable, head-strong fourteen-year-old? Or three months of sex with her best friend?'

He was taken aback to hear it, but recovered to hiss, 'Why not a moment too far with *you*? Why *Elizabeth*?'

'Because she wouldn't believe it of me.' And he knew it was true. I'm no fourteen-year-old girl – never was, in a sense; never had the luxury – and nor am I a woman for whom a moment could ever simply get out of hand. There'd have been more to it than that, Kate would realise.

He sat back on his heels. 'Have a heart. Not Elizabeth.'

A heart for whom, I wondered. 'I'm afraid it has to be Elizabeth.'

He saw it: 'It's not so much that you don't want it to be you, is it. You want it to be Elizabeth. You want Elizabeth in trouble, don't you. You want her – what? – chaperoned? Is that what you want? Or sent away? And you want Harry to think Elizabeth is capable of –' He stopped, as if offended beyond words. '*Oh*, no. No, no, no.'

I reiterated, 'I will tell her,' and put it to him: 'What have I left to lose?' and believed it, utterly. 'Her friendship? I don't deserve her, Thomas; I deserve to lose her. I've ruined it all, already; it's already ruined. And my "good name"?' Me? Good name? How laughable. 'If I have to sacrifice my good name – such as it is – to save my son from the mess he's made for himself, then I will. You know I will.'

Oh, he knew. He tried, though: 'Cathy, listen, there are other ways to save Harry.'

'Not that aren't patchy, leaky, and that's not good enough. And not that will keep him on my side.' I shook my head. 'No, this – the Elizabeth situation – will do it. And, anyway, he needs to see Elizabeth for what she is.'

'But she *isn't*,' he protested, horrified. 'And how *could* you? How could you do this to Harry?

Oh, Thomas, come on! We all have disappointments, in life.

He said, 'In any case, what do you think Elizabeth's going to say?'

Not much. She wouldn't get the opportunity. I'd advised Kate: when you talk to Elizabeth, keep it general, keep it to the 'overfamiliarity', don't get dragged into specific instances and details because then she can argue with you and you'll get tied up in denials and it's not about what she did when, it's the whole situation, the situation that's developing. To Thomas, I said, 'Elizabeth will know that she's allowed you to overstep the mark too often and that it's upset her stepmother, and she'll feel very sorry.'

He rose, slowly, and began to pace. 'Elizabeth's second in line. If I'd been messing about with her, I could be had up for treason.' He gave me a cool, frank look. 'I have enemies, Cathy.'

Yes, I know, and whose fault is that? But I said, 'Not here, you don't.' I got to my feet. 'As for further afield, well, who's to know? Kate's hardly likely to make it known, is she? Nor is Elizabeth.'

'And Harry?'

'I'll deal with Harry.' As best I could. Truth was, I didn't fancy my chances. Hurrying on, I reapplied the pressure to Thomas, appealed again to his self-interest: 'Think: which is Kate more likely to forgive you?'

He was weighing it up, I could see. He couldn't resist. Self-interest was winning. *I* was winning. He switched to, 'And what happens to us?'

I'd been hoping he'd ask and give me a chance to make it clear. 'Nothing. I made a mistake, Thomas.'

This, of all, seemed hardest for him to believe. '*What?*' He laughed aloud – there, in chapel – and came towards me, stopped only just in time, standing too close. 'Again and again and again? Face down over a bolster?'

I didn't dignify it with a response; turned, and walked out.

Thirty-five

The next day, we left. I insisted to Kate that she and Thomas would need time to themselves, and, despite her protestations, she did seem relieved. Charlie was merely puzzled and a little disappointed. Harry was initially furious at the news, but I gave him the impression that our hasty departure was for his benefit, as part of a plan, a strategy. He was unaware that we wouldn't be accompanied by his and Elizabeth's letters. We were taking no evidence, nor leaving any behind. Even as I spoke with him, those letters were flaking to ashes in my grate.

Harry was surprisingly unaware of just about everything that was happening. Clearly, Elizabeth hadn't yet come to him. Perhaps she had enough to do, placating her stepmother, and Harry was one complication too many; Harry could wait. Harry, as her rock, in her opinion, would understand; there was no rush to explain herself to him. Perhaps that was it. Or perhaps she had been half persuaded of her guilt, or was examining the possibility of it and avoiding Harry while she did so. Whatever the explanation, she retreated to her room, into the care of Mrs Ashley. But this retreat from Harry, I knew, wouldn't last. Time was of the essence.

Kate had told me what had happened with Elizabeth. She hadn't needed to, because in a sense I already knew. I'd guessed what Elizabeth would feel, do and say, because she was me all over again. Her life had been lived under the care of many different people, good people, kind people, but no one had ever understood her and placed her first. And then, just in time, just as Elizabeth was almost grown up, just before it was too late, a wonderful woman had taken her on as a daughter. How horrible, how unthinkable for Elizabeth: the accusation that she had betrayed Kate, had tried to take something of Kate's own belated happiness.

That I'd anticipated, and used. Only in retrospect did I realise that there had been far more in the situation that had worked in my favour. Elizabeth's life was like mine, yes, but also nothing like mine and nothing like anybody else's. Yes, like me she had seen at fourteen that there was a good life to be had, and she longed for that good life for herself, but above all she wanted a life which, unfortunately, for her, was no given, not as the royal bearer of bad blood. She had to be very, very careful at all times and had developed a nose for danger. Two when her mother was disgraced, she'd grown up the offspring of a woman executed for adultery with her husband's best friend and her very own brother. It was a lot to live down, a lot to try to escape. Accuse Elizabeth of being involved with someone else's husband, and accuse her of keeping it in the family, and no doubt she felt that her fate had come to claim her. In short, it was no more than she'd expected.

She would have said and done anything to try to make amends. According to Kate, Elizabeth did plead her innocence, but didn't dare contradict her. In other words: if she had behaved improperly, then that hadn't been her intention (nor Thomas's, she was quite sure), and she was more sorry than she could ever say. She couldn't bear to argue, couldn't live with herself if she caused Kate any more distress. Begging to be forgiven, she cried and, according to Kate, seemed terrified. 'Heartbroken, too.' Kate sounded surprised. It was no surprise to me.

Kate decided to send her away for a while, into the care of our friends Jane and Anthony Denny in Hertfordshire. The real reason was kept from them; they were told that Elizabeth needed to concentrate on her studies away from the hectic preparations for the baby and then its arrival. Elizabeth pleaded with Kate to allow her to stay – *You need me here!* – but Kate didn't waver. We need some breathing space, she told Elizabeth, we need some time for reflection. It's not for ever, she said.

All that I could have predicted. What I hadn't been able to guess was whether Elizabeth would mention Harry. In fact, she had. 'D'you know,' Kate said, 'she told me that she's in love with Harry. *Your* Harry. Seems to think she wants to marry him. *Did* you know, Cathy?' The question was genuine.

'*Harry?*'

Kate offered, 'Well, it's an idea . . .' but then seemed to lose interest, adding only, 'She really does need some time away, doesn't she, to think, to calm down.'

'Oh, yes,' I said. 'Definitely.'

'We all do,' she added, quietly, which made me shiver.

And Thomas? Thomas had done as I'd said. Kate quoted him inexpressively, as if what he'd said was barely worth relating: 'It was nothing, a bit of silliness, he was drunk and it was just a moment that got out of hand, just a kiss, and, yes, he's been stupid, and it's been a difficult time for him' – her hands to her belly – 'what with the pregnancy.' At this last, she raised her eyebrows, disparagingly. She clearly didn't believe a word of it, although what exactly she *did* believe about this supposed situation between Thomas and Elizabeth, I didn't know.

Thirty-six

It was spider season when I returned to Sudeley, webs everywhere in the garden, spanning paths and veiling windows, each bearing a single dark fruit. Eerily blind to us, those spiders, squatting there, clutching their lace. I walked with care, head bowed, flinching.

It was the end of the summer, late August, and I'd come to Sudeley for the impending birth. At last came the opportunity to make amends as best I could, to do my utmost for her. To be everything to her, I hoped. My boys, of course, had stayed home, because this was women's business. Harry had said nothing. What he knew of what had happened to Elizabeth, and what he made of what he knew, I had no idea. He hadn't said if she'd written, and I hadn't asked. He didn't seem himself, though. He often didn't hear me when I spoke to him and when he did, he often didn't seem to understand. Time, I told myself: it'll take time.

Me, I hadn't missed Thomas once, not even for a heartbeat, since I'd last been at Sudeley. As for missing what we used to do together, well, I'd begun to think differently; I'd begun to think how it might be to be married again. That was new for me. I had no fear of facing Thomas again, because I'd managed it fine before, hadn't I? Been civil to him when I felt anything but. Indeed, that was how it had almost always been between us. In any case, he'd be keeping out of my way, I knew, because Sudeley was about to become no place for a man.

I hadn't missed Thomas, but I'd been longing for Kate. Dignified Kate, who always knew what to do for the best. That was how she was, again, in my eyes. Gone was the dumpy, befuddled woman who'd briefly crept into her place. She was untouched by the mess of the past few months – she *didn't* know the truth, did she – and moved with grace and confidence towards the future. We now had something to do together, she and I: get this baby born and cared for. I was determined to be of the most use. I knew I could do it. Not because I'm tough – although of course I am – but because while the other women would fuss, I could make her laugh. It seemed a simple enough hope at the time, although now, when I look back, it seems breathtakingly audacious, that optimism of mine, and hopelessly naive.

I was shocked when she came to greet me in the courtyard: she was even more swollen. Her smile, though big and genuine, looked painful, splitting her face; her hands, taking mine, didn't look like hers, didn't look like anyone's, could have been stone-carved, all features subsided beneath the swelling. No rings on her fingers. My concern showed, because she begged, 'Don't look at me like that!' but was laughing. And quite a roar it was, for her, sweeping me up so that I laughed, too, and did indeed shake off whatever look had come over me. 'I'm sorry,' I said, 'I'm sorry, it's just –'

'Oh, I know! I'm *huge*!' She was trying to hug me but couldn't get close enough, which, of course, had us laughing harder. She said, 'There's this great big baby, and then, tagging along, there's me.'

I broke the bad news: 'That doesn't stop when it's born.'

'Ah, but then Thomas can do some of the hefting.' This first mention of Thomas so early on, placing him firmly here with us. My heart, stubbed. I'd been thinking – stupidly, stupidly – that he was over with, that he'd not trouble us and we'd not have to trouble ourselves with him. Kate enthused, 'Let's go and see him,' but I hesitated, a hand on her arm, ready to make excuses. 'No,' she urged, 'no, it's fine,' although the hurried, whispery delivery belied this. 'It's fine, it's . . . *fine*,' this last word ringing with surprise but also clearly meant to be conclusive. She raised her hands only to drop them back to her sides: *there's nothing more to say*.

'Good.' I hoped she didn't hear my scepticism. How could it be fine? It would never, ever, be fine, with Thomas; of that, I was sure. 'Good,' I said again, for want to something to say.

There *was* more: 'He's been trying very hard.'

He always did, though, didn't he. That was never his problem. The problem was that he could so easily be up to no good elsewhere. I longed to tell her what I knew about him and had to remind myself that at least I'd told her something, even if it hadn't been the actual truth. She had had her warning.

She said, quickly, 'We don't talk about it.'

Well, I can't pretend I wasn't grateful to hear that, can I.

Then she said, 'Elizabeth writes,' her determined cheerfulness back as we walked arm in arm towards the house. 'Lovely letters. Chatty, just . . .' she shrugged, 'telling me what she's up to, asking after me. She's a good girl.'

'And you write back to her?'

'I do.' She kept the smile in place and didn't meet my gaze. There would be no discussion.

I concurred, moved on, but took the opportunity to ask, 'Does she mention Harry?'

'Nothing like that.' Still the smile, still no eye contact. Clearly she didn't want to think about any romance of Elizabeth's.

Thomas had changed, too, I found, when we did at last see him, at supper, and his change was the opposite of Kate's: there was less of him. He'd had a glow, but now it was as if a scrubbing brush had been wielded because not only was there no glow, but there was something raw in what remained. His manner, too: the politeness and attentiveness were there, on duty, working as hard as ever, but there was none of his usual leaping in. He limited himself to responses, and they were perhaps a little slow, as if to echoes.

The midwife, Mary Odell, was exactly as I'd remembered her; I doubted she was ever otherwise, *could* ever be otherwise, doubted she could ever be ruffled. Which is how people think of me. She was genuinely serene, though, whereas I just stand my ground. As soon as I arrived, I paid a visit to the newly finished nursery. 'Go on up,' Kate had urged me, claiming to be too pregnant to tackle the stairs, and that was how I came to be up there alone, pushing open that door.

The room covered with tapestries. No walls, no panelling, but floor-to-ceiling depictions of the twelve months of the year. Not merely the seasons, not four panels but a full twelve, the top border graced at appropriate intervals with the signs of the zodiac. Facing me was an espaliered tree, among its leaves some blush-hued globes that were probably supposed to be peaches. Better and more plentiful peaches than I'd ever seen on any tree, however well tended and however sheltered. Circling its base, a twinkling of ripe strawberries – heart-shaped rubies, green-capped, bowing their delicate stalks – and, nestled amid them, a basket piled with blood-red blobs on wishbone stalks. In the same panel were two doll-like – distant – figures, two halves to make a pair of arm-in-arm ladies. I wondered, were they supposed to be us? In the foreground, a substantial boy depicted mid-stride, bowling a hoop. My boys never bowled hoops, no child I have ever known has been the least interested in bowling hoops, yet that's always how they are in illustrations. This one, though, for all his enthusiasm for a simple hoop, was no common, carefree child. He was gorgeously dressed, from his plumed cap down to the firmly squared toes of his slippers. His doublet was draped in gold, his cuffs lost in lace. And all of it – except the lace, the gold, and that feather – was purple, the colour of royalty. This one was every inch the little prince.

And there he was in every panel that I could see, involved in the usual childish pursuits, sometimes alongside other, smaller playmates but always subtly depicted as a prince. Skating on a pond stitched from silver thread, his cold-ruddy little face peeking over an ermine collar: that, too, marking him as royal. Obscuring a couple of spring months for me was the room's other major piece of furniture: a massive, gold-canopied chair – the cloth made of threads of pure gold – like a chair of state, a throne. Actually, it *was* a chair of state, I realised. A chair for a queen: Kate was still queen, I had to remind myself. Married to a man who couldn't behave like a husband, let alone a king, and stuck out here at Sudeley, but still, if only in name, England's queen. This room had been done by the book for a baby of the queen, for this first-born, latecoming child of England's queen. And it was a room fit for a prince or princess, although that was a step too far – let me guess: a step taken by Thomas – because a prince or princess was something this child of this queen could never be.

Kate's own rooms were stunning, but – being beyond Thomas's influence, presumably – were sumptuous rather than grand. They were to be our home for the coming weeks, both before the baby's birth and afterwards. A luxurious retreat for us, the ladies of the household. Less 'ladies' than girls, of course, this being Kate's household; and there were fewer of us, too, than I'd envisaged. There was the usher's wife, Susan, with Marcella, Agnes, and little Frankie Lassells who, recently married, was now allowed to attend a confinement and lying-in. Bess Cavendish would have come but for it being too soon after the birth of her own daughter; and Jane Denny couldn't leave Elizabeth, who, apparently, hadn't been well. Kate's sister was too pregnant to leave home, and her brother's wife wasn't yet recovered sufficiently from a fall from a horse.

Luxury, but a confinement all the same and I wasn't sure I could do it, stay cooped up for so long. I'd never had to, before, except for the birth of my own babies and that, of course, was different: that, I remembered, had been welcome.

When it came to it, though, I surprised myself by taking to it. We did the things ladies are supposed to do, and did them with relish so that, somehow, there never seemed to be quite enough time in the day. We played card games with increasing skill, and higher – and higher – stakes. Susan was the surprise, here: daring. We played instruments – our own, and then, tentatively, sometimes badly, others' – and sang, finding our voices together. We learned new songs from each other; and old ones we reworked, gave new twists. Some days, we spent hours dressing ourselves elaborately, experimenting with one another's clothes, jewellery, hair, make-up; but other days, we lolled in our shifts. The rooms, too, became giddily dressed: our flower arranging, intended for no one's eyes but our own, became ambitious, then overambitious, then unhinged. Kate's doing, principally. 'And everyone thinks I'm so restrained,' she said once, shoving a plum-bearing branch into an already overstuffed vase. Late afternoon was when restraint tended to win the day and we'd write letters or settle to our books, reading and reading and reading: the new ideas in Europe percolating into a room of sleepy-eyed, shut-away women. We'd raise our heads, stupefied, at the arrival of our evening meal. Oh, we ate: that goes without saying, doesn't it. We sleepy-eyed, shut-away women ate a lot, ate everything that was presented to us, and, usually, more: sending down, every mealtime, for more.

When everyone else had gone to bed, Kate and I had time together. Too uncomfortable to be able to sleep, the baby keeping her awake or waking her, she'd beckon me onto her immense bed, behind its hangings. And there we'd lounge, those hangings drawn around us and the lamp above extinguished, whispering for hours about nothing much. I was happy; I've never been so happy with anyone except my boys. Surely she could know nothing, suspect nothing, of what had happened between Thomas and me. She and I were recapturing old times, we were girls again. And we were lucky to enjoy such freedom: once, she whispered, 'Imagine if this had been a royal birth,' and her relief was audible. It was indeed hard to imagine. If we were at court, her door would be hard to force shut against the frenzy of expectation. On the other side would be councillors and their families and staff, physicians and theirs, various dignitaries of the church, and a royal-appointed astrologer or two. Not to mention a king who was in no way to be disappointed. Below the window would be messengers ready to ride, and, beyond them, across London and across the land, bells ready to peal.

Instead, outside Kate's door, there was a silent, night-watched hallway and staircase, and then deep Gloucestershire darkness. We were getting away with something, was how I felt; and I knew she felt it too. After all that we'd been through in our lives, we'd made it, we'd made it here, where the birth would be Kate's occasion; this baby, Kate's, not England's. We were on the dark edge of the world with nobody looking over us but the stars, and if we chose to tell no one about this birth, then no one, for a long time, would know.

Another night, she confided to me, 'I'm not scared,' and then sounded scared when she added, 'D'you think I should be?'

There was only one answer to that, to be truthful: 'Well, it wouldn't *help*, would it.' And although I knew very well that disaster could strike any birthing woman, I couldn't imagine Kate running into trouble. Statuesque, capable Kate: surely a baby would slip from her with ease. And, anyway, just about every woman I'd ever known had survived. The exception was Thomas's sister, Jane Seymour, but her fate seemed like a story, had an inevitability to it: the new, doomed queen sacrificed for the longed-for prince.

Kate said, 'We've a good history, we Parrs. My mother survived, so did my sister.' She added, 'And I'm so lucky that I have Thomas: if anything goes wrong – for me, I mean – he's there for our baby.'

What a prospect, was my immediate reaction: he'll lead him or her astray.

'And I know he'll be marvellous,' Kate whispered.

But she didn't mention any possible role for me. Names, too: I wondered for whom this baby – if a girl – would be named. 'Catherine' was unlikely, though, being her own name and also being rather old-fashioned, a name of our mother's generation. So clearly a saint's name. *The* saint: the 'bride of Christ', no less. When Kate and I first knew each other, we shared our hatred of our name, sniggering together over that pathetic old prayer: *A husband, St Catherine, A handsome one, St Catherine, A rich one, St Catherine, A nice one, St Catherine, And soon, St Catherine.* St Catherine, patron saint of unmarried girls. Well, we were hardly that: me, married from girlhood; Kate, married already several times.

I did wonder if she'd call a girl baby 'Elizabeth', but that, now, perhaps, was doubtful. No word, either, on who would be godmother. I hoped she'd know that I'd do my very best for her child. She knew I was good with boys. And girls? Well, a girl, I would champion; I'm all for girls. I said to her, as a kind of prompt, 'I've been lucky, knowing' – because we'd talked it over, many times – 'that you'd step in for my boys, if anything happened to me.'

But she just said, quite flatly, 'Nothing'll ever happen to you, Cathy. You're invincible.'

Thirty-seven

Kate went into labour a week or so earlier than we'd expected, and the onset was gradual. The heaviness of which she'd been complaining for days – staggering around, almost – became, she said, a downwards draw. She began to pace, pausing every few minutes to clutch a bedpost and exhale slowly. For the first few pacings, the first few puffings, she was denying it could be labour – 'It's in my back' – but Mary Odell managed to catch her and unlace her sufficiently to feel her belly. A slow smile from Mary, a flush to her cheeks. 'Oh, yes,' she enthused, 'feel,' and grasped one of Kate's hands, flattened it beneath hers on the bump.

'Oh, yes,' echoed Kate.

And so there they were, the two of them, begun on their adventure.

Progress was slow, though. Labour kept coming and going, over a day, a night, another day and another night. For want of anything else to do, and cajoled by Mary, we attendants followed the old routine – the card-playing, the instrument-playing – albeit half-heartedly, distractedly. Mealtimes, none of us managed much, and Kate declined to join us although sometimes Mary could tempt her to a snack. During the nights, we dozed; Kate for the odd hour or two at a time. I got up on the bed with her and rubbed the small of her back, which was where, she said, the pain was. When her labouring began to pick up pace, she'd disappear down into her gown – she was still dressed, still insisted upon being dressed – crouching down and folding over, humming a single note, until the contraction passed. It was all so calm and under control, nothing like what I remembered of my own labours.

And then, quite suddenly, her labour intensified. After all that time waiting for it, I somehow missed the actual crucial change. In the blink of an eye she was kneeling up, facing the headboard and gripping the top of it. She was out of her gown and into her nightdress. Mary Odell was wearing an apron. Kate looked wide-eyed and . . . well, *studious*. Not 'serious', there was no solemnity to it. *Studious:* ready, rapt.

I, too, was taken up, now, in the excitement. Kate groaned through her contractions and I swear there was considerable satisfaction in those groans. Her round eyes shone, blank, inwardly focused, as she anticipated the next contraction and prepared herself to sail on the crest of it. I stood at the side of the bed and held her hand, which seemed to me a useless gesture; but she held on hard and groped after my hand when briefly – on some errand – it went missing. I was thinking, *This is going well, this is going well.* Daring to think it. Unable to stop myself, even if I'd wanted to.

Once – only once – I glanced in the direction of the window and there, astonishingly, was the outside world, just as it had always been. The ripe, lazy sunshine of early autumn.

Sooner than I'd expected – and perhaps I'd never expected it, perhaps I was expecting that we'd go on and on like this, that this was our life, now – Mary Odell announced, thrilled, 'The head's there.' Presumably she'd done one of her almost magically discreet examinations. This news was good to hear, but it was Kate who mattered to me and I couldn't think of anyone else. The baby, to me, was practically an irrelevancy.

For Kate, though, the news did the trick, buoyed her up, and she began to smile as if winning at something. And now, although our handholding continued, the delivery of the baby became shared between her and Mary Odell, and I was glad of it, ready to step back. We women urged her onwards and after a couple of false finishes – 'One more push, just one more,' said more times than she'd have liked to hear – Mary was talking herself through easing the baby free: 'Here we are, here . . . we . . .' Suddenly Kate screamed, 'Somebody help me, please,' but no one did, there was nothing anyone could do and no time to do it because here was the baby, in a gush of blood.

'It's a *girl*, Thomas,' Kate wailed in mock commiseration when he arrived to see them. She couldn't care less that she hadn't produced a son, so obviously relieved was she to have a healthy baby, so obviously delighted to be cradling her. Thomas, too: 'Oh, well, a boy next time,' he said as he approached them, but only because he was expected to; said it self-consciously and apologetically, to amuse, which he did. For once, he didn't irritate me, and I even warmed to him. His brother, for all his good points, wouldn't have been so pleased had his first-born been a daughter. Perhaps – a flash of optimism – this was how it would be for me, from now on. Perhaps, sometimes, if only sometimes, I could like Thomas as other women do. Perhaps I could accept him for what he is, and like what's likeable.

It was nice to be just another lady in a roomful of ladies, a relief not to have to meet Thomas's eyes or avoid them. Unconventionally, he had been admitted to the room, at his own request and at Kate's bidding, but naturally he'd had to come unattended. So, he was on his best behaviour, subdued and deferential, eyes only for his wife and child. And what a perfect picture they made, over there in the bed. And what a lot of work that had taken, of which – I was proud of us – he'd be unaware. Before we'd got busy, blood had been pooled and splashed around the bed. We'd taken away bedclothes and carpets, we'd wiped and scrubbed floorboards. Kate was sitting on a deep pile of cloths, which Mary was checking at intervals and changing.

Having placed a kiss on Kate's forehead, Thomas turned his attention to the baby, whose red face was closed in sleep. I could see him move nervously as if to touch her nose, couldn't see if in fact he did. Then he looked up from the baby into Kate's eyes and she took it as a question.

'"Mary", I think,' she replied.

He nodded, then said it, savoured it: 'Mary.'

Well, well, well. I'd never have guessed: *Mary*, the ultimate catholic name for this, the ultimate protestant baby.

Thomas said to the baby, as if announcing it to her: 'Mary.'

There were appreciative murmurs from the women around me, and Mary Odell laughed a little, bashful. Smiling, Kate reached for her, put a hand on her arm and said, 'My elder stepdaughter's name, too.' Neatly done, freeing Mary from any embarrassment, any obligation to feel honoured. There was now no telling if the baby was named for our princess or for the midwife, or both. We could think as we liked. Both seemed likely to me. Kate, the diplomat, naming her baby for a woman whom she loved but who persisted in cold-shouldering her, and making for that woman – England's head catholic – a grand gesture. And Kate, unconventional, giving credit to a servant of whom she was fond and who had helped her.

Thirty-eight

I don't remember much about the following couple of days; I'd say they were unremarkable – nothing much happening, routine tasks – but it's also true of course that they were remarkable, there being a new, tiny, noisy person among us. We women were busy checking on Kate and the baby: busy, busy, busy keeping them clean and comfortable, changing their clothes and linens, maintaining the fire and the room's supplies of ale and milk, apples and bread. We'd try to settle the baby, and to reassure Kate whenever it all became too much for her: a fretful baby, aching breasts and stomach cramps, weakness, weariness, and other people's expectations as to what news they were due or visits they could make. (Jane Grey came dolefully to the door several times every day for news, and one or other of us would talk to her – usually other, if I had anything to do with it.) We introduced the baby to her wet nurse – Alys, wife of one of the carters

– and to her nursery, and often took the baby there to allow Kate some much needed rest. We, too, had breaks, going off at intervals; twice I returned to my room and slept for perhaps five or six hours, which was both blissful and disorienting. Kate's bedroom, peculiar and exhausting though it now was, had become the centre of my world.

And then everything began to go wrong. Kate was sleeping and I was fitfully doing some needlework, meaning that whilst doing nothing I was working a threaded needle down a pillowcase seam. Agnes was boring Marcella with her marital difficulties. Kate groaned. I looked over – it was daytime, the bed's hangings were open – to see her face tightened in pain. She was very pale; I wondered whether the pallor was new, or whether she'd been like this before her sleep but I'd only now, belatedly, noticed. Mary Odell, to one side of me, tensed. I asked Kate if she was all right. 'Just a . . . pain,' she managed, blowing into her cheeks and raising her eyebrows to signify its intensity. Then, immediately, again a groan, and this time she tried to curl up, curl over, clamp herself shut. Mary and I were both up and over to her in the same instant. One of Mary's hands went to Kate's forehead, as always, and the other eased back the bedcovers as she murmured assurances: *Now, let's see . . .* Reaching down to Kate's belly, she asked, 'Would a rub help?'

Kate nodded meekly but then the pain came again. 'This is *bad*, Mary,' she gasped. '*Oh*, this is bad,' and was suddenly overwhelmed, despairing, crying. Crying? I was taken aback, actually stepped back. Mary, though, continued, checking with those capable hands of hers – 'Here? Here?' – while keeping up the comforting murmurs, promises of 'a nice poultice', and 'something settling to drink'. Kate resisted her, doubled over, eyelids screwed up. I noticed with habitual irritation a bloodstain on the back of her nightdress – it happened whatever we did, however well we padded her – but then noticed something else, a smell. Not the usual flat smell of her blood, which had wafted towards me from time to time in the past couple of days when I'd been attending to her, but something . . . well, something twisted, complex, dark.

Mary Odell had noticed it, too, and she was concerned: this I realised later not from what she said, because carefully she said nothing, but from the different manner in which she took the bundles of linen away – indeed, she bundled them away – with the instruction that they were not for laundering but for burning. As if it were a dead baby, I couldn't help but think with a shudder as I watched one load despatched. What with Kate's pains, and the dreadful smell, I did begin to fear in my bafflement that the cause of all this could be another baby, a small, forgotten twin come away too late.

Kate stayed doubled up, crying out and crying, for hours and hours and hours. I rubbed her back, which was all I could do and all I could reach although I knew I was nowhere near the pain. She didn't want to hold my hand now; she wanted handfuls of bedlinen, which she seized and held fast. I rubbed and rubbed but she remained beyond my reach – there was just a hot, hunched back below my hands. Me, I became nothing but those hands of mine, then nothing but the circles they made. A constant wondering: *when will this pass?* Her Doctor Huick came, frowning at her from the end of the bed and asking questions that went unanswered by her and guessed at by us. Then he spoke with Mary Odell outside the door. When she returned, I dared to ask her what was wrong. I was still thinking, at the same time as not daring to think, that perhaps something was trapped, or perhaps something had come loose. 'Bad humours,' was all she said, confiding it solemnly. She didn't need to say more; I understood: Kate had some badness inside. She said that Thomas would have to be informed. He wouldn't – yet – be allowed into the room, of course. I didn't know whether to envy him for that, or pity him for it. It was dreadful being in that room with her when she was so distressed, but it might be worse, mightn't it, not to be. Kate hadn't asked for him, I realised, but she hadn't asked for anyone or anything. Unable, no doubt, to think through the pain. Me, too: only when Mary mentioned Thomas did I remember that there was also a baby, away in her nursery.

Sometime later an apothecary – or perhaps his assistant – came to the door with two jugs of infusions and several pots of ointments which were greeted by Mary as if they were old friends. She seemed to know what to do with them, slathering the glimmering grease onto strips of linen. Kate's pains seemed undiminished; she had taken to baying through them, her face no longer pale but livid. Surely this was the worst of it now. Eventually I was up on the bed with her – me, too, down to my shift – doubled over her, cradling her, although tentatively because she was burning. This was when she began to say my name, and for some reason, no reason, I'd say, *I know, I know*, although of course I didn't; how could I? I'd never known anything like this. Mary Odell seemed aware of Kate's fever: the ointments were made into cold compresses for Kate's forehead, although they were almost impossible to administer, Kate twisting away from us; and no doubt one or both of the infusions – hard to help her to take – were to cool her down. I was burning and I didn't have a fever. The room was stifling. I was sick of it, the room: that sickening room, stuffed with carpets, coverlets, cushions, and crammed with hangings. Outside was a garden, lavender heads fussing in the breeze. I was sick of the candle gloom, the shutter shadows, the fire growling in the grate. And the smell, that vile smell.

I said to Mary, 'She's very, very hot.' Stating the obvious, having to start somewhere.

'She is,' Mary agreed, gravely, as if it were to be accepted.

Again, I had to go with the obvious: 'We need to cool her down.'

'We're trying.' Mary's gaze took mine to the jugs, the grease-plastered dressings. She'd spoken patiently, as if indeed I were her patient and she was doing her best to deal with my distress.

'But the fire,' I despaired, looking over at it.

Mary joined me: 'The fire?'

'It's *hot*,' I insisted.

She looked blank; would have looked startled, probably, if she'd had the energy. I watched her struggle with something she took to be self-explanatory, hard to put into words. 'But it's purifying,' she tried. 'Burning away the bad in the air.'

I do understand, but . . . My mother, I remembered, had been derisive of fires in English sickrooms. Regrettably, I had been derisive of *her*, thinking of her as Spanish, as peculiar, as, well, *wrong*. Sometimes during her final illness she'd asked me to open her window and I'd refused, but, then, we were in Southwark and the air was foul, full of contagion. This, here, though, was Sudeley: outside Kate's room was the sweet air of Sudeley. What harm could it do? Think of lavender, the scent of it: the heat of it in the air and yet its coolness.

A memory from childhood, one that was new to me: I was in bed, I'd been coughing and coughing, had had long nights of coughing. My mother told me that the doctor had arrived to see me and I was puzzled because he'd only just visited. This, though, turned out to be a different doctor; this one spoke incomprehensibly to my mother, and she to him. A Spanish doctor, it occurs to me now, and he could only have been Catherine of Aragon's own, the Queen's Physician. My mother opened the window – oh, the lovely sound of it opening, the wrenching of the catch, a shove and then its squeaky give – and it was as if my lungs themselves had been opened.

So, me, who'd considered myself as English as a solid oak door, as English as a sopping hedgerow: the fleck of Spanish blood that had been sunk somewhere in me was welling up. I was going to get that window opened. I put it to Mary: 'We should open the window.'

'She could catch a chill.' There'd been a heartbeat of hesitation; she wasn't comfortable contradicting me. It crossed my mind how odd her position was, in a household. Her arrival for the hour of need, as bringer of the best news or the very worst, and then she was gone, moved on, leaving no trace. She *had* no position in a household, despite briefly being at the very centre of it. She was a kind of visitation. And, indeed, here she was, acting as if she were Kate's guardian angel. As unworldly as one, too. A chill was a risk worth taking, as far as I was concerned.

'If it's Thomas you're afraid of – answering to him if something goes wrong – I'll take full responsibility.'

A mistake, I saw: she was offended, her lips pursed, her eyes unblinking. 'I'm *afraid* of her catching a *chill*.'

I tried again, a different approach. 'Listen, Mary, this can't be right, can it? To leave her like this?' I gestured at Kate. '*Can* it?'

She sighed, regretful. 'But that's how fever *is*.'

'But she's burning up,' I persisted. 'How must that feel? We have to *do* something. This is something we can *do*, Mary. I can't bear to stand by and see her suffering like this.'

I was sure I detected the unspoken response: *This isn't about what* you *can or can't bear.* What she said was, 'She's in God's hands.'

I was getting nowhere; I had an urge to yell, *This is Kate!* And if they'd have understood – if I could have been calm and clear and made them understand – that's what I'd have done. *Kate*, who'd been so busy making differences for the better in ways no one else was able to do; so much to so many people. She'd touched so many lives. And *my* life. She was my best friend. She was the best friend any woman could ever hope to have. I couldn't begin to think how I'd come to betray her as I had. It was as unthinkable to me now as it would be to her, if she knew.

She was hot and I was going to cool her down. Defying Mary, I'd be acting alone, I knew. A useless lot, they were, in that room; they'd never speak up. Not even Susan, whom I'd considered the most companionable of the women. *Women*: that was it, wasn't it; that was the problem. These were *girls*. No one to give any real help, should Kate need it. And she needed it now, didn't she.

I opened the window. Outside was dark. The garden had been surprised by rain into giving up its fragrances.

Thirty-nine

It was later, morning; first thing, judging from the shallow light. Kate – still kneeling, still doubled up – had quietened, moaning and rocking. I wondered: was this good or bad? Could be either. Good – *so* good – that the pain was diminished, but bad that she, too, seemed diminished. I was doing what I sensed she wanted: leaving her alone. Doing nothing, by the still-open window; a breeze in a nearby tree. Dozing, perhaps. Someone touched my shoulder: Mary Odell. Telling me that Thomas was at the door. For news. She seemed to think that I was the one to give it. I didn't have any, though, did I. When I said, 'But I don't know what to say to him,' she misunderstood me: 'Say she's in God's hands now.'

But we're all in God's hands, aren't we, Mary? Every minute of every day. What I want to know is: what is it that He's doing with Kate?

I headed for the door. Mary tapped my arm, stopping me,

reminding me that I was undressed, nothing over my petticoat. I shrugged her off. Not that she'd know it, but Thomas had seen me rather less dressed than this. On the other side of the door, I did glimpse Thomas's surprise to see me so dishevelled; saw, too, though, that he barely registered his own reaction. 'How is she?' was all that concerned him. There were men in the background, keeping back; I didn't look, didn't see how many – three, four. Thomas himself looked hastily dressed, not fully dressed, although I couldn't have said what was missing. His eyes were less blue; that I did see. They were no more luminous than glass.

'Her pain seems lessened,' I said.

'Oh.' He nodded, desperately hopeful, grateful, and looked around at his men as if to share this with them. The scent of him was scribbled into the air and I shocked myself by drawing it down into me, unable to desist.

'Yes, she's quieter,' I said in an effort to come up with something of more substance.

'Quieter,' he echoed, less convinced. 'And the fever?' I heard how he made himself say the word, *fever*, having to leap at it, refusing to be cowed by it, a man whose own sister had died of childbed fever.

I wondered what to say. 'Well, that's still there,' I admitted. Even to me, it sounded as if I had something to add. But actually there was nothing. Well, no: there *was* something, coming bubbling up . . . *I don't* know, *Thomas. I don't* know *if she's going to survive this.*

Until then, I hadn't considered that she might die. I hadn't had to. What I'd had to do was hold Kate's hand, rub her back, offer her a drink, help change her dressings. Now Thomas's arrival at the door had raised the question, and I had to stifle a loathing of him for it. Having realised there'd be nothing more forthcoming from me, he nodded again, although this time understandably grudgingly. He didn't turn towards his men – who must have heard – but kept it to himself. 'Does she,' he tried, 'does she want anything? Need anything?' *Me?*

'Just rest.'

A nod: reluctant, disappointed. We two should perhaps have been able to comfort each other. We two, who could have claimed to be closest of all people to Kate and who had on occasions been so close to each other. But there was nothing between us; there never had been.

'The baby?' he checked.

'Very well, apparently. Feeding ferociously, I'm told.' For the sake of form, we shared a wistful smile.

Then, 'Should I see her? Kate, I mean.' *Let me see her, Cathy.* 'When should I see her?'

There was – as he knew – only one answer I could give him: 'We'll let you know if you're needed.' My expression – my eyes – asked for his understanding. The bitterness in his own, as he turned away, was frightening.

A little later, Kate did ask for him. Or, at least, asked his whereabouts. 'Where's Thomas?' Nothing from her for hours – impossible even to rouse her for the doctor's latest concoctions – and now this, loud and clear. Clearly afraid, too. Immediately, I was up from my chair, glad to be able to do something for her, if only answer a question. Her eyes found mine but I was unconvinced she was seeing me or seeing that it was me; the surface of her eyes was somehow flesh-like. Unlike her lips, which were cracked, and the fissures were bloodied. How – when – had that happened? I made a mental note to get some wax for them. 'Thomas is here,' I said. 'I mean, he was at the door, not long ago, asking after you, and now he's . . . well, he's probably in his room.' Thomas, night-wanderer: who on earth knew where he was? *She* hadn't known, half the time, had she. *A law unto myself.* Had he ever – or would he ever – do with other women what he'd done with me? It struck me as incredible, the trust I'd placed in him.

Kate's breath was foul, really foul: how she'd hate it if she knew, and how she'd hate that I'd noticed. To what I'd told her of Thomas's possible whereabouts, she said nothing more and gave no reaction; I couldn't know if it was the answer she'd wanted or expected. In the following hours, I was never sure if she was awake or asleep. Neither, quite, perhaps. Breathing alone seemed to be all she could do.

I tried to pass those hours by writing to my boys, or trying to write to them. There'd been no time, earlier, and now there was endless time but so little that I could say. Whenever I looked up – which was often – I found myself silently imploring the figure in the bed, or willing her, perhaps even threatening her: *Get well, can't you? Can't you get well?* The others seemed to keep their entreaties for God: they prayed often, judging from the distinct stillness that I observed, from time to time, coming over one or other of them. I was always intending to pray, I was always just about to do it. Somehow, though, it never got done. It had never quite yet happened.

I soon discovered I'd been wrong about Thomas: he wasn't in his room, but outside, below our window, in Kate's own private garden. As close as he could get, in an important sense; closer to Kate than if he'd lurked a mere few paces away, on the other side of the door but in the impersonal, ancestor-hung hallway. From one side of the window, I could watch him. Sometimes he paced, kicking at stray fallen leaves; sometimes, he rested on a bench, ankles crossed, face turned to the sun. Whenever he looked up, I'd snap back into shadow. I watched him with longing, but the longing was for the sun that warmed his face. For him, I felt the same fury as when he'd first singled me out and kissed the back of my neck. That same feeling: something having been done, and my being left with it. If he'd never done it, never made that one small, stupid move, none of what ended up happening would ever have begun.

Forty

Kate had been asleep – and so, probably, finally, had most of us – but then, some hours later, came a sudden, awful wailing. A calling for: *Mary*. Mary was there, as if she had known this would happen. Kate snatched at her and gabbled – *I'm so scared, I'm so scared, please, Mary, help me, you have to help me* – while Mary stroked her head as if this outburst were entirely expected and indeed even necessary. She murmured, *It's fine, you're fine, don't worry, stop worrying.* To me, she mouthed, 'This can happen with fever.' Rather than being a reassurance, this chilled me: Mary Odell claiming Kate as one of her cases. Kate was saying. 'He's not to be trusted; he's not to be trusted, Mary'; she said it fierce and fast, and I paused, only then aware that I'd been moving towards her. This, from her, was new. Was she referring to his ambitions? There I stood, conscious of the women's eyes on me, before making myself go on, stepping up. To do or say what, I didn't yet know.

'Kate?'

She buried her face away from me, I swear it. Again, the scrutiny from the girls, their expectation – I knew it – that if Kate was troubled, her confidante should be me. Their puzzlement piled on top of my own. All I could do was try again: 'Kate?'

In her delirium, 'he' could of course be anyone – a member of staff, her brother or Thomas's, the late king, even God or the devil – but I knew he was Thomas. Kate began again, to Mary: 'I don't know what to do, don't know what to do. He's cruel, Mary, a cruel man.' My stomach twisted. Not, then, his ambitions. Something more personal.

Mary whispered, 'Hush, you're safe here. This'll pass, this feeling frightened.' And to me, again, whispered, apologetic: 'It happens.' For Mary, this was the fever talking. But I knew better. Or worse, you might say.

Why now was understandable: Kate's defences were down, and any face-saving was abandoned. Why Mary, though? Why tell Mary? If this was how she felt about Thomas in the light of what he was supposed to have done with Elizabeth, she could have addressed those fears to *me*. Because I *knew* all that, didn't I. As far as Kate was concerned, I *knew* about Elizabeth. I'd have understood. Was this not, then, perhaps, about Elizabeth?

She began to cry for the baby. 'We'll fetch her,' promised Mary, looking at me, probably only because I was nearest. But I couldn't go, could I. Not with Kate as she was, saying what she was saying, not knowing what she was saying. I passed the request to Susan, who was keen to oblige. While we waited, Mary talked to Kate about the christening, which was due to take place later that day. As the mother, still lying in, Kate wouldn't, of course, in any case, have been attending. Me, though, I'd have had to go, but for the circumstances; now, though, my absence would be excused. It wasn't as if I was to be godmother. That honour had been bestowed – before Kate's decline – upon Jane Grey.

When the baby arrived with Susan, Kate was unable to take her. What on earth had happened to her hands? Horrid, claw-like. She'd only been ill for a day or two: how had her hands wasted away? Mary held the baby for her, and the baby's apprehensive gaze found Kate's before drifting over her face and giving equal attention to each feature. 'Look at you,' Kate wondered, although in truth the baby was nothing much to look at.

'She's beautiful,' I made sure to chip in.

Kate began whispering to her – *Well, here you are, my little girl, here you are* – but almost at once became distressed: 'What will happen to us, little one?' Panic prickled over me. Kate wouldn't die of this, would she? She was getting better, wasn't she? Mary moved away with the baby as if this latest outburst, too, was entirely expected, and as she did so, Kate begged of her, 'Why did I marry him? What future is there for us, with that man?' My prickling burned now. Kate wasn't thinking about dying, she was thinking about having to live the rest of her life with Thomas. She knew something, didn't she: something *more*. This wasn't about Thomas's supposed silliness with Elizabeth. This went deeper. We were perilously close to something damning being said, but what, exactly, I couldn't foresee – and anyway I'd have to stand there and take it when it came. And I didn't know – still don't – what scared me, or scared me the most: that I'd have to hear it; that others would hear it; that Kate was thinking it; or that it would be the truth.

'There's no man.' Mary had misunderstood. 'Don't worry.'

'*Thomas!*' Kate managed, and we all jumped; even me, and I'd been expecting it. '*Thomas!* That *liar!*'

My heart seemed to spin in my chest.

Mary spoke clearly and evenly, as if merely fulfilling another duty of her job in saying it: 'He's a good man, your husband, a lovely man, and he'll make an excellent father.' Precisely the manner in which I'd talked to my boys when they were toddlers: acknowledging what they'd said but setting down the truth against them and resisting a discussion.

Kate rasped, 'I could tell you.' And then she looked at me, those big eyes an open confrontation. 'Tell her, Cathy. *You* tell her. Tell her what we both know about Thomas.'

Instinct whirled me to Mary, to see what she'd heard, but she was shaking her head – *It happens* – and I saw that it didn't matter if Kate named Thomas, it didn't matter what she said about him: no one would believe her. Oddly, I felt no relief; absurdly, I felt defensive of her. *This is Kate*, I wanted to impress upon them: queen, thinker, diplomat. *Don't you dare be dismissive of her.* Instead, though, to Kate, I urged, 'You must rest.' No platitude: she was exhausted.

But, 'Rest?' she sighed. 'How *can* I "rest"?'

And then I made the mistake of trying to appeal to her, leaning close – breath held – and whispering, 'Kate, this does no one any good.' Again, it was no platitude: I did believe it.

Suddenly her distress was gone; in its place, a look of cool appraisal. 'And lies do?'

She knew, *she knew*. Didn't she? I retreated across the room. The baby was taken, to be returned to the nursery. Kate, having said her piece, had fallen silent. I tried to think. I could do as she'd asked and tell her the truth. *The* truth, not *a* truth. Because, of course, I did have it: the whole truth. Only Thomas and I had it, and I was the one who was here, and the one whom she'd asked. But did she really want to hear it? *What* exactly did she want to hear? They were two different things: her wanting me to say it, and her wanting to hear it.

When Kate started up again, it was as if she was in the middle of a conversation, and indeed her tone was peculiarly conversational. 'I don't trust him, Mary,' she said, as if she were answering a question. Mary, sitting at the bedside, snapped to attention. Wearily sing-song, she summed up: 'I don't trust him, and he disregards me: it's deadened me.' I made myself get up, made a move towards her with some vague notion of putting a stop to this, of getting her to settle back down and rest. Kate's face was worryingly discoloured, as if her skin had been somehow discarded in the sun.

'I'm done for,' she informed Mary.

Mary approached her with a drink.

'A distrustful, deadened mother,' she announced herself to Mary, turning from me. 'What use am I to my daughter? My mother was strong. Sharp, bright.' She recoiled from Mary's drink, and again, when Mary persisted. 'She wasn't warm,' she murmured into her pillow, head averted, 'but anyone can come up with kisses, can't they?' She turned back to Mary. 'My friend Cathy' – speaking of me as if I weren't there – 'she's stayed a widow. She's no fool, Mary. She's long known the truth about Thomas, but how could she tell me? My best friend.' And now she did look at me, but to look me over, as if from a distance. 'That must have been hard.'

This was unbearable. 'I need some air,' I said to no one

in particular, to anyone who was staring at me: at a guess, everyone in the room.

Kate's composure was gone again in a puff. 'He's a liar,' she complained.

Jesus Christ! I might have said it aloud.

Mary said, 'I think we should fetch him.'

Inexplicably, I took her to mean the doctor – he hadn't been for a long time – and gestured, infuriated, at the array of potions. 'What? So he can just –'

Mary stood straight-backed and expressionless, stood her ground, facing me with my mistake.

I queried, '*Thomas?*'

Mary said, 'I think we should.'

Kate wailed, 'I don't want that man in here!'

'Oh, Mary!' I flung up a hand in the direction of the wreck in the bed. 'How on earth would that help?'

'He could reassure her,' she said.

'*Could* he?'

Susan's voice came up behind me: 'She might be right, Cathy.'

Behind Susan was Marcella. Beside Marcella: Agnes, Frankie. All of them with that eerie lack of expression in the face of my rage. Susan tried, 'What else can we do?'

'Do it, then,' I hissed. 'Do whatever you want, but I'll have no part in it.' Once outside the room, though, I stopped dead, and not only because I had an attack of the shakes. I'd realised that, like it or not, I was in the middle of this. And that's where I needed to stay; it was crucial that I stayed there and sorted this out. I turned back, re-opened the door and said into the room, 'If he has to come, I'll be the one to go for him.'

Forty-one

He was a wreck, capless, his hair ruffled and his clothes askew: hook-and-eyes unhooked or mis-hooked. Scrambling to his feet, he looked ready to ask, *What news?* but then said nothing, probably didn't dare.

'Just you,' I made clear, and he complied, not so much as glancing at his retinue. As soon as we were alone together in the hallway, I told him, 'You're wanted. She's raving.'

He was horrifed. 'What do you mean, raving?'

'You're a liar, I'm a liar.'

'Oh,' he breathed, wounded.

Oh, stop the display, Thomas.

'So, she knows.' He sounded amazed.

'She knows nothing, Thomas,' I snapped. 'How would she know? Did you tell her?'

His lips hardened. 'I told her nothing. I told her what you told me to tell her.'

'Then she doesn't know, does she,' I said, ignoring my own qualms. And, away from her, away from that room, I did just about believe what I was saying. Because how *could* she know? What had I been thinking? If she'd known, how could she ever have been with me as she had, up on her bed, during those long nights before her labour and then during it?

Thomas and I began to hurry. 'What do I do?' he asked me.

'Nothing. Just be there. Just . . . reassure her.' As if that were possible.

'Reassure her,' he mulled it over: keen, by the sound of it, but just as unconvinced. Then he dared to ask, 'Is she getting better?'

'I don't know,' I admitted. She did seem stronger: all this urgent confiding and protesting. But *better*? How could what I'd witnessed be said to be 'better'?

Thomas halted. 'Cathy? Is she worse?'

'I *don't know*,' and fury shot through me, fury at being left like this – all of us – in this house, flailing around helpless while these bad humours did their dirty work on her.

He resumed walking; me, too, alongside. He asked, 'Should I . . . talk to her?'

I looked at him, kept looking at him.

'Tell her,' he clarified.

I asked, 'Tell her *what*?' Which shut him up.

'Oh, it's you,' she managed, when he reached her bedside; she sounded surprised. Shocked, he'd have been, to his core. Me, too, suddenly seeing her as he did. I saw now that her face was little more than a skull; her glorious, golden hair incongruous, her eyes so big that they themselves looked somehow painful. *When did you go?* Because I saw it now: she was on her way and she wasn't ever coming back. My heart flared and plummeted. She was on her way, leaving me, and there was nothing I could say to her to change it. Somehow, it had already happened; it was happening. *How?* A mere week ago, she'd been as healthy as I was. Pregnant, so – yes – she'd been struggling, but underneath, strong-boned, strong-hearted. She should have been fine. She *had* been fine. What had *happened*? God was making a mistake, a stupid, awful mistake and there was nothing I could do but watch.

I made for the others, who'd settled – or were making the appearance of being settled – on cushions in a corner of the room. I tried to avoid the eyes of my companions, which – sleep-deprived – were so small in comparison to Kate's. Susan made a stab at a smile, for me, as a greeting. In her hands, her lap, was some embroidery of dazzling delicacy. A distraction for her. For Marcella, *I* was the distraction, if only for a heartbeat: she watched me sit down. I sat shakily, my heart in all the wrong places in my body: in my mouth, my legs, my head. More embroidery was laid beside Marcella and could have been hers or Frankie's, but Frankie was holding open a prayer book and merely glanced up, eyes red, before returning to it. Agnes was fingering the chain on which her own book of hours hung from her waist, but staring into space, chewing her lower lip. Mary Odell sat straight-backed, to attention, observing Thomas and Kate. Improper, it seemed to me, that attentive gaze, and I itched to slap it away. She was attending to Kate, though. As we all were, I reminded myself.

We wouldn't be able to avoid eavesdropping on Kate and Thomas, and I dreaded whatever we might be about to hear. Now was not the time; there *was* no time. Thomas was holding one of those newly bony hands of hers.

'It's no good, Thomas,' she whispered, resigned, wretched.

My throat began to ache. I focused down on my own hands, pretended to myself an interest in my rings, in the story of each of them, *This one from Charles, when Harry was born . . .*

'Sweetheart?' Thomas, all kindness and concern. 'What's no good?'

Sweetheart. How odd to think of Kate as someone's sweetheart. That tall, strong woman with her cool, clear eyes and the wry turn to her mouth: how had he managed to turn her into a 'sweetheart'? Or was it only now that he could do it, now that she was small and helpless there in that bed?

'You and me,' she breathed. *No good.*

'You and me?' Gently incredulous.

She accused, 'You did me a wrong, Thomas.'

This one, rubies, inherited from my mother, come from Spain; Spanish treasure, as I used to think of it when I was little . . .

'I know I did, darling, I know I did, and I'm sorry, you know I'm sorry.' *Sorry.* Was that how he felt about what he'd done with me? Was that all – that time in the bower, the times in those two rooms – something for which you could be *sorry*? Was he sorry that, between my thighs, his lower half would gallop like something with a life of its own? Was *I* sorry? Sorry was useless, and, as such, was an insult to Kate. What mattered was that it had stopped. Beyond that, what was done was done.

With his free hand, he was stroking her head, her hair.

'And I know "sorry" isn't enough; I *know*. But I don't know what else I can say.' Pleading, he was placing himself in her hands. Weak as she was, though, what could she do with him? He was a fool, the man was a fool, in fact he was a bastard to be asking anything at all of her. 'Oh, darling,' his voice was hoarse with disappointment, 'I thought this was behind us.'

Bringing me up sharp, a flash of how it might have been for them over the past few months, only a flash but as vivid and affecting as if I'd been there: they were in her private garden for a stroll, making a point of appreciating the flowers, making sure to keep smiling. *Oh, leave her be, Thomas.* Don't plead with her, or bargain with her, don't even discuss anything with her. *And aren't you, really, asking for more lies?* If it's not behind her, it's not behind her: *don't make her agree that it is.* My scalp was prickling under my hood; I adjusted the hood, Marcella watching me as if it were something worth watching. I couldn't stop a sigh, which came out shudderingly and seemed to have taken more air than the room had to give. I was going to have to watch Kate die. I'd just watched her labour, seen her rise to it with such spirit and to such a good end, and now I was going to have to watch death grind and grind her to nothing.

I thought this was behind us. Kate said, 'So did I,' or I think she did. She'd spoken so quietly, and I'd been trying not to hear but, in trying not to hear, I'd been holding my breath, and into that tiny silence of mine had seeped the words, *So did I.* Then she said, 'I *want* it to be'; that I did hear, and heard the misery in it, too. 'I *want* to forgive you, and I *hate* myself that I can't, and it *scares* me that I can't, Thomas, it *scares* me.' My heart was caving in, because how dreadful, how dismal: Kate invaded by ill-feeling, at this time of all times, when she'd never before – I'd lay my life on it – had a single uncharitable notion cross her mind. And it was me who had reduced her to this. She was crying, 'There are so many lies, Thomas, that I don't know what to try to forgive.'

Could you not just let them be, these lies? Is there no chance at all that we could just get on with our lives? But no: a jolt, the realisation afresh; the horror of it keen. *No, not in Kate's case.* She wasn't going to live long enough now for what I did to become an aberration; stupid and disgraceful, but an aberration. She knew what I'd done – that, again, was my suspicion, my belief – and surely she distrusted and despised me, and would die distrusting me and despising me. Leave me distrusted and despised. Which, of course, was nothing less than I deserved. I'd wanted to make amends – be a good friend – and now there was no time.

Thomas said, 'There'll be no more lies from now on, I promise you.'

She managed a reproachful 'Marriage was a promise,' *and look what you did with that.*

He turned helplessly to us, and I saw that the same silence – the silence that had hold of me – was clamped over him. He couldn't tell her now, could he, and there was only ever going to be now; and if he couldn't tell her, there was nothing else to say.

An unfolding beside me: Susan, rising. She laid one hand on Thomas's back, the other on Kate's shoulder. 'Lie down beside her,' she whispered. 'Just . . . be with her.'

He looked at her in fear and I understood it: fear that this couldn't really be true, that he'd misheard or misunderstood or that she'd withdraw her offer – because that was what it was; she had taken it upon herself to bestow our permission, our blessing. 'Go on,' she confirmed. 'We'll draw the hangings and leave you in peace.'

There was no peace for some time. Kate didn't let up. Unable to fight death, she railed at Thomas. He stayed there and took it until she could no longer keep going and subsided into a kind of sleep. A couple of hours later, she suddenly asked to dictate her will, which she then did in no time by making Thomas sole beneficiary. Then we left her inside the bed's hangings with John, her chaplain, for five or ten minutes of whispers. Then, last, her daughter: it was to be Thomas and the baby with her behind those hangings, for their goodbyes. That I couldn't bear to witness.

Chapel seemed the obvious place – the only place – to go. Knowing where Kate kept her key, I let myself into her covered walkway, but some way down the passage, I came to a stop. Stood there. There, on the clean terracotta tiles, in that place which was neither inside the house nor outside it. How long should I give her? She'd be doing it now: wishing her baby well for the rest of her life. How could she do that, knowing how hard life can be? She'd be handing over that perfect, tiny person who looks to no one but her. I just stood there in the walkway until I didn't any more; until I found myself walking again, my back turned on the distant chapel door.

Forty-two

As I slipped back into the room, Susan caught my eye and shook her head: a quick, furtive shake, not the slow one that would have told me Kate had died. Thomas had relinquished the bedside, though; he was at the fireplace, frowning at the incongruously lively flames. No one had taken his place, and the vacancy drew me to it. My instinct, too, was to check back with Kate after my absence. As if to say hello. Except that her bedside was for goodbyes now, wasn't it. But even if that was what I wanted, even if there was anything to say, I was too late. There she was, what was left of her: a fleshed skull, and the lovely hair that looked to have so little to do with it that it might come away all of a piece. Her eyes were sunken, and stuck shut. They'd never be opening again, I now knew; I'd seen the last of them.

Gingerly, I laid a hand over one of hers, doming it to avoid much contact. The chill of her fingers confirmed how little life remained. A single, silver-grey thread, I imagined it, deep inside her skin. I announced myself in a whisper, because I felt I should: 'It's me: Cathy.'

Nothing, as I'd expected. But then there *was* something. She'd *said* something. Or something, certainly, had come from her disappeared lips, and it was more than an exhalation. Something articulated, if barely. Flotsam, probably, from her sinking mind, but in case it was a request, I leaned closer. 'What, Kate?'

She breathed, 'Elizabeth was pregnant.'

Clear this time, but nonsense. This, then, was the depth of her confusion, and I, too, was puzzled: how had she got to this? 'No,' I whispered, to reassure her. I could at least tell her the truth of this. 'No, Kate, that's not what happened.'

Something else, now: she said something else, but I missed it. *Jenny said?* Who was Jenny? And again, something, this time sounding like *Jane didn't.* Jane . . . Jane . . . Was this something to do with Jane Grey? Elizabeth . . . Jenny said . . . Jane didn't . . .

No: *Jane Denny*. That was what Kate had said.

Jane Denny said.

Jane Denny, who was looking after Elizabeth.

Jane Denny said.

Elizabeth was pregnant.

Dread slithered from the crown of my head down my back, like something dropped. 'No,' I said, instantly; just said it, no thinking behind it; just had to.

Nothing from Kate.

Delirium, surely, this. *Surely.*

Not impossible, though. I was thinking now. Thinking fast. Jane Denny would know, wouldn't she? She'd be the one to know. And she'd tell Kate, wouldn't she. Kate would be the one she'd tell. And Elizabeth had indeed been ill this summer: that was what Kate had told me, *ill*.

Elizabeth *was* pregnant? Those had been Kate's words. Why *was*? What did that mean? What had she meant by *was*?

Was *any* of this true? Thomas was turning half awake from the fire, starting back to resume his deathbed duties; he was a mere three or four steps away. No time for me to ask questions and anyway she wouldn't have the strength to say nor perhaps the presence of mind to know the answers. She'd said what she'd needed to say and now *I* had to say something. One more step from Thomas before he'd be in earshot of my quietest whisper. All this time, I'd been fearing that she suspected *me*. And perhaps she had, on occasions. Perhaps on several occasions. But not now. I couldn't let her die thinking that her husband had impregnated her fourteen-year-old stepdaughter. Not when I knew otherwise. (But *did* I? What, really, did I know?)

'Kate,' I hissed into her ear, 'listen to me. *Kate, listen*. That would have been' – say it, *say it* – 'Harry.' *Say it*, because it was safe with her: 'My Harry.' (*Was* it, though? How did I know, really?) 'Not –' *your husband*. Tried again: 'Not Thomas,' was all I said. And didn't dare say more. What had happened between Thomas and me couldn't be the last thing she'd ever know. She gave no indication that she'd heard any of what I'd said, and died a few minutes later.

Forty-three

January again. There are two views of two-faced Janus himself, aren't there. Poised Janus, looking both backwards and forwards, properly both reflective and optimistic. And then there's two-faced Janus. Perhaps, though, it's just that he doesn't know where to look. There's nothing much to see, is there, in the dark days of January.

I heard Ed Seymour arrive; or heard a small party of riders, didn't know who, hadn't been told to expect Ed and the view from my Barbican window was choked with household smoke and river fog. Ushered unaccompanied to my room, chill clinging to him, he made a stab at looking cheerful as he administered the usual kiss. Only when he stepped back to register surprise and reproach did I realise I'd endured it with my arms folded. Letting them fall, I indicated the fireside.

'It's dismal out there,' he agreed, banging his gloved hands together to shock feeling back into them.

No request for milk, this time, but instead something stronger: malmsey. And dates, I added, sending Bella to the kitchen: a plate of dates stuffed with marzipan. My ladies, too, I sent from the room.

Following polite enquiries after my own health and that of my boys, stepdaughters, godchildren, senior household and chapel staff, Ed began on his baby niece as if he had at last arrived at the reason for his visit. I went along with it, but the fact was that since the baby came to me – when Thomas was arrested – Ed had steered clear of her. He'd said, at the time, that Thomas had claimed it as Kate's wish: if something happened to her widower, the baby was to come to me. And who was to know the truth of it? No doubt Kate wouldn't have wanted her to go to Ed and his awful wife, but they wouldn't have wanted her anyway: child of a traitor, and a traitor so close to home. And where else could she have gone? Kate's sister is ill and her brother is a mess, Council having decided that his divorce was illegal and given him the choice of going back to his first wife or to the block. His is no household for a child. So, she came to me.

I knew the real reason for Ed's visit. I'd known he'd come sooner or later to ask me about Thomas, about the rumours that have led to Thomas's arrest on suspicion of – among many other things – plotting marriage to an heir to the throne. Those rumours about his pursuit of Elizabeth don't come from me. Indeed, their spread – the speed and extent of it – has horrified me. I can't pretend that I wouldn't prefer Thomas not to be around, but nor do I want his supposed approaches to Elizabeth to be investigated. What I want, I suppose, is for him never to have existed. For none of this ever to have happened.

And it so nearly didn't: that's how it seems to me. I think back to Kate as the newly widowed dowager queen in that lovely old manor at Chelsea and it feels no more than a matter of months ago. As if I haven't seen her for a while but could get in my boat and go there now and there she'd be and none of it would have happened.

I'd known Ed would come, but nothing I can tell him will make a difference to Thomas's fate. What matters to me is keeping my family out of it. Thomas is as good as gone, he's a lost cause. Council has long been out to get him, and lately he's been making it very easy for those men. Doing deals, first, with the pirates against whom he – High Admiral, still – is supposed to be protecting us: that's one rumour. Then complaining to others as if to suggest that they join him in some unspecified move against Council: that's another. Then there was the bungled attempt to kidnap the little king: no mere rumour that one, because he was found outside the king's bedroom – chasing an interloper, he claimed – and panicked into misfiring his pistol, killing the boy's dog. Since Kate's death, much of what he has done has been inexplicable, rash, desperate. Suicidal. As if he has only his own life to destroy, as if he has no child to consider.

Having taken so much of Ed's new-found concern for his niece, I cut him short. We should address the state of her finances, I said, before he left. Clear enough indication that I knew there was something else to be discussed and we should get on with it.

I'd succeeded in shutting him up; when he began again, he did so in a different tone. 'So, here I am,' he admitted, 'investigating my own brother.' Adding, ruefully, 'It has to be done.'

'It does?'

'I'm told it does.' Drily. Oh, how times have changed: Ed, under orders now. *And done well, too*, he didn't say. Conveniently for Council, this can be made a test of Ed's loyalty, but, inconveniently for Ed, it's probably not one that he can pass, whatever he does and however well he does it. Because this is how it happens in our world: people smell blood. One Seymour down and just one more to go, then that's the end of the Seymours and your own family is a step nearer the king. No matter that Ed's a good man. These days, a good man has as many enemies as a bad man. Which Ed must know. The shadowing under his eyes suggested so. His dreadful wife will know it, too. I doubt she's much comfort to him when he returns home after a day of this kind of work. She's probably already packed.

'What with everything else' – gesturing at the door: his niece? – 'we haven't actually ever talked, have we, you and I, about what happened at Sudeley last summer.' He looked down at his hands, flexed his frozen fingers. 'I do appreciate that you might not want to. Might not want to have to think about it.' With a sigh, he gave up on his fingers, looked up at me, frank and sad. 'You might prefer to put it behind you, dreadful time that it was.' He added, unnecessarily, 'The loss of your dear friend.'

Not *our*. He could have said *our*. He was distancing himself. Even here, in front of me. And that would be the doing of his wife, is my guess. Done at the urging of his wife. *Distance yourself from the tragic dowager queen, the mess she made of her life in the end*. Done at the urging of his appalling wife, perhaps, but done nonetheless and in front of *me*. He should reconsider his loyalties. He leaned forwards, for me to confide in him. 'What did you witness, Cathy?'

I wondered what he wanted me to say. Not so long ago, I would have been able to ask him, just ask, but that time has gone. Was he hoping to build the case against his brother, or undermine it? Or did he perhaps want the truth, if only just for himself? The truth of what his errant brother had or hadn't been involved in. Because, after all, Thomas was his brother, his boyhood companion, even if – I imagined – they hadn't in fact been great companions. Thomas was the man with whom Ed shared his own history, and now Thomas faced a pitiless, vengeful death. Wouldn't Ed want to know what his brother was really about to die for?

He wasn't asking, though, and anyway I couldn't tell him; I had to stick to my story. 'Nothing.' I made sure to sound surprised.

He echoed me: 'Nothing?' Same tone: 'You don't think Thomas did what he's accused of?'

'That's not what I said.' He was playing into my hands. I stressed the crucial distinction, the one through which my boys and I could slip to freedom: 'I said I *saw* nothing.'

He was genuinely incredulous. 'You were at the very heart of that household, and you saw nothing?'

'*Ed*' – my turn to lean forwards, for emphasis – 'what I *saw* – *who* I saw, *all* I saw – was *Kate*. I had no interest in Elizabeth, in what she was up to.' Never a truer word. 'And as for Thomas . . .' I shrugged to imply that it was much the same for Thomas, but then threw in, 'What I saw was no more than the usual.'

He bit. 'The usual?'

Gently does it. 'Oh, you know . . .'

He cocked his head: *Go on*.

'Thomas being overfamiliar.'

'With Elizabeth?'

'Yes' – who else? – 'with Elizabeth.' A flash of anger at Thomas. He certainly hadn't helped himself. He should have been more cautious. But that was Thomas, wasn't it. Thoughtless towards those around him, careless of the consequences for others. Why should I care about the consequences for him? I can't afford to, not with my Harry at stake.

'How, exactly?'

So I listed some instances: the early-morning river walk, making no mention of tag-along Jane Grey; the hair-plaiting session, omitting Mrs Ashley's inept supervision; Elizabeth sitting in Thomas's lap as if it was something that I, alone, had come across; and the chasing around the bedroom as if I'd witnessed it for myself.

He remained expressionless, then asked, 'Was Kate concerned?'

'She said not.'

'She *said* not? You discussed it?'

Witheringly: 'Of course we discussed it. We were best friends, weren't we.'

He was chastened, uneasy, apologetic: 'I mean, she raised the subject?'

'She did.'

'How? Why?'

'Mrs Ashley had concerns.'

'About?'

'About what I've just told you,' and that was all he was going to get from me. What I'd told him was fairly common knowledge, so I was on safe ground. To go any further would lay me open to doubts, to questions.

He frowned, puzzled. 'But Kate did send Elizabeth away.

Why would she have done that, unless she was worried?'

I repeated the explanation that Kate had always offered. 'A baby was about to be born in that household. Elizabeth had to go away so that she could get on with her studies, free from distraction.'

'But she didn't send Jane Grey away.'

'Jane Grey is never distracted.'

He couldn't help but half smile at that. He couldn't dispute it. After a pause, he stopped the questions and instead told me something. 'Thomas was trying to contact Elizabeth again, just before his arrest, you know.'

My blood ambushed my heart. 'I didn't, no.'

'We can only presume that it was a renewed attempt to get her to marry him.' Fingertips to his temple, as if calming a pain. 'He never learns, does he. He'll never stop.'

'No,' I agreed, although of course I knew differently. He'd have been trying to get to her to square their stories. Whereas me: he hadn't tried to reach me, to negotiate or plead with me. He'd given up on me before he'd even started. Probably his only wise move ever. I asked Ed, 'What's Elizabeth saying?' He'd tell me, I knew. In his view, we were old friends, and although I might bristle at being questioned, we were on the same side. He'd share what he knew.

'Nothing,' he said. 'Absolutely nothing, and I don't think she ever will.' He shook his head in wonderment. 'She's smart, that one.'

I'd been right to rely on her saving her own skin. In that, we're alike; in that, we understand each other.

'Some performance, she's giving us,' he said. 'Icily polite, but outwitting us all.'

'Maybe there's genuinely nothing to tell.' Made to sound

like musing, but in fact a probing to see how much he knows. 'Maybe they really were just friends.'

'No, *something* went on.' He spoke as if this was a mystery for us to share. '*Something* was going on, Cathy.' The faintest of smiles appeared in his eyes. 'Don't forget, I've a lifetime's experience of my brother, and I can tell you that whenever there's any suggestion that he's been involved in some wrongdoing, it'll be true. And what's more, it'll be worse than you imagined.'

Determined to return the smile, I found myself unable to hold his gaze.

'Mrs Ashley will be the one to tell us. She's done her best at maintaining a silence – I have to say, she's done admirably for Elizabeth – but she'll be the one to crack.'

What does Mrs Ashley know? Nothing, has been my guess, my gamble, but – crucial, this – she *thinks* she *does*. That will have been Elizabeth's doing, to keep her much loved but fusspot governess at bay.

'You know she's in the Tower?'

I nodded. I'd heard. Mrs Ashley, busy with her embroidery in one of the Tower's riverside rooms. Nowhere near Elizabeth, thank God, for any belated confidences.

'Well, now she's in a dungeon.'

'A *dungeon*? Mrs Ashley?'

He held up his hands: *Not my decision*.

Unfortunately, I could believe it: Ed, excluded now from decision-making. 'That's *repugnant*, Ed.'

His hands came together as if in prayer, then to his lips, then they opened and he dipped his face into them. Looking up with red-rubbed eyes, he continued, 'As I say, I think it'll get them what they want.' Then, apparently as an afterthought, 'I'm expected to talk to your boys.'

Was it an afterthought? Why mention a dungeon and, in the next breath, my sons? *Steady*, I warned myself. *You're doing it again: you're imagining it, the threat you heard*. 'Why? They were never there.'

He corrected, patiently: 'They were *sometimes* there.'

'Almost never,' I countered, but reined myself in, aware that I was protesting too hard. 'It'll be pointless, your talking to them. They're *boys*, Ed, they're just boys: they're oblivious. We've talked about it, of course, the three of us.' A lie. 'We've talked about what's happening to Thomas and why, and frankly they're as puzzled as I am. Interviewing them will be a waste of your time and,' I reminded him, a touch brutally, 'time is something you don't have.'

He allowed it with one sharp nod, then stood, giving me a tight little smile. 'And with that . . .'

I said it for him: 'A quick look in at the nursery.' He seemed surprised to be directed there alone, but I explained that Mary is a fearful child. With good reason: losing one parent within days of her birth and now, four months later, the other. I explained that she doesn't like a lot of people around her, and he huffed at what he judged to be absurd. 'But you're not "people", you're her . . .'

Yes, indeed, 'Her what? I'm nothing to her, Ed, I'm no one. She doesn't know me. Her various members of staff' – and God knows there are enough of them – 'are family to her.'

And so now he's over there, across the courtyard in the wing of my house that the baby and her nursery staff have practically taken over, and he'll be keen to do what's expected of him. Playing up to the ladies, in his awkward way, and cajoling the little girl. Hoping to prove himself – not least in his own eyes – to be the good uncle, the family man. And in a few minutes he'll be back over here, exhilarated by his efforts, exclaiming how she looks like one or the other of her parents. I can't see it, myself. She might have no connection to either, for all that I can see.

Perhaps that's how her questions will start. It's something she'll want to know one day, isn't it? Do I look like my mother, do I look like my father? By then, there'll probably be something I can say: *You have your mother's smile*; or, *You have your father's eyes*. She'll want to know about her parents and it'll be left to me to tell her. Kate: well, that's easy; there's plenty I can say about Kate, all of which will have her daughter feeling special and proud. Thomas, though? He felt that we understood something about each other, didn't he. He felt that we recognised something in each other. But Thomas, I'll tell her, I barely knew, and there's some truth in it.

Epilogue

Catherine, Duchess of Suffolk was indeed Katherine Parr's closest friend, but her relationship with Katherine's husband as depicted in this novel is of my own imagining. In every other aspect, I have aimed for historical accuracy.

At the time of Thomas Seymour's trial, there were rumours that Elizabeth Tudor had been pregnant and had had a miscarriage or stillbirth or a baby. She'd been ill and unable or unwilling to leave the Dennys' Hertfordshire home during the summer of 1548. A local midwife, it was said, had claimed to have been taken to a secret location to deliver a baby of a young noblewoman who was in disguise. Such rumours persist to this day, the most recent claim (in 2006, exciting the attention of the British press) being that William Shakespeare was the child of Thomas Seymour and Elizabeth Tudor.

Thomas Seymour was indicted on thirty-three counts of

treason and beheaded in 1549, on the day his daughter was seven months old. (His brother, Edward Seymour, suffered the same fate in 1552, on trumped-up charges.) He had been described by one of his contemporaries, Sir John Hayward, as 'Fierce in courage, courtly in fashion, in personage stately and in voice magnificent . . . but somewhat empty in matter.' Hugh Latimer (Catherine of Suffolk's chaplain, and Katharine Parr's close friend) attended his execution and said that he died 'very dangerously, irksomely, horribly'. There is no mention of his daughter, Mary, beyond infancy; she is believed to have died as a small child, although a popular myth held that she had survived into adulthood, married Sir Edward Bushell and had descendants. Historians consider it extremely unlikely, though, that the daughter of a dowager queen could disappear from public record.

In 1551, when they were students at Cambridge, Catherine of Suffolk's two sons died suddenly on the same day from 'sweating sickness', an almost always fatal flu-like illness, specific to the Tudor period, which killed within hours of the first symptoms. Catherine reached the bedside of only one of them – the younger, Charles – in time.

In 1553, Catherine married one of her own staff, her gentleman usher, Richard Bertie, and theirs was a long and happy marriage, despite having to escape into exile in the Low Countries during Mary Tudor's reign. Catherine had two more children, Susan and Peregrine, both of whom survived into adulthood. Peregrine grew up to be a happily married father of six and a valued member of Queen Elizabeth's court, but he had a troubled and controversial early adulthood (not least when he backed away from a marriage with one of Bess Cavendish's daughters in favour of the tempestuous Lady Mary Vere) and his relationship with his mother was fraught. They were estranged at the time of her death in 1580. She is buried (with Richard Bertie, who died eighteen months later) in the fourteenth-century church at Spilsbury in Lincolnshire. Her biographer, Evelyn Read, describes her as 'singularly modern in the midst of the sixteenth century, modern in her quiet assumption that in addition to home-making and caring for her children a woman could and should make a contribution to the spiritual well-being of her people, in her courage and outspokeness, and, above all, modern in her refusal to accept beliefs and customs simply because they had always been accepted.' (See *Catherine, Duchess of Suffolk*, Jonathan Cape, 1962.)

Sudeley Castle was beseiged and wrecked during the Civil War, and remained ruined for two hundred years before new owners began restoration. The mediaeval buildings of the inner court, including the banqueting hall, have been left evocatively as ruins. During the Second World War, Sudeley Castle was used as a prisoner-of-war camp and shelter for part of the Tate's collection of paintings. Nowadays, it is open to the public (Katherine Parr's apartment only by special arrangement), and on display there – looking as good as new – is princess Elizabeth's christening gown and cradle-canopy (discovered at Sudeley Castle, with other of Katherine Parr's belongings). The Tudor formal garden was uncovered in front of the banqueting hall during the 1860s, and the grounds have been extensively restored.

For the ruined chapel, John Ruskin recommended 'no restoration; a pile of mossy stones a fitter monument for Queen Katherine Parr than the most gorgeous church that wealth could erect'. In 1782, a man discovered her lead coffin among the ruins, and opened it to find her undecayed; he took a sample of the red cloth of her dress and a lock of her auburn hair. Over the next ten years, the coffin was unearthed and opened on three occasions by curious locals, before being reburied upside down by drunken labourers. Public dissatisfaction with the situation led to a successful search for it in 1817, and a skeleton and a mass of ivy roots was discovered inside. It was placed into a vault in the restored church of St Mary's (Ruskin's advice had been ignored), and in 1861 a new and magnificent altar-tomb was designed by Sir George Gilbert Scott and carved by S. Birnie Philip, who were also responsible for the Albert Memorial.

Katherine Parr's biographer, Anthony Martienssen, credits her with having rescued Elizabeth Tudor from obscurity and educating and encouraging her to develop into the politically astute young woman she became. He claims, 'It is, I believe, no exaggeration to say that without Katherine Parr, Queen Elizabeth would not have been the Queen she was nor her reign the epic it became.' (*Queen Katherine Parr*, Secker & Warburg Ltd, 1973).

Historians have noted that despite all they shared (their protestantism, their loving memories of Katherine Parr), relations between Queen Elizabeth and Catherine of Suffolk were only ever cordial at best.

Acknowledgements

Many thanks to my agent, Antony Topping, without whom this novel would never have got off the ground in any sense; Venetia Butterfield for taking the novel on, and Clare Smith for then taking it over and making me feel so welcome as one of her writers; Annabel Wright and Essie Cousins, my editors at HarperCollins, for a job beautifully done; and Jo Adams and Carol Painter for so often lending me their cottage, which has made such a difference to my life.

THE HISTORY BEHIND THE STORY

Tudorspeak

When the idea for the first of my so-called historical novels came to me—Anne Boleyn's story in her own words—I immediately dismissed it. I don't do historical fiction. Then came another idea: Well, don't write it as historical fiction. But what did I mean by that? I wasn't even a *reader* of historical fiction, so how could I presume to know what the new generation of historical novelists was up to? "Prithee" and heaving bosoms were what I meant, but to be honest, I knew that "prithee" was long gone. Characters in historical fiction do, though, still talk in a stilted fashion—"do not" instead of "don't"—and even that was enough to put me off. And this business of the bosoms: it's not bosoms that I mind, it's that they're heaving. Historical fiction is too often costume drama, it seems to me, rather than real—human—drama.

Character is what I go for, both as a reader and a writer. My characters have to be more than the stuffing for some eye-catching dress. They have to feel real: really, really real. And a big part of how someone *is*, is how he or she speaks: that, too, has to feel real. Perhaps novelists who use "do not" instead of "don't" are trying to remind us that their characters lived in a world very different from our own. And if so, fair enough: that's certainly one way to do it. But it's not my way. It's not what I want. It's exactly what I don't want.

That's how I've ended up with readers asking me why I don't write dialogue as it was spoken in Tudor times (and that's when they sense it's a conscious decision; some seem to think it's an oversight). I have to contain my sarcasm: "Oh, and you know how people spoke, then, do you?" Because although we know how people wrote (correction: how *some* people wrote—those who could write), that would've been different from how they spoke. We all write differently from how we speak, much more so than we realize, and if you don't believe me, look at a transcript of speech: it'll be practically unintelligible. Consciously or unconsciously, we all do a lot of tidying up to make our words clear on a page. We translate the spoken word into the written word. Cod olde English is just a fashion in translation. No more than that. Just an idea. Take it or leave it. Well, I decided to leave it. Look at it this way: it's acceptable (indeed, de rigueur) for translators not to give us a literal, word-by-word translation and instead to phrase things so that they're as faithful as possible to the original but—crucial, this—give us the flavor. The problem, for me, is that the flavor of characters who say "do not" rather than "don't" is one of quaintness. And the people I write about were anything but. Take Catherine, Duchess of Suffolk, who narrates *The Sixth Wife*. My reading had given me a clear picture of a woman who was thoroughly modern for her times, an outspoken woman with a disregard for formality and tradition. That was the impression I needed to give my readers, and no amount of "prithee" was going to do it. Oddly enough, truth matters above all to me as a reader and writer of fiction. Most often when I put down a novel unread, it's because I don't believe in some or all of it. I'm thinking, "But he/she wouldn't do/believe/say that!" My job as a writer, as I see it, is to get to the truth of something or someone and then enable you, the reader, to see it, too. To that end, I'm always stopping myself as I write and asking myself, checking, "Would he/she really think this/behave like this?" And, now, with historical fiction, "*Did* they. . . ?"

Because, of course, I'm now dealing with people who did live, who were once real. It matters to me that I do them justice. Reading as widely as possible gives me a picture of them that's both broad and detailed. Yes, historians differ in their accounts, but usually not too much. I can weigh up what they say and come up with something that feels believable. I'd assumed that Katherine Parr was nice but dull, but a bit of reading around showed me that she was a lot more interesting than that. Which, happily, in turn, makes for a more interesting read.

What's hard for me, funnily enough, is making things up. That's my job, too, though. I need to tell you more than you know, and more than you could possibly ever know even if you read all the history books. I'm not a historian, and I should do something other than merely retell history. I have to go beyond or behind what's known and come up with a story. In *The Queen of Subtleties*, my invention was the king's confectioner—not her existence (her surname and the kind of work she would have done is what we know of her) but her unwitting, tragic involvement with the innocent young man who was executed as the alleged lover of Anne Boleyn. In *The Sixth Wife* the sad truth is that cautious, clever Katherine Parr survived her marriage to Henry VIII only to make the all-too-common mistake of falling for a man who wasn't worthy of her and who messed around with her fourteen-year-old stepdaughter. My invention is a central role for Katherine's best friend in this sorry tale.

A Conversation with Suzannah

What was your childhood like, and can you see any connection between it and the work you do now?

It was economically unstable, in that my father was self-employed, and I can certainly see that connection with my own working life. It was noisy and crowded, in that I am the eldest of four children, and the work I've chosen requires quietness, space, solitude. So, yes, a connection there. The flip side of living in a fairly large family is that the attention is often necessarily elsewhere, particularly, of course, when siblings are younger, so, actually, paradoxically, I also had a lot of space and solitude and was able to be day-dreamy. Being the eldest child, I was much confided in by my very talkative mother, and she has a keen interest in the stories of other people's lives and an excellent memory for the details. I think that influenced me. I'm very grateful that my primary school education was in the 1970s and gently progressive, with an emphasis on creative writing.

What are you aiming to do in your novels? What reaction are you trying to evoke in your reader?

It's quite simple, really, nothing fancy. I think the highest praise would be something along the lines of the reader having felt that he or she was "really there."

How important is it to you to be historically accurate, and how do you decide when to invent?

It's extremely important to me, more than it should be, in fact. I'm not very good at letting go of the facts or accepted accounts, but in a sense, being a fiction writer, it's my job to do so. I feel inhibited in that respect. Not only do I feel an obligation to the reader to be historically accurate, but I also feel an obligation to try to do justice to characters who were once real. With both my historical novels, it's been my agent, whose judgment I trust, who has encouraged me to do some invention. I go to him, all excited with the real story that I've come across, and his line, both times, has been: "Don't just retell the story that we all know; contribute to it something that's solely yours." Both times, I've fought shy of doing so, and he's pushed me, making some suggestions, and then I've felt able to go for it, as if I've been given permission.

How much research do you do for each novel and how do you go about it?

I don't read original documents, perhaps because I lack confidence in the face of Tudor English, perhaps because I'm lazy. I stick to secondary sources: books written about the period. Of those, I read as widely as possible—often irrelevantly, it'll seem at first, but there's always the odd fact, in any Tudor-related book, that's useful—getting further titles from each bibliography. I treat myself to field trips, too. I visited the obvious places such as Hever Castle and Sudeley Castle, but as with the books, anywhere that dates from the period turns out to be useful in some way.

What was your biggest challenge in writing *The Sixth Wife*?

The sex scenes. They're always a challenge. The first challenge being, of course, to avoid sounding ridiculous, laughable; the second, to strike a balance between suggestion and explicitness. But then there's the business of Tudor details: underclothes and the mechanics of undressing, and I found it hard to know or imagine how nobles, attended all the time, could hope to ensure secrecy. Added to that, I had recently had a baby and was therefore, shall we say, working from memory, distant memory. Another challenge with this particular novel was being inside the head of someone I didn't quite like—the narrator, Catherine, Duchess of Suffolk—for the eighteen months it took to write it. That was grueling.

Do you identify closely with any of the characters you have written about? Are there any that you particularly admire or dislike?

When writing *The Queen of Subtleties,* I identified with Anne Boleyn's outspokenness and lack of compromise, and I admire it. However, I am that peculiar Libran mix: a lot of the time I say exactly what I mean and believe I'm right to do so, but at other times, I realize I'm infuriatingly elusive, noncommittal, which I see as diplomatic but non-Librans probably see as two-faced. I identified with Katherine Parr having a first baby late in life, and I admire her for the excellent relationships she built with her many, various stepchildren and the other young people in her life. I feel ambivalent about Catherine, Duchess of Suffolk. She was definitely a big character, a strong woman with lots of steadfast friends and influential contacts and a few enemies. She was set on reform and averse to compromise, all of which I admire. However, she refused to testify in favor of a good friend of hers when, it seems, it wouldn't have harmed her in the least to do so, and she complained long and loud (in letters) of the cost of caring for the orphaned infant daughter of her best friend. Interestingly, I can't say I dislike what I know of Thomas Seymour. He seems to me to have been a silly man, that's all.

Are you religious?

I was raised as an atheist, and I don't mean agnostic. I think atheism is a position of faith, too, and I find it hard to shake it. Ironically, I've ended up focusing on the Reformation and loving the subject. I wonder if my lack of religious faith enables me to have that interest, looking on from the sidelines.

What are you writing now?

A novel about Mary Tudor's reign at the time of her marriage, which was late in her life, her protracted phantom pregnancy, and her relentless, horrifying persecution of so-called heretics. We English tend to shy away from Mary because—understatement—she's not glamorous; indeed, she's pitiful and repugnant. Her sister, Elizabeth, was glamorous, and we have loads of books and films about her, but Mary, no. That was challenge enough, initially, for me. Then there's the fact that she was England's first ruling queen and had to try to find her way through the unexplored territory of being both queen and wife. I'm telling the tale via a Spanish man who arrives in England as part of Mary's husband's retinue. He also has his own tale to tell from his time here.

What would you like to be remembered for?

I don't want to be remembered. Life goes on. Once you're gone, you're gone. Having said that, I would like to be remembered by my son with warmth and humor.

When do you write?

Any time I can find to write. Actually, that's not true. I rarely write in the evenings because I'm not sharp enough then or, usually, at weekends, which comes from having lived for years in my early adulthood with a junior doctor whose off-duty weekends were sacrosanct.

Why do you write?

It's how I earn my living. But, yes, of course, there are many ways of earning a living, and I made this particular one my own. I knew at the age of nine that I'd never be able to work full time at a normal job. I need to work for myself, by myself. My father and his father and grandfather were all self-employed, so perhaps it's something that runs deep in my family. I tend to claim that I wouldn't write if I didn't have to, but I suspect that's not the truth. I like the exploratory aspect of writing fiction. I want to get under the surface of characters, to find out what happens and why.

Pen or computer?

Both. Pen first, for rough notes; then computer, to tidy it into sentences.

Silence or music?

Music. Radio 3, or a CD if I've been organized enough to choose one before I sit down.

How do you start a book?

I don't know. Each one is different. I think I do usually start at the beginning, even if I'm not entirely linear after that.

And finish?

I find finishing impossible. I always feel that I'm doing the bare minimum, in my finishing, and hoping to get away with it (i.e., "Will this suffice?").

Do you have any writing rituals or superstitions?

No.

What or who inspires you?

If I knew, I'd always be inspired, wouldn't I? And I'm not. Broadly speaking, people's stories, the stories of their lives, inspire me.

If you weren't a writer what job would you do?

See above.

What's your guilty reading pleasure? Favorite trashy read?

Harlan Coben novels (sorry, Harlan! no offence intended). Love 'em.

The lighter side of HISTORY

*** Look for this seal on select historical fiction titles from Harper. Books bearing it contain special bonus materials, including timelines, interviews with the author, and insights into the real-life events that inspired the book, as well as recommendations for further reading.**

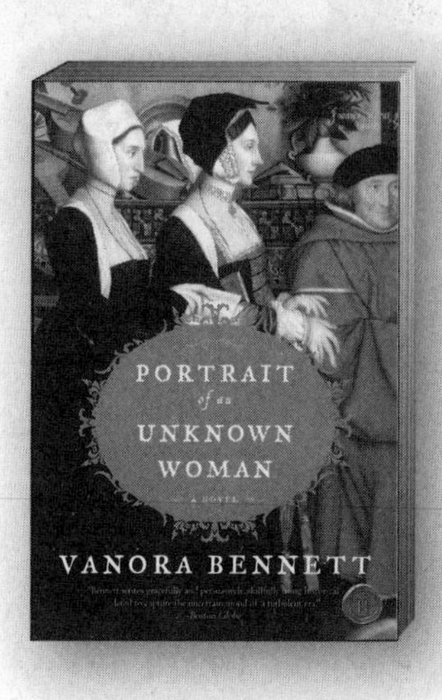

PORTRAIT OF AN UNKNOWN WOMAN

A Novel

by Vanora Bennett

978-0-06-125256-3 (paperback)

Meg, adopted daughter of Sir Thomas More, narrates the tale of a famous Holbein painting and the secrets it holds.

THE SIXTH WIFE

She Survived Henry VIII to be Betrayed by Love...

by Suzannah Dunn

978-0-06-143156-2 (paperback)

Kate Parr survived four years of marriage to King Henry VIII, but a new love may undo a lifetime of caution.

A POISONED SEASON

A Novel of Suspense

by Tasha Alexander 978-0-06-117421-6 (paperback)

As a cat-burglar torments Victorian London, a mysterious gentleman fascinates high society.

THE KING'S GOLD

A Novel

by Yxta Maya Murray 978-0-06-089108-4 (paperback)

A journey through Renaissance Italy, ripe with ancient maps, riddles, and treasure hunters. Book Two of the Red Lion Series.

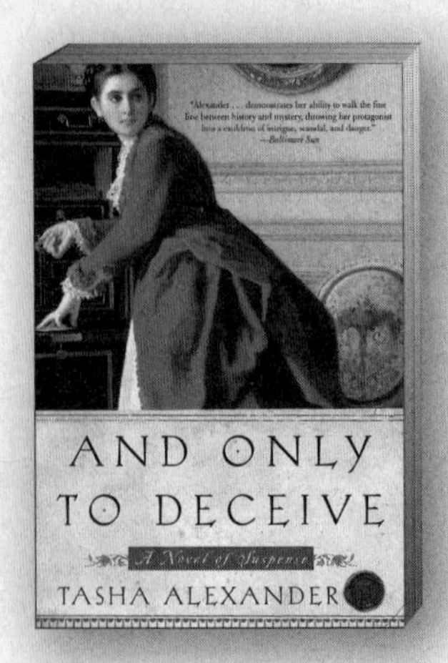

AND ONLY TO DECEIVE
A Novel of Suspense

by Tasha Alexander
978-0-06-114844-6 (paperback)

Discover the dangerous secrets kept by the strait-laced English of the Victorian era.

TO THE TOWER BORN
A Novel of the Lost Princes

by Robin Maxwell
978-0-06-058052-0 (paperback)

Join Nell Caxton in the search for the lost heirs to the throne of Tudor England.

CROSSED
A Tale of the Fourth Crusade

by Nicole Galland 978-0-06-084180-5 (paperback)

Under the banner of the Crusades, a pious knight and a British vagabond attempt a daring rescue.

THE SCROLL OF SEDUCTION
A Novel of Power, Madness, and Royalty

by Gioconda Belli 978-0-06-083313-8 (paperback)

A dual narrative of love, obsession, madness, and betrayal surrounding one of history's most controversial monarchs, Juana the Mad.

PILATE'S WIFE
A Novel of the Roman Empire

by Antoinette May 978-0-06-112866-0 (paperback)

Claudia foresaw the Romans' persecution of Christians, but even she could not stop the crucifixion.

ELIZABETH: THE GOLDEN AGE

by Tasha Alexander 978-0-06-143123-4 (paperback)

This novelization of the film starring Cate Blanchett is an eloquent exploration of the relationship between Queen Elizabeth I and Sir Walter Raleigh at the height of her power.

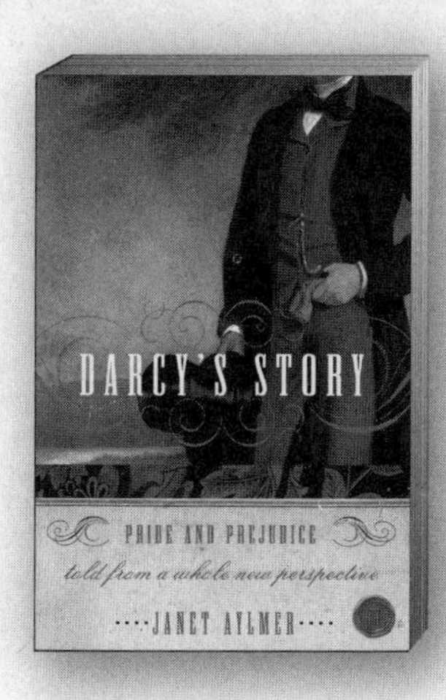

DARCY'S STORY

by Janet Aylmer
978-0-06-114870-5 (paperback)
Read Mr. Darcy's side of the story—*Pride and Prejudice* from a new perspective.

THE CANTERBURY PAPERS

A Novel
by Judith Healey
978-0-06-077332-8 (paperback)
Follow Princess Alais on a secret mission as she unlocks a long-held and dangerous secret.

THE FOOL'S TALE

A Novel
by Nicole Galland 978-0-06-072151-0 (paperback)
Travel back to Wales, 1198, a time of treachery, political unrest...and passion.

THE QUEEN OF SUBTLETIES

A Novel of Anne Boleyn
by Suzannah Dunn 978-0-06-059158-8 (paperback)
Untangle the web of fate surrounding Anne Boleyn in a tale narrated by the King's Confectioner.

REBECCA

The Classic Tale of Romantic Suspense
by Daphne Du Maurier 978-0-380-73040-7 (paperback)
Follow the second Mrs. Maxim de Winter down the lonely drive to Manderley, where Rebecca once ruled.

REBECCA'S TALE

A Novel
by Sally Beauman 978-0-06-117467-4 (paperback)
Unlock the dark secrets and old worlds of Rebecca de Winter's life with investigator Colonel Julyan.

REVENGE OF THE ROSE

A Novel

by Nicole Galland

978-0-06-084179-9 (paperback)

In the court of the Holy Roman Emperor, not even a knight is safe from gossip, schemes, and secrets.

A SUNDIAL IN A GRAVE: 1610

A Novel of Intrigue, Secret Societies, and the Race to Save History

by Mary Gentle

978-0-380-82041-2 (paperback)

Renaissance Europe comes alive in this dazzling tale of love, murder, and blackmail.

THORNFIELD HALL

Jane Eyre's Hidden Story

by Emma Tennant 978-0-06-000455-2 (paperback)

Watch the romance of Jane Eyre and Mr. Rochester unfold in this breathtaking sequel.

THE WIDOW'S WAR

A Novel

by Sally Gunning 978-0-06-079158-2 (paperback)

Tread the shores of colonial Cape Cod with a lonely whaler's widow as she tries to build a new life.

THE WILD IRISH

A Novel of Elizabeth I & the Pirate O'Malley

by Robin Maxwell 978-0-06-009143-9 (paperback)

Hoist a sail with the Irish pirate and clan chief Grace O'Malley.

Available wherever books are sold, or call 1-800-331-3761 to order.